ABOUT THE AUTHOR

Ian Mathie spent his childhood and early school years in Africa and Asia. After a short service commission in the RAF, he returned to Africa as a rural development officer working for the British government and a number of other agencies. He continued visiting Africa and Asia for work and personal interest until health considerations curtailed his travelling. He now lives in south Warwickshire with his wife and dog.

By the same author

The African Memoir Series:
BRIDE PRICE
MAN IN A MUD HUT
SUPPER WITH THE PRESIDENT
DUST OF THE DANAKIL
SORCERERS AND ORANGE PEEL
THE MAN OF PASSAGE

KEEP TAKING THE PILLS

For Suzy Bubbles & Jonesey,
a bit of excitement
for you!

Chinese Take-out

中餐外卖店

All best wishes

Ian Mathie

Ian Mathie!

MOSAÏQUEPRESS

First published in the UK in 2014 by
MOSAÏQUE PRESS
Registered office:
70 Priory Road
Kenilworth, Warwickshire CV8 1LQ
www.mosaïquepress.co.uk

Front cover design by Melissa Brayford

Printed in the UK.

ISBN 978-1-906852-31-3

DEDICATION

For my Dad, who always loved the saxophone,
even after injury forced him to stop playing one himself.

AUTHOR'S NOTE

THIS IS A WORK OF FICTION, inspired by the defection of Fang Lizhi, a Chinese physicist, who took refuge in the United States Embassy in Beijing in 1989. This happened at the time when China was experimenting with democracy, with Tienanmen Square as the focus of its expression, particularly among the student masses. At the same time there were several sources of international tension and world leaders were conducting missions of shuttle diplomacy to stop the global pot from boiling over.

Fang Lizhi eventually managed to leave China and took up an academic post in UK, later moving to the University of Arizona in Tucson, where he died in 2012. He was brought to the UK in an American military plane, although his actual arrival was a long time later, and the circumstances were a little different from those described in my story.

All the 'active' characters in the story are fictional and any similarity to real individuals is entirely coincidental. The historical facts are on record.

Ian Mathie

Chapter 1

THE FLAT CRACK of a rifle brought Green instantly awake. The sound lay dead on the frozen air and it was impossible to say from which direction it had originated. It was just after dawn, overcast, with thick gray clouds hanging so low he felt as if he could reach up and touch them. Down by the shore a thin trickle of smoke was beginning to curl up from the rusty flue sticking out at a crazy angle from the wall of the border post.

Green wanted to stand and stretch his cramped limbs, but that would be a mistake. The small hollow in which he lay, and the rock that had sheltered him from the wind the night before, were the only cover for several hundred meters. He shifted a leg instead, and pulled a heavy pair of binoculars out of a padded white bag that lay beside him. He raised them to his eyes and began to scan the ground below.

It had snowed again during the night. Once the wind had died the snow had fallen in fat, heavy flakes, covering the low bivouac tent and making it shapeless. The weight of the snow pressed down on Green's legs as he lay on his stomach watching. Nothing moved.

Green lowered the binoculars and looked at his watch. There were still at least two hours to go, provided the agent was on time. He was about to pull out a self-heating ration pack when a movement down by the building attracted his attention.

A soldier came round the side of the hut, a rifle slung across his chest. He stopped in front of a deep drift, opened his fly and relieved himself into the snow. It was deep everywhere down there, almost up to the soldier's knees. He buttoned his clothing and looked around. As he turned towards where Green lay he paused, staring intently. Swiftly he raised his weapon, aimed and fired. Green winced as he saw the muzzle flash, followed immediately by the flat report. There was a grunt above him, the snow in front of his face splashed red, and he felt the weight of something heavy landing in the snow beside him. He froze and held his breath.

Slinging his rifle over his shoulder, the soldier headed purposefully towards where Green lay. Another uniformed figure came out of the hut and shouted something. The soldier turned and shouted back, but the distance was too great for Green to hear their words. The soldier turned back and continued trudging up the slope. The other man went back inside the hut.

Green would certainly be discovered. He wished he had a rifle, but there had been no way of bringing one. He reached inside his parka and pulled out a heavy Remington automatic pistol. He had no silencer, so he wrapped the padded binocular bag round it and pushed it out in front of him, under the snow, pointing it upwards slightly.

He waited.

It seemed to take forever for the soldier to arrive. He was looking down at the snow as he trudged upwards. He looked up once or twice to check his direction, but did no more than glance before looking down again. When the soldier was only a couple of meters away he slowed and looked up, straight into Green's eyes. He hesitated for barely a moment before his rifle began to swing down.

With a muffled roar the snow in front of Green erupted. A red flower blossomed where the soldier's face had been. He was thrown backwards into the snow. Green lay still and watched the hut. For several minutes he waited.

Nothing happened.

When he was satisfied that the other man was not going to come out, Green eased himself forward, out of the slim tent and turned, expecting to find the body of his agent. A young stag, still breathing, lay bleeding into the virgin whiteness.

Green thought rapidly. If the soldier did not return to the hut soon his comrade would surely come looking for him. Reaching into the bivouac, he pulled out his rucksack. He dragged the dead Korean border guard by the feet, pushed him into the tent and brushed snow over the entrance. With the butt of the Korean's rifle he hit the stag hard across the neck. There was a soft snapping noise, the beast sagged and its breathing stilled.

Green slung the rifle over his shoulder, hung his binoculars round his neck, and holstered his pistol. Then he took hold of the stag. It was heavier than it looked, and with muscles sluggish from hours of chilled inactivity he found it difficult to lift. At the third attempt he got it across his shoulders, and started down the slope towards the hut.

The noise as Green dropped the dead stag onto the wooden porch brought the other soldier out. Green was ready for him as he opened the door. The

Korean's eyes widened in disbelief as he saw Green, and felt the long steel blade slide between his ribs. He sagged soundlessly to the floor and lay still.

Green made sure the guard was dead and then pulled him to the end of the boards. He did not bother to search the man, but simply rolled him off the end and into the snowdrift that had formed against the side of the hut. Then he went inside.

There was plenty of fuel and the old stove was remarkably efficient. Green stoked it up and began to thaw himself out. He looked around to see what supplies the former occupants had left but was disappointed. The Korean rations were disgusting and he was glad to have the fresh meat.

It was two more days before his agent arrived.

Chapter 2

THINKING BACK TO THE events on the border brought them close. Was it really only nine weeks ago that he lay on that distant frozen frontier? He mused.

Malcolm Green sat in the unfamiliar office chair and stared moodily out of the window. Bright spring sunshine was bathing the immaculate lawns and flower borders, kept in regulation order by an unseen army of Uncle Sam's gardeners. Patches of dappled shade shimmered slightly as the light breeze ruffled the fresh canopies of ornamental trees. A squirrel looped its way across the lawn. The sounds of the traffic beyond the gardens were muted by the heavy double glazing and the low hum of the air conditioning.

Green had not wanted this assignment and had argued strongly against taking it, almost as if he had sensed that something momentous was about to happen in his theatre. Unwilling and mildly resentful, he had sat here for the past three weeks. For the last nine days he had been seething. All his calls to the Chief had been blocked. It was as if the man didn't want to admit he had goofed by moving Green just as things turned critical in the field.

With a sigh he turned back to the office and drained the last of his coffee. It tasted bitter and matched his mood. He launched the empty paper cup at the waste basket in the corner, and missed. Turning back to the pile of files on the table beside him his eyes caught the headline on the daily newspaper his staffer had placed beside the action tray.

REVOLUTION IN CHINA
MILLIONS PROTEST IN BEIJING FREEDOM RALLY

The heavy black type intensified his resentment at being transferred to sort out the Indian Ocean Section just as things began to move in his own back yard. Green had been working his way up the China Section for sixteen years, with many good field operations to his credit, and they had to choose this moment to pull him out to sort out some other bastard's snafu. Things are happening out there in the world, he thought bitterly. Momentous, terrifying things; history in the making. Stupid cliché that, but true none the less, and I've been goddam sidelined. Why? Oh, why did those stupid bastards have to go and screw up just now? And why'd the Chief have to dump me in it to mop up the mess?

He picked up the newspaper and read, for the twentieth time, the grizzly details made electric by the press hype. They don't even know half of it, he thought, with the reporting restrictions the Chinese would have imposed. His eyes scanned the text while his mind drifted over the details that had been streaming into Langley from field agents over the last few months. Many of them were his agents, people he had selected, trained and placed during the past nine years. It galled him to be isolated from them now.

His brooding was interrupted by the telephone and he snatched it from its cradle to silence the insistent warbling.

"Green," he said, trying to keep the frustration out of his voice.

"Word just came from the Senate, sir," the staffer's voice said. "They have scheduled the first hearing for two thirty on Tuesday week."

"Hell! They ain't even giving us time to do the prelims before starting to burn asses," he grumbled. Someone up on the Hill must be real jumpy. After the scandals of Watergate, Iran-Contra and all the muckraking into the private affairs of the new President's nominees for public office, which had resulted in several embarrassing disqualifications, it was hardly unexpected. Now just a sniff of something irregular was enough to start a witch hunt. A few lousy guns in the hands of some bunch of Tamil rebels in Sri Lanka and they want to start an investigation that would make the Salem Witch Hunts look like a high school debate.

"Mr Green?" The staffer's voice sounded tentative.

"Yeah. I heard you. Thanks. Call Hal Johnson, Penkowski, Mitch Sullivan and Joe. Set up a meeting here for four thirty. No stenographer. Come in yourself and take notes."

Green never heard the staffer's reply as he dumped the phone back on its cradle. He folded the newspaper, tossed it onto the side table, and turned his attention back to the task in hand. Pulling the pile of files towards him, he opened the first one and began to read. For the next two hours he worked rapidly through the pile, making notes on a pad and occasionally flagging pages with small adhesive tags numbered to correspond to his notes. He was a meticulous researcher, with a unique ability to organize information and spot inconsistencies. That was why he was in intelligence and probably why the Chief had assigned him to this investigation. Green had a record of getting to the root of things several steps ahead of everyone else. As he worked his way through the files the first indications of a pattern began to coalesce in his mind.

The internal door opened and the staffer came in with the rest of the files Green had requested the night before. Without a word he placed them on the side table and left. Moments later the staffer returned and placed a cup of coffee on the corner of Green's desk. He glanced up as the young man left and noticed him pick up the fallen paper cup and drop it in the waste basket before quietly closing the door. He was surprised to see the coffee had been brought in a real cup and saucer. He picked it up. Black, no sugar, his mind registered as he drank. That young man is pretty quick off the mark, he thought. I must find out about him. Better than the jerk they sent first time, who couldn't even tie his shoe laces properly.

The Assignments Secretariat had sounded shocked and slightly hostile when Green had demanded that they replace the man they had assigned, saying that he was highly competent with a good track record. They had nobody else available at the moment. Green did not waste time arguing, he simply sent the staffer home and rang the Chief's secretary.

The Chief came into Maureen's office while Green was on the line telling her what he had done. Maureen had dealt with Green for years and was familiar with his foibles. Even so she frowned and her lips puckered in disapproval as she listened to his description of the man's failings and what he would do to him if he returned.

"What's burning him now?" asked the Chief. "Still grumbling about having to play Sherlock Holmes?"

"He's fired the staffer. He says the man is an incompetent jerk and he'll shoot him if he comes back."

"Oh yeah? Better get him a good one then." The Chief grinned, imagining what Green had really said. "Anything new in from Walker?"

"Not yet, sir. I expect it'll be an hour or so before we hear."

"Hmmm!" The Chief grunted and turned to leave as Maureen called the Appointments Secretariat.

The new staffer arrived at Green's office twenty minutes later.

GREEN NEVER ATE LUNCH and was finishing the second batch of files when the staffer buzzed him to say that the team had assembled.

"OK. Bring em in here, and get that anti-bugging unit turned on," he said.

The door opened immediately and the team trooped in followed by the staffer with a tray of coffee and mineral water, which he placed in the middle of the conference table as they all sat down.

"You've all heard the schedule," Green said, taking his place. "Someone must have one granddaddy of a burr under his saddle to give us so little time, so let's get going."

The meeting broke up at eight and Green asked them to meet again at eleven the following morning. By that time the members of the Senate Committee would have been nominated and they could begin planning how to present the initial outline.

As they left Green was standing by the window looking out over the floodlit gardens and wondering what was going on at the far side of the world. The staffer came back with a sheaf of papers.

"I thought you might like to see these, sir. The latest reports off the wire from Beijing."

Green's face registered his surprise as he turned and took the papers. "Thanks. That's just what I was thinking about," he said with a smile.

"I guess most of us have it somewhere in our thoughts, sir." The young man said with a grin. "May I lock these files away now?" He indicated the pile Green had been working on.

"Sure. There's a list on the pink paper of those I want first in the morning. The notes you took this afternoon need to be distributed to the team so they have time to read them before tomorrow's session. I would prefer that none of the typists see them, so just Xerox and pass them out yourself." Green said, with half his mind on the teletype sheets. "I'll just read these and then I'm off. My wife has invited some neighbors over and will surely skin me if I skip again," he looked up with a lopsided grin.

"I'll just order up these files and secure everything here, sir. Will you want the computer again tonight?"

"No thanks. I'm done for the day." Green handed back the teletype sheets. "G'night," he headed for the door.

The staffer tidied up the office, shut down the computer and returned to his own office next door. Just Xerox and distribute the notes, he said to himself. If time were not pressing and Green were not Green that might be fun. I wonder how many of those guys read shorthand? He sat down at the word processor and began to type fluently. When he had finished he locked the disk in his safe, to be printed in the morning, and cleared the machine. He lifted the telephone to call the registry with Green's list of files, but hesitated. Perhaps it would be better to let that wait until the morning, just in case someone was watching what files the investigating team called for. If there really was anything suspicious about this affair it would be better not to give too many warnings. The tentacles of treachery could reach into the most unlikely places.

The staffer cleared up, made the office secure, and went home.

Chapter 3

THE EVENTS IN CHINA had been world headlines for two weeks. After thirty years of isolation following the communist take-over in 1948, one fifth of the planet's population was largely unknown to the rest of the world. Of course the political people had their sources, and occasional items of news came out with the few foreigners privileged enough to visit, but after the Cultural Revolution the lid had been screwed down tight.

The thaw was slow and comparatively recent. The first tentative steps had been taken when President Nixon made an historic official visit. But following that little seemed to happen for a long time. Word that the British were negotiating with Beijing over the future of Hong Kong when their ninety-nine year lease expired received only short lived coverage, and news that an agreement had been reached was given little attention outside the colony and Britain. In Hong Kong itself the agreement received intense scrutiny as three and a half million people in one of the world's most dynamic economies wanted to know what sort of future they would have under communist rule.

Word leaked out to the rest of the world that Mao's successors had been purged. Then the New China News Agency released some film of the trials that followed, in an attempt to show the world that justice and reform did exist behind the inscrutable bamboo veil. The Chinese regime was still made up of geriatrics, as the tradition of reverence towards age had never weakened in the circles of influence. Old men clinging to power when they should have given way to a younger generation, said the rest of the world, but the mandarins closed their ears and continued their secretive processes behind firmly closed doors.

Despite the rest of the world's lack of awareness, changes were being made, and several experiments were tried into what was called democracy. Some of these were even allowed to continue so long as they posed no threat to the established order. Somewhere in the hierarchy the need for more contact with the outside world was recognized and slowly small doors opened. Western businessmen were invited to trade, particularly in high technology goods.

Carefully vetted tourists were permitted managed access, even to some of the hitherto most sensitive parts of the country, and the trickle of news coming out became a regular flow.

The CIA took full advantage of this improved access to fill in gaps in their knowledge jigsaw, and established a rudimentary network of contacts and sources.

The rest of the world had been skeptical about alleged reforms in China, but most were finally convinced that the leadership were sincere when the Queen made a State Visit. The press corps of the world flocked to follow the tour and was most hospitably received. Even countries like Bolivia, which could make little claim to any direct interest, were represented in this scrum. For the first time since modern communications became widespread, the world was able to peek behind the veil and marvel at what was to be seen. This sudden openness made a major impact.

As businessmen from every western country jostled for a share of the new market China crept tentatively out of its shell into the glaring daylight of the twentieth century. The Roman Catholic Church, so long suppressed, was again permitted to exist openly. Foreign teachers were invited to work in several provincial cities. International mountaineering expeditions were organized to conquer unscaled peaks, previously known only from satellite pictures and from legends. Even the conservationist movements were permitted to participate in efforts to save the giant panda from extinction.

The initial flush of popular interest eventually subsided but news of new reforms in China continued to be received by many with enthusiasm. The man in the street thought China was a bit quaint and rather backward, but at least they were making progress at last. If only they did not breed so fast; the size of their population was frightening and somewhat unimaginable, but so was the size of their country. Few took much notice of those who expressed doubts in chic drawing rooms, bars, or smoke filled working men's clubs.

In time events in the Soviet Union and Poland took the limelight. Words like glasnost and perestroika caught the imagination. The Soviets had finally abandoned their fossilized leadership and given power to a man in his fifties. Mikhail Gorbachev was full of charisma and charm, and seemingly competent to pull the country out of its constipated economic stupor. He shunned personal publicity and thereby increased his charisma and credibility. With his beautiful wife, Raisa, at his side the new Soviet leader visited the West in style, making agreements right and left to support and fuel his reform programs.

The world heaved a great sigh of relief when the first nuclear missile treaty was signed with the United States and again when the Soviets made a unilateral cut in their conventional forces. International alarm over radiation leaks when the Chernobyl nuclear power plant blew up soon subsided to the level of mutterings off stage. Ethnic unrest in several of the minor Soviet Republics, and industrial unrest in Poland, were accepted as part of the teething troubles of change, and soon forgotten in the wave of international sympathy following the Armenian earthquake, and the enthusiasm with which the world watched the formation of the new Soviet parliament and its very public debating.

The world may have been taken in, but not Malcolm Green and his ilk. They had been brought up in the years of the Cold War and trained in the profession of suspicion. While the rest of the world marveled at the new Soviet openness, free elections in Poland, and speculation about the possible demolition of the Berlin Wall, Green, and so many others like him, continued to poke into dark recesses, peering behind curtains and lifting the corner of carpets to see what had been pushed out of sight.

Chapter 4

JUST AFTER SEVEN THIRTY the next morning Green reached his office and was surprised to find the staffer already there. As Green was hanging up his coat, the staffer put a copy of the previous day's meeting notes on the desk and said he was going to the registry to collect the files Green had requested.

Green had woken refreshed; his dark mood considerably lighter than it had been yesterday. Finding the staffer already in the office set him in an even better mood, but this took a jolt when he looked at the notes and found they were typed. He had wanted them kept within the team since necessarily everyone else in the section was under the shadow of suspicion. Too late now. He started to read the notes and again his mood improved. This staffer took good notes; missed none of the detail. Green was impressed.

The young man came back with a bundle of files under one arm and a cup of coffee in the other hand. Green looked up as he put them on the desk.

"Ah, coffee. Thanks."

The staffer simply nodded and turned to leave but Green called him back.

"Er… I thought you were going to distribute the notes hand written. These are typed." Green waved the paper as he spoke.

"Yes sir, but you and the other gentlemen don't read shorthand," the staffer replied, "so, well…" He dried up as he saw the look of amusement on his boss's face.

Green could not contain his laughter for long.

"I wondered how you caught so much detail, but I didn't want any of the typists to read this. Which one did it?" His smile died.

"I did it myself on the machine next door, sir. Last night before I went home. Then I locked the disk in the safe and printed it this morning just before you came in. I did not want to leave sensitive material lying around."

The smile returned to Green's face.

"Smart thinking. So you found out that I like my coffee black, no sugar, in a real cup; you write shorthand and use a word processor proficiently. Anything else that I should know about?"

"Well, sir, I decided that I won't order files from the registry. Better to call for them myself when they are needed. It stops anything going astray."

"Do you think it might?" Green asked.

"I don't know, sir, but if it should turn out that there is something to hide someone might try to do just that if they have warning which way our enquiries are heading. If there's nothing then no harm will have been done."

"Good thinking. Any more?"

"Yes sir. I have requested, in your name, the exclusive use of the adjacent three offices for the rest of the team. I thought it might focus things and make our work more efficient."

Still smiling, Green leaned back and ran his fingers through his hair.

"Just go right ahead," Green said. "You seem to have things very much under control, so I'll leave all that sort of thing in your capable hands. Now, nobody ever got round to introducing us properly and it has been kinda busy, so what's your name?"

"Ashkhenarahov, sir." The staffer watched carefully for Green's reaction.

"Sit down." Green waved him to a chair. "Russian?"

"A long way back, sir. My paternal grandfather."

"First names?"

"Mikhail Tan, sir."

Green nodded. "So what do your friends call you?"

"The family calls me Misha. Most of my friends call me Mike, sir."

"Mike, then. Now give me a short bio sketch," Green said. "And please stop calling me sir all the time. My friends call me Malcolm. You just joined that exclusive group. Now go ahead Mike."

"Yes sir. I mean Malcolm." Mike smiled at his slip. Green ignored it and drank his coffee.

Mike's grandfather was born on Sakhalin Island, the son of a shipwright, and followed his father into the trade. He joined a whaling fleet in his teens and, after a couple of years, jumped ship in San Diego, married a Japanese immigrant and settled down to raise ten daughters and a son. The son had an aptitude for things mechanical and got a job on the railways, moving around the country and eventually settling in San Francisco. He had married late in life and a year later his wife died in childbirth. He married again two years later, a woman who was twenty years his junior and of mixed Japanese and Canadian origin. She produced a son in each of the first four years of the marriage, to the delight of her husband who doted on the boys.

Green had been wondering about the slightly Asiatic cast to Mike's features. This explained it. There must be many like him on the west coast.

Mike's father had had very little formal education although he was a first class engineer. He made toys for his sons and spent long hours in the basement teaching them how to make things for themselves, talking all the time about places that he had visited and about his father's home. Mike's mother had also spent plenty of time with the children and they all grew up fluent in both the Japanese and Russian languages as well as English. Their father had made enough money to ensure that they all received a good education and helped all four through college.

The eldest son took over the family workshop and was joined two years later by the second son who had a talent for electronics. The third son developed a passion for flying and joined the Marine Corps. He was now a helicopter pilot on a carrier.

Mike showed a flair for languages at college and also a remarkable organizational ability. One of his tutors had been with the CIA before he turned to teaching, and brought Mike's potential to the attention of a former colleague who was still in harness. He passed the word along and the Company set about the cat and mouse game of recruitment. They paid for Mike to have further language training, adding Cantonese and Mandarin Chinese to his repertoire and took him into their own training system to learn the intelligence trade.

His ability to plan and organize kept Mike desk bound for several years, but recently he had carried out a series of short field assignments. His superiors had soon noted the economy and quality of his work and the future looked promising. Mike enjoyed the work and took pride in doing things well. Two years ago he thought that he had put a blight on his career after his appendix blew up. The Company took him into one of their own clinics and made repairs, then suggested that he combine convalescence with his annual leave which was due two weeks later. Mike agreed and headed for Europe.

After two weeks loitering around continental Europe he crossed the channel to Dover, more for the thrill of riding the hovercraft than because anything particular drew him. He found a small hotel and then walked around the town that evening. In a pub, situated in a quiet side street just off the town center, he was accosted by a loquacious Welshman whose lyrical description of his homeland's beauties both amused and attracted Mike.

The next day he rented a car and set out to tour. Mike fell in love with the Brecon Beacons the moment he set eyes on them, and decided to spend some time walking in the hills. Mountains, the drunken Welshman in Dover had called them. He had seen bigger, but none more beautiful. They made him want to sing. It was whilst doing just that, sitting in the sun admiring the view from the top of Fan Fawr, that Cupid loosed his second arrow.

The view reminded him of family walks in the hills to the north of San Francisco, when he was a small boy. His father had told the boys stories and the whole family had sung Russian folk songs. Remembering that time, Mike began to sing one of the songs learned all those years before, then stopped suddenly when a second voice joined in the chorus. It was a warm, light, female voice in perfect harmony with his. Turning round, half afraid he was dreaming, he found a dark haired girl with brilliant blue eyes standing close behind him.

"Are you real?" he asked, almost to himself. Since he had been thinking and singing in Russian his words came out in that tongue.

"Da!" said the girl with a bright smile as she moved towards him.

"Come and sit down, you must be tired after that climb."

She sat down beside him, arms around her knees, and they introduced themselves.

The girl had just completed a language degree and was supporting herself for the summer by singing in pubs. She had come out for the day to climb some of the mountains that she had never climbed, despite being surrounded by them throughout her childhood. They sat there in the sun all afternoon talking, until she realized that she was going to be late at the pub where she was to sing that evening.

They raced each other down the hill and Mike drove her to the pub, stayed to listen, and even sang a couple of Russian folksongs with her. Two weeks later Siobhan accompanied him back to the States.

The girl was on the dumpy side compared to Mike's mother, but about the same height. The two women became instant friends when his mother failed miserably in her attempts to pronounce Siobhan's name and announced that she would call her Chevvy. Mike said it fitted, since she was built for comfort, and the whole family killed themselves laughing. The name stuck.

THE COMPANY WERE decidedly cool when Mike announced his impending marriage and asked if he had told Chevvy anything about his work. He said he had told her he was an interpreter for the government. They quizzed him for two days and were then silent for a week. Then Mike's boss called him in and told him to go home and bring Chevvy to the office. Chevvy didn't ask why, she just came and smiled demurely at Mike's boss when they were introduced.

"Go ahead Mike, tell her what you really do for a living," he said, to Mike's surprise.

"I am an agent with the Central Intelligence Agency. That means that sometimes I'm a spy, a trade official, a courier, all sorts of unsavory things, Most of all I'm a servant of Uncle Sam."

"So?" Chevvy looked Mike's boss right in the eye. "Is that supposed to make a difference to us?"

The boss spluttered and turned red.

"Young lady, you have to appreciate that the job can often be very dangerous. With some of the things that Mike may be asked to do he could easily get himself hurt or killed. He will have to go away for indefinite periods without notice, and you'll never know exactly what he is doing, where, or for how long. A lot of wives can't handle that sort of life."

"So? You can get killed crossing the road, but you still have to do it." Chevvy said defiantly. "Mike loves what he does, and I expect he does it very well. It's not for me to tell him what work to do, and if it makes him happy then that's good for us both. My Da was a miner. We all knew it was dangerous, but he loved it and because he was happy we had a happy home. When the mine collapsed we grieved, but that's what it's all about. I accept that to make my life here with Mike I have to support what he does, and I don't intend to keep looking under stones just in case there is something nasty hiding there. With all your investigations you don't seem to have found out very much about me, do you? Perhaps you should have let Mike do it for you. You can't seriously expect me to run home in tears. I'm staying, and that's that!" Her voice was light and even, but the challenge was clear.

The boss was stunned, but recovered after a moment.

"Dammit Chevvy, you're a hell of a woman!" He roared with laughter and hugged her. "You better marry her quick, Mike. If I'm invited I'll come and dance at your wedding. Now get out of here, both of you."

Two weeks later the boss danced at their wedding. The following week he sent Mike off on a four week trade mission to Tashkent, Omsk and Leningrad.

"Chevvy's now eight months pregnant." Mike ended his account.

"Your first?" Green asked with interest.

"Yep," said Mike with evident pride.

"Great. Why don't you both come over to supper tomorrow and Betty can tell Chevvy all the horrors of raising kids. I'm asking the rest of the team, but it's strictly social and informal. Come about eight."

"Thanks. We'll be there," Mike nodded. "Now the rest of the team will be in and I must pass these notes round and phone the Hill to see who has been put on the committee."

As Mike got up to leave Green stood and shook his hand.

"Welcome to the team Mike. You're doing a fine job. Helluva lot better'n that jerk I sent home."

"Who was he?" Mike asked.

"Some idiot by the name of Connor Morton Swingate," Green said with distaste.

"Sort of thin, rat faced, with his shoes always coming untied?" Mike asked.

"Yes. Know him?

"Er. Not really. Seen him around," Mike said, his thoughts a long way off. He left and Green wondered why Mike had looked vague when he had told him about the jerk. Have to ask him, he thought, and opened the first file.

Chapter 5

WHEN MAO TSE TUNG unleashed the Cultural Revolution and sent his Red Guards to sweep through China the rest of the world looked on in horror. They watched, mute and impotent, as if transfixed like a frightened rabbit under the glassy stare of a hungry snake. The West was fearful the unrest would spill over and further destabilize the rest of South East Asia, already over populated, economically destitute, and ravaged by wars.

Mao, however, was not interested in the outside world. He had seen the seeds of decadence germinated by outside influence and growing rampant like weeds in the fertile fields of Chinese society. Traditional moral values had been eroded, nepotism and corruption were rife, and the feudal system that had been displaced in 1948 was threatening to reassert itself. Communism was under threat, so Mao took action to secure its dominance.

The action was swift, bloody, and all encompassing. Atrocities were brushed aside in the name of the revolution and the terror instilled by marauding bands of Red Guards soon ensured compliance with the new order. Office workers and functionaries were forced to serve time in the fields or factories. Intellectuals and dissenters were either summarily killed or forcibly re-educated, many ending up exiled in disgrace to isolated provinces and obliged to work as laborers.

It would be wrong to see the whole period as just destructive, although the destruction left no aspect of Chinese life untouched. After the initial wave of turmoil, Mao pulled in the reins on his Red Guards. The commune system was reorganized so that even the lowliest peasants had some voice in their own destiny, provided it fitted with the new ideology. The barefoot doctor system brought basic health care to regions previously untouched. Wages and prices were controlled to create economic stability. Equality was imposed on the population, although the select few remained significantly more equal than the masses. China closed her frontiers and took a long step back from the rest of the world. For years the bamboo curtain hid the world's largest nation and the rest of the world turned its interest to new pastures.

CHONG TSE DO WAS a child when the Cultural Revolution began. His father had been an administrator in the port of Shanghai and was killed in the first wave of the purges. The rest of the family was split up and young Chong was sent to a farming commune fifty miles away. He had grown up with the waterfront as his playground. Amid the international hurly-burly of the port, Chong had come under many diverse influences and had developed a passion for jazz that he heard blaring out from the waterfront bars, eating houses and brothels. He hung around the musicians and begged his father for music lessons. One night his father came home with a saxophone, acquired from a drunken foreign sailor who could not pay his fine when he was arrested. Chong was ecstatic, and not the least put off by the fact that his hands were still too small to handle the instrument properly. His enthusiasm was infectious and he soon found players in the bars who were willing to teach him.

A Jesuit priest who ran a mission near the port agreed to teach him to read music if Chong's father would allow him to attend the mission school. Chong's father was not a Christian and at first he hesitated, but eventually gave way to his son's pestering and the boy went to school for four hours every morning and had music lessons in the afternoon.

Chong proved to be a remarkable pupil. A year later his father received a visit from the priest begging to be allowed to send the boy to the Jesuit school in Macao where there were many teachers who would help him develop his academic potential. The old man had been impressed by his son's progress at the school and wanted him to have the best possible education. He was, however, enough of a traditionalist to be wary of the influence the Christian priest might exert, and he hesitated again. The priest was willing to be patient and said he would come back in two weeks.

Two days later the Red Guards stormed into Shanghai. Chong's father died a shameful death in the first few hours. The mission was burned down and the priest was expelled. Chong was now twelve and considered responsible for his own actions. His saxophone was held up as a symbol of western imperial decadence, and he was then forced to smash it in public before being severely beaten and shipped off to the countryside to mend his ways through honest toil.

Along with the rest of the community he was forced to attend cultural re-education sessions and chant the Party slogans. Chong bitterly resented what had happened and at first he resisted. The punishment was swift and savage but he soon developed protective camouflage by pretending to join in willingly.

Eventually, as order was established out of the chaos, Chong was again sent to school. The groundwork done by the Jesuit priest had been good and made him stand above his peers. There were several occasions when this proved uncomfortable as some of the priest's concepts were contrary to the new ideology, but it did not take Chong long to sort this out in his mind. He was sent to a town where there were bigger schools and the Party officials could keep a better eye on him. Chong often wanted to rebel but realized that he would lose the opportunity for more education, so he curbed his impulses, worked hard at his lessons and waited.

At about the time Chong was coming to the end of his school days, it had become apparent to those in authority that China needed educated people to develop the country's industrial base. Those with potential were given further education and training and Chong was sent to a university to study science. He showed promise in biology and chemistry and was steered in this direction. After graduation he was sent to a research establishment north of Beijing where his ability flowered.

WITH THE EASING OF restrictions in the aftermath of Mao's death, small luxuries began to appear. Chong managed to obtain a radio on which he would listen to western music programs, particularly those playing jazz. As well as being able secretly to indulge his passion in this way, he also began to learn English from the radio.

From foreign broadcasts he learned that much of the research on which he was working had already been done by others and he began to pester the authorities for access to western scientific papers. At first they viewed his requests with suspicion, and refused, but eventually a few arrived. Chong devoured them and then wrote to their authors asking for more information. His letters were all intercepted and he faced an inquisition from the Party about why he was writing to Western Imperialists. Chong showed them the papers they had previously permitted him and showed that he could more usefully be engaged in doing original work rather than simply repeating what had already been well researched by others who were more than willing to share their results.

The flow of material soon increased and Chong was permitted to write to scientists in other countries with only a few overt restrictions. He was aware that all his letters were censored and that some were never forwarded. This annoyed him but there was little he could do about it. From time to time he would complain but this was simply met with denials and he was told that dissent would not be tolerated. After each such protest he found petty restrictions being imposed. On one occasion he found his radio mysteriously stopped working. On examination he found one of the transistors had been crushed and spares had suddenly become unavailable.

Chong decided he would play his faceless masters at their own game. He could not just stop his periodic protests for they would become suspicious and investigate more closely. From now on he would tailor his protests and time them carefully whilst exercising his freedom through a variety of subtle activities. The first thing he needed was direct contact with foreigners.

FOLLOWING MAO'S DEATH and the purging of the Gang of Four, the new leadership in China made tentative advances towards the outside world. In particular they approached the West to replace much of the technical base that had been wiped out in the pogroms. Chong was never told that his continual protests had contributed to this awakening, but he gradually became aware that more information was becoming available.

From time to time a piece of western made equipment would arrive at the research center without either warning or explanation. Where these items came from nobody knew, and none save Chong ever dared ask. He heard that a delegation of foreign businessmen had made a visit to China and that others were going to come. There was even a rumor that an international trade fair was to be hosted in Beijing or Shanghai. The news thrilled him. This was the access to outside ideas for which he had been yearning.

Providence smiled on Chong and his secret campaign. Less than three weeks after he had made his decision, he heard that two foreign English teachers had arrived to work in the local school. They were a young American and his wife. Chong was about to rush off and visit them when he thought about the likely reprisals that such an action would cause. He stifled his frustration and made a formal application to be allowed to attend their classes.

There was an enquiry into why he wanted to learn English and he was accused of subversive activities. His radio vanished from his quarters. He pondered long over whether or not to report it and eventually decided not to in case its possession was seen as further evidence of counter revolutionary revisionism and made things worse. Chong explained that he needed to be able to read English at an advanced level since most of the scientific papers were in that language. The next day an interpreter arrived at the center. Chong's hopes slumped until he met the woman and realized that she actually spoke less

English than he had learned from the radio. Luckily one of the other scientists at the research center complained about the interpreter and she vanished as suddenly as she had arrived. Two days later Chong received permission to attend the English classes. His radio reappeared.

The classes for people from outside the school were held each evening with the teachers alternating. Only approved students could attend and an official scrutinizer was present at all times to ensure that nothing subversive was said. Chong soon noticed that there were six different observers, who took the duty on a rota. Two were very attentive but the other four sat through the two hour classes looking bored. He wondered how many of the watchers spoke English, and if so how well.

The next evening when one of the bored looking watchers was on duty Chong contrived to walk a short distance with him when the class broke up. He asked the man what he thought of the classes. The watcher said they were boring and that English was a disgusting sounding language. He could not understand why anyone would want to learn it. Chong said something in English and the man looked blank. Over the next few weeks he tried the same thing on the other watchers. His guess was right, only two of them spoke any English.

Occasionally the teachers collected their students' notebooks and corrected their work. Chong thought about writing something in his notebook that would invite further contact with the teachers. He had almost resolved to do so when fate saved him from a calamitous mistake. It came in the form of one of the English speaking watchdogs who arrived at Chong's laboratory one morning with the notebook he had handed in the previous evening. He told Chong that his spelling was poor and his writing was worse. He should make more effort or he would not be permitted to continue attending the classes. Chong dropped the idea of a written invitation.

For a month he made no move and then fate intervened again. The local political committee, in their wisdom, decided that the foreign teachers should themselves be educated and taught to appreciate the ideology and practical benefits of the Cultural Revolution. A series of visits to farming communes, factories, local markets and other places was arranged. One of these visits brought the couple to Chong's research center and, because he was the only scientist with any proficiency in English, he was instructed to be their guide for the day. In the evening they were entertained in the mess hall. The duty watchdog that day was one of the four who spoke no English.

CHONG'S ENGLISH WAS much better than he had allowed anyone to understand. He had put the long night hours of listening to the radio to good use and had managed to obtain a good dictionary with official approval. He used the opportunity afforded by the teachers' visit and their response, if guarded, was entirely positive. They explained that their activities were carefully watched but they would receive visits from the American Consul at three monthly intervals. When he came again they would try to do something for Chong.

They must have done something immediately because within a week the Consul arrived and insisted on sitting in on the classes and meeting some of the students. The watcher that evening was one of the four bored ones. At the end of the class the teacher introduced each of his students. Like many Americans the Consul insisted on shaking hands with everyone. He told Chong he was delighted that the United States was able to offer its help and managed to palm a note whilst shaking his hand.

When the teachers returned home at the end of their year they were replaced by a CIA man who spoke fluent Chinese and could teach a lot more than English. He made himself well liked by the local Revolutionary Committee but at one stage alarmed them by conducting open debates with his students in which he encouraged them to disagree and argue before carefully steering them back towards the approved view. Chong immediately saw the potential of this technique and set about mastering it. The teacher calmed the committee's fears with revolutionary platitudes and continued sowing the seeds of free speech right under their noses.

The standard of English in his class improved dramatically and the committee approved. Under the guise of helping Chong and making the lessons relevant to his working needs, the teacher brought in a steady stream of scientific papers. Chong received them with open arms and the committee thought the man must be naive to pass over so much valuable material so freely. They completely failed to notice that Chong slipped copies of his own work into the notebook every time he handed it in for marking. Chong realized that the papers he received were old and not very advanced, but they brought him new ideas and it was the exchange that he relished most. He had the sense not to hand over all his best work, but wished that he was free to do so.

Trouble came when a paper written by Chong was published in the West. It had been passed through channels to a group of western academics for evaluation. Whilst the work was not new, some of the ideas were. The professors felt that the paper was worthy of publication and without thinking of the possible consequences to Chong, they submitted it under his name and affiliation to one of the most prestigious scientific journals. It was accepted and a copy was sent to Chong along the channel through which his original had been received.

When his teacher handed the published copy to Chong he was apologetic. He had never thought that anyone would publish any of Chong's material, and immediately understood the risks. Chong was not in the least put out. He was delighted. This was tangible proof of the exchange of ideas that he loved so dearly.

"Today is the best day of my life," Chong told his teacher proudly.

"But won't the authorities be upset?" the teacher asked.

"Yes, I expect they not like but someone have to stand up tell them they wrong sometimes. I just telled them," Chong replied with delight.

"You realize that they will expel me?" the teacher asked.

"They not that smart. I tell them I send paper myself." Chong was not going to let anything spoil his moment of glory.

"But you said they censor all your mail."

"This just show they make mistake sometime!" Chong said, dissolving into a fit of laughter.

The teacher shook his head in amazement. This was a facet of Chong that he had not expected.

It took two more weeks for the news to reach the authorities. The Director of Chong's research center was at once pleased that one of his staff had achieved world recognition and alarmed that he had known nothing about it. He would certainly have to answer for his failure. He was right; they shipped him off in disgrace to a farming commune in Singkiang.

Chong was brought before the local Revolutionary Committee to answer charges of subversive activity. They passed him on to Beijing, where bigger men began to investigate his activities. The whole catalogue of Chong's misdemeanors was brought out and he was branded as a reactionary dissident. They made him broadcast a public apology for his actions. He was kept in prison for three months while the investigations continued. After a summary tribunal he was sentenced to three months hard labor on a building gang, and then sent back to the research center.

He found his radio had disappeared again. All his papers had been rifled and thoroughly searched but none were missing. A watchdog was assigned to monitor his every move. The watchdog turned out to be an attractive girl, full of revolutionary zeal, well educated, and fluent in English. Chong was locked in his room at night and protested that he could not even go out to relieve himself when he needed to. He was told to knock until the watchdog let him out. Chong objected and was told that if he could not behave himself he would have to put up with the inconvenience. He was not going to give in that easily and started knocking to be let out every twenty minutes during the night. After four days he was moved to a larger room with an adjoining bathroom and a second bed was installed for the watchdog. Chong still felt that this was unacceptable and set about seducing the girl.

To his surprise this proved remarkably easy. The girl found his quick mind fascinating and when he discovered that she had had some scientific education the two spent many happy hours in technical discussion. Soon she was not just watching Chong at his work, she was helping him. With this she began to appreciate his desire to talk freely and share ideas. She turned a blind eye to his passing papers to the teacher provided he wrote 'not for publication' across the top. She even persuaded Chong to control his periodic outbursts. She began to share his bed, and life settled down again.

CHONG FOUND ANOTHER discreet ally in the new research director who built contacts with other centers in China and actively sought funds for new work. If he was aware of Chong's new domestic arrangements and the contribution his watchdog was making to the work he said nothing.

Chong was fascinated when the central government permitted students and others to hang posters and public notices on a wall in the capital. He believed passionately in the right of everyone to think and speak out when they had complaints. The name 'Democracy Wall' appealed to him and he wished that he could go and see it. Things were definitely improving, but the country was still in the grip of suspicion and fear. One could be denounced at any moment for counter revolutionary activity, often by relatives or colleagues seeking to divert suspicion from themselves. Even so this new liberty was a dramatic change.

At first the posters hung on the wall were tame and bland, but within a few weeks more critical comments began to appear. There was open and harsh criticism of the authorities, with pictures of the wall shown on national television. Then, after three months, the wall was cleared of its posters and a number of people were arrested for subversion. The privilege was withdrawn and the democratic voice was silenced.

Chong had been thrilled by the experiment and was saddened by its termination, but by Chinese standards the clamp down had been gentle, and talk continued in squares and market places across the country under the watchful eyes of the police. Provided things did not get out of hand and the crowds remained small they just watched, listened and, no doubt, reported back to the old men.

In minor ways restrictions had begun to be eased all over the country. Chong was permitted to attend meetings of scientists from other research centers, and he continued to receive some information from abroad.

When the American teacher left he took a lot of material from Chong with him. He was replaced by a Chinese teacher from the south and Chong wondered how he would maintain his contact with the outside world. It had been almost too easy before. He began to feel isolated and frustrated.

A group of European scientists were invited to the next scientific congress that Chong attended. He saw this as an opportunity to vent his feelings. After years of patient work Chong had risen to prominence in his field and, apart from his periodic outspokenness, he was considered to be one of the top biochemists in China. He was to deliver a paper on his current research into the artificial synthesis of endorphins. For weeks before the congress Chong spent long hours preparing his paper, including all his latest results and ideas. He was helped in this by his watchdog assistant, who had now become a valued colleague. The Director and the local Revolutionary Committee had officially approved her participation in Chong's work, thinking that it would enable her to keep a closer watch on his activities and save the cost of another scientific assistant. Little did they realize that San Kiu had been completely converted to Chong's way of thinking.

At the congress, Chong was given a prominent position, and placed at the top of the list of major speakers. To everyone's surprise he delivered his paper in English and stated at the outset that it contained the results of his latest work. The European delegates sat up and paid careful attention. They soon realized this work was far ahead of anything being done in the West and were astonished that Chong should make such a complete disclosure of his ideas, methods and results.

They were delighted when he sent San Kiu round the auditorium to distribute copies of the paper. Most of the other Chinese delegates spoke no English and were outraged that Chong did not deliver his paper in his own language. There were interpreters present to translate for the foreign delegates and to censor any material they considered ought to be withheld. Chong had effectively made them redundant, but gave them copies of his paper in Chinese so that they could read it over the headphones as he was speaking, for those who only spoke Chinese.

When he came to the end of his prepared speech, Chong launched into another of his rebellious outbursts. He loudly condemned the secretive system that prevented the free flow of information. He demanded the freedom to share ideas in open debate and severely criticized the country's policy makers, claiming that they were distorting the ideals of true communism, preventing equality and progress by the suppression of free speech and the sharing of ideas. He said that the leadership were stifling China's growth as a modern nation, and called for major changes.

The audience rose in uproar as Chong resumed his seat. The foreign delegates were cheering loudly. Some of the Chinese scientists, fearful for their own positions, cheered less loudly, but with inward enthusiasm. The organizing officials and Party observers were outraged at such blatant sedition by one of the country's top researchers.

As officials tried to clear the auditorium, one of the foreigners managed to get close to Chong and asked if he was going to publish the paper in the international journals. Chong explained that he had access problems and would probably be in trouble for what he had said today, but if the German delegate would submit a copy for him he would be grateful. The man instantly agreed and thanked Chong for such an exciting session. By then the officials had moved in and hustled their rebellious speaker outside to a waiting car. He was rushed back to his own institute and told to stay in his quarters. A guard was put on the door to prevent him leaving. San Kiu was ushered in an hour later looking worried.

San Kiu expected instant reprisals, but Chong had timed his outburst well. The Royal Visit was in progress and their research center was to receive a visit from the Queen in two days time. It would be hard to explain why the top scientist had suddenly become unavailable. There had been many foreign journalists at the congress who would surely report what had happened and tie it in to the fact that the man at the center of the controversy was to meet the Queen during her visit.

THE CHINESE GOVERNMENT were working hard to make the tour an international showpiece, and any overt repression at this time could result in a major embarrassment. Action would be taken, Chong felt sure, but not until after the visit was over. San Kiu was not so optimistic. Her doubts were reinforced later when the guard brought their food. He told them the center's director had been removed and sent to the provinces.

The Chinese authorities were also capable of subtlety as subsequent events were to prove. A television was delivered to Chong's quarters that evening and he was told to watch the news bulletin. The first half hour was coverage of the Royal Tour, but the next item had him and San Kiu on the edge of their seats. He had not been aware of any cameras in the congress hall, but there on the screen was Chong delivering his impassioned speech before the eyes of the world. He was speechless.

The report went on to show views of the center where Chong worked and to praise the work that was done there. The advanced state of Chinese research was loudly proclaimed and the people were proud that their foremost scientist would be presented to their distinguished visitor in two days time. Chong's outspoken plea for a free exchange of views and ideas was held up as a symbol of the new liberalism that was reaching all sectors of Chinese society, and it was announced that the Government was inviting visits to their technical institutions from prominent international specialists. The voice of democracy in the world's largest nation was being heard across the world.

THE GOVERNMENT'S REACTION disconcerted Chong and he wondered what hidden retribution was in store. His puzzlement increased the following day when an official arrived from the Ministry of Technology and informed Chong that he had been appointed Director of the center. He was also told that his actions had been shameful and that he should not have spoken without approval. Since San Kiu had proved so unreliable she was to be replaced and sent elsewhere to mend her ways.

Chong protested that she was too valuable a worker for the center to lose, but the official insisted. Chong said in that case they had better send him away as well since he had taken San Kiu as his wife. He refused to let her be removed from the center without him. The official was confused by this. San Kiu, to whom it was an equal surprise, was impassive but confirmed, when challenged, that she was now Chong's wife.

The man stood glaring at the two rebellious scientists for a long time before he shrugged and, with great reluctance, eventually agreed to rescind the order. But, he informed them, every action would be very closely monitored in future. They must give up this senseless behavior or expect severe penalties. A team of three new watchdogs arrived later that afternoon.

CHONG WAS AMAZED at the incompetence of bureaucracy, for he soon discovered that only one of the three new watchdogs understood English. All three were very attentive and stayed close to Chong. Since San Kiu was never far away they were able to keep her under surveillance equally well. As soon as Chong found the weakness he set about exploiting it. Whenever the English speaker was not on duty he spoke to San Kiu only in English.

The watchdogs demanded to know what they were talking about and told them to speak Chinese. Chong explained that English was the language of science. They were talking about technical matters for which there were no words in Chinese. The watchdogs had no option but to accept this, though they were clearly unhappy. San Kiu expected reprisals, but Chong was confident. As insurance he spoke English all the time whenever the conversation had anything to do with work. At night, when they were alone in their quarters, Chong and San Kiu laughed about the guards' stupidity.

SIX WEEKS AFTER the convention there had still been no comebacks. Chong began to wonder why not. China was still in the spotlight of world interest and the authorities were again making tentative experiments with democracy. He decided to conduct an experiment of his own.

Several of the research staff under his charge now spoke reasonably good English, and most had a basic understanding, having attended the evening classes run by the American teachers. Chong decided to hold weekly seminars at which one of the staff would present a short paper followed by a group discussion. The watchdogs were immediately suspicious and wanted to know why he was doing this. He told them that it was to increase awareness among his staff about each other's work and to make the researchers think more clearly about what they were doing. His explanation was accepted, but the English speaking guard made sure that he was always in attendance.

To start with, Chong kept the discussion sessions to the straight and narrow. He made sure that the subject matter was technical, very complex and non-controversial. As a result the guard understood very little and soon became bored. Some weeks after the seminars started, the watchdog mysteriously got food poisoning and was taken to hospital. That week one of the others took his place, and Chong seized the opportunity to introduce some controversy into the discussion.

He had learned well from the CIA man and had become quite adept at managing and steering the conversation. Gradually he allowed more and more contentious issues into the talk and built the trust of his staff. They in turn became more willing to express their views and some of the seminars became quite lively debates that reached well beyond the confines of science. Everyone enjoyed them and welcomed the chance to talk openly.

DISCOVERY OF CHONG'S heresy did not come for almost eight months. It happened one day when a member of the local Revolutionary Committee called unannounced at the center, hoping to enlist the help of one of the electronics specialists to fix his television set. He asked someone in the workshop and was told that the man most likely to be able to help was at the seminar. Knowing nothing about these seminars, the official demanded to be taken there at once.

His arrival was not noticed at first, and he stood at the back of the room listening. Because the discussion was in English he understood nothing that was being said, but Chong's tone and the attentive look on the faces of the audience told him that this was irregular. The official strode to the front of the room and challenged Chong. He demanded to know what they were all talking about. Chong told him. The committee man's face went purple with rage. He demanded that the meeting be ended and Chong accompany him to his office to account for the affair.

At the door Chong found the workshop helper who had brought the committee man along, and asked him what he wanted.

"The committee member was looking for help to repair his television," the man explained. "The technicians were all at your meeting, so he asked to be brought here." The helper looked uncomfortable.

It was Chong's turn to be angry. He turned on the petty official.

"You come here to abuse a government institution for the benefit of your personal luxuries and have the effrontery to challenge me for taking the views of my staff? You and your kind are the ones who are evil, decadent and corrupt! Get out, and do not come back!" With that he grabbed the man by the ear and dragged him to the door. He pushed the man out with such force that he stumbled and fell.

Chong turned back to the workshop helper and asked about the television in question.

"It is in the workshop, honorable Director," the man shuffled nervously as he answered.

"Please go and bring it here," Chong said, and the man ran off down the corridor.

The ejected committee man was back on his feet, standing outside the door yelling imprecations at Chong when the workshop assistant returned. Chong took the television, opened the door and hurled the set to the ground at its owner's feet. It landed with a satisfying crash. Chong quietly closed the door and turned back to the frightened assistant.

"You were not at fault in this. Go back to your work and forget the matter," he said gently.

The assistant looked relieved, bowed quickly and hurried away.

Half an hour later Chong was sitting in his office attending to the daily pile of administrative records when the police came to arrest him.

"Arrest me? What for?" he demanded.

"The People's Revolutionary Committee Member has accused you of conducting illegal discussions and spreading counter revolutionary doctrine," the policeman said stiffly.

"This is a research institute," Chong answered frostily, "where every week we discuss our work as a group in order to improve its quality. We do this work on the instructions of the government for the benefit of the People and the Revolution. The reason that our work is so good is that we have good staff, who work together by discussing the work with their colleagues. You see that out there?" He pointed to where the wreckage of the television still lay on the path. "That flea ridden creature came here to abuse the facilities of this center and the skills of a respected government technician to repair his personal luxury. Do you consider that to be correct behavior? I do not, so I threw him out. He and his kind are continually doing such things. How can they dare to make accusations?"

"But he said that …"

"But nothing," Chong interrupted him. "He and his gang are all corrupt. They are morally degenerate; leeches feeding on the blood of the people. They are only interested in flexing the muscles of their own self importance. It is time that they did some real work instead of continually interfering with other people's honest efforts. If you want to arrest someone then go and lock up those pariahs on the People's Revolutionary Committee and make your enquiries into their activities. I will have that evidence put into a box for you," he pointed out of the window, "and you can take it with you."

Chong rose and moved towards the door to show the policeman out. The officer looked doubtful, but after a few moments shook his head and followed Chong out of the office.

THE WALLS OF THE OFFICES were thin and it did not take long for news of this interview to spread through the research center. Many of the staff lived off site and by late that evening the news was all over the town. By midnight those with grievances against members of the Revolutionary Committee and many onlookers had gathered in the square. Soon posters were produced denouncing the whole Committee and demanding their arrest. A chant began and was soon taken up by every voice.

The demonstration was orderly and the police made no move to disperse the crowd. They were, in any case, vastly outnumbered. The crowd took this as implicit evidence that their protest was just.

One of the Committee came out to address the crowd and tell them to disperse. His words, despite being amplified by a bullhorn, were completely drowned by the boos and jeering of the crowd. The demonstration continued all night and into the following morning. Factories were at a standstill because all their workers were in the square.

At ten thirty a convoy of police vehicles drove into the square and pulled up outside the offices of the People's Revolutionary Committee. A company of police disembarked and formed a line between the expectant crowd and the office building. Everyone waited.

A squad of police went into the building. They came out some time later with the whole Committee in handcuffs and loaded them into a bus. The crowd went wild with delight, hugging one another and cheering. The line of police re-embarked and the convoy departed.

The next day Chong was summoned to the Ministry of Technology in Beijing. He was faced with an investigating board who grilled him for seven hours about his part in the affair. At the end he was reprimanded and warned that if there should be any more incidents of this sort he would suffer the severest punishment. The three watchdogs were removed from the research center and replaced with nine new ones who all spoke good English.

Chong was by now firmly branded at least as a dissident, if not actually a counter revolutionary. Had it not been that he was the country's leading research scientist, continuously producing significant advances in his field, he might have been removed altogether and sent away for re-education. Moves were then made to remove several of his staff because they had taken part in the discussion groups. The fact that nobody from the research center had taken part in the demonstrations leading to the arrest of the People's Revolutionary Committee, and that they were all engaged in urgent development work on projects important to the central government, enabled Chong to forestall this. The situation, however, remained less easy than it had been for some time, and the level of watching increased to the point of interference.

BEFORE THE NEXT CONGRESS Chong and some of his colleagues were due to attend, they were obliged to submit their material several days beforehand so that it could be vetted. When the time came, Chong was escorted to the hall, his papers in the charge of a watchdog. This man led Chong onto the podium, placed his notes on the lectern before him and then took a seat a few feet behind the speaker.

When he saw the notes, Chong was furious at what had been done to his paper. He loudly declared to the assembled scientists that his work had been emasculated by petty bureaucrats with no understanding of either science or the needs of the nation. He refused to present the paper at all and strode angrily from the platform followed by an alarmed watchdog.

The audience rose as one, shouting. Some cried shame and demanded that Chong deliver the paper. The majority yelled their enthusiastic support for his defiance, tearing their agenda papers in half and throwing them in the air in protest.

The auditorium was cleared and only those who had opposed Chong's action were allowed to return. Of the seventeen papers due to have been given, only three were eventually delivered, and these to an audience of only eleven out of an original one hundred and ninety eight delegates. Only four of the eleven were scientists, the others were all government officials.

Back at the center, Chong was again confined to his quarters. His radio disappeared again, but curiously the television was still there. He did not turn it on, but simply went to bed and slept. Next morning a new Director was appointed. He sent for Chong and the others who had attended the congress and delivered a stern lecture before sending them all back to work. The whole affair was then quietly swept out of sight.

THE GENERAL POPULATION knew nothing of these and similar events. Some experiments into new forms of democracy were still being tried, but most were comparatively short lived. It appeared that at least some measure of reform was still present in the minds of the old men in Beijing. Their problem was to find reforms that would satisfy the groundswell of popular desire whilst maintaining, in essence, the status quo.

News coming into the country about reforms in the den of the Soviet bear kept hope alive that change would one day come in China. This hope was given a boost when it was announced that the Soviet President would make an official visit to China.

For more than thirty years the two great powers had maintained a grumbling friction over their common border in Mongolia which periodically flared into open conflict. The Soviets had recently withdrawn most of their forces from the region. It appeared that they were making a positive effort to end the dispute that had kept the two greatest Communist countries from the warmth of each other's hearths for so long.

A week before the Soviet leader was due to arrive in Beijing, a few hundred students began a good humored demonstration in front of the Great Hall of The People, asking for reforms similar to those that were proceeding in the Soviet Union.

Chapter 6

GREEN BEGAN THE morning meeting briskly, going round the table to see what each of the team had discovered, starting with Penkowski. He was a heavy-set man, nearing retirement but full of energy. His features were almost Neanderthal, with heavy brow ridges under thick black curls and the blue shadow of a beard that needed shaving twice a day. However serious the situation, his deep brown eyes always sparkled with amusement and the wrinkle lines surrounding them showed the frequency of his smile.

"The men on the Hill are not going to be happy with this one," he began. "Everything I have looked at so far has been straight by the book, all procedures followed to the letter, and I have found no indication that anyone has either done anything irregular or tried to hide something."

"You don't think there is anything in this, then?" Green asked.

"Not from our people. I think this will turn out to be a blind. Who started the scare in the first place anyway?"

"Word apparently came through from the Indians that their peace keeping force in Sri Lanka was capturing a lot of American weapons from the Tamil Tigers. They put through a request to know how they were getting the weapons," Mitch chipped in.

"Then how the hell did the men on the Hill get involved?" demanded Green. "That request should have come through military channels."

There were blank looks around the table. Mike cleared his throat. "Some Senator was asked on the quiet by an Indian General at an Embassy bean feast while he was junketing in Delhi," he said.

"That's all we need," muttered Green. "Which one?"

"Senator Jefferson Stanley Swingate from Idaho," Mike said. "He has also been appointed Chairman of the Senate Investigating Committee."

"That jerk!" spat Hal Johnson. "The man is nothing but a two bit potato farmer with as much discretion as a farmyard rooster. Just wants to see his name in the papers to impress his electorate."

"OK, Hal, leave that. What have you got?" Green asked seeing Hal's views mirrored in most of the faces round the table.

"Very little. There are no records of any arms shipments to that part of the world in the last twenty months, either from manufacturers, dealers, or the Company. In fact we are not on record as ever having sent anything to that island. My enquiries to the Indians, apart from suggesting that the weapons are American, have produced absolutely zilch. They have not identified what the weapons are, and no hardware has been shown to anyone. The whole thing seems highly suspicious and speculative to me. Unless they start producing a load of hardware, fast, I agree with Penkowski. It's a blind."

Green nodded as Hal spread his hands and fell silent. "Mitch?"

"Same thing. It's a blind," he shook his head sadly.

"I agree, and I think it's been set up to cover something else," Green agreed. "However, I have something. Seventeen weeks ago a shipment of irrigation pumps left Corpus Christi in Texas for Colombo. Several weeks later four crates labeled as irrigation equipment were found lying in a port warehouse in Corpus Christi. There was no documentation to show what vessel the crates were consigned to, no destination was painted on any of the crates, and no indication of who the shipping agent was. The manufacturer's label was the only marking, so the port authorities contacted them. The pumps were made by Soper Pumping Inc. of Chicago. They had been bought as an export batch by a Sri Lankan holding company, through agents in Houston. They were shipped to the port by Soper, apparently properly labeled, to join up with other unspecified equipment from elsewhere. The shipping agent was Shandar Freighting of Dayton, Ohio. The pumps were all paid for by bank drafts raised in Dayton by persons unnamed. The bank confirmed this morning that the drafts were issued to a customer who telephoned to arrange them. He walked in and handed over thirty seven thousand dollars in cash to pay for them, then quietly walked out without even giving his name. I have asked the FBI to run a check on the freight company and to interview the bank clerk. They are also making enquiries with the Customs Department in Corpus Christi," Green explained, looking round the ring of astonished faces. "It's OK; I'm not blaming any of you for drawing blank. I just happened to have the right batch of files."

"The hell you did," snorted Joe, who had so far said nothing. "It's your nose again. Never been known to fail, just like a hound dog sniffin' out jackrabbits."

Green smiled at the compliment and continued. "I regret having to bring in the Bureau, but with the Customs Department involved there is really no choice.

I don't like those guys poking their noses in any more than you do, but there it is. We'll just have to keep their involvement as limited as possible. I have no real interest in any funny business between commercial enterprises here, that's the Bureau's business and they're welcome to it. What I want to know, and fast, is what's the tie in to the Company, and whether something else went out on a ship in the guise of these pumps. We have had very little activity in that part of the world for some years, so it better be easy to trace what all our people have been doing. Joe, you get onto that. I also want to know what weapons the Indian Army have captured. Mitch, that's your job. We require not only a full and detailed list with serial numbers, but hardware on this table, yesterday if not sooner."

Mitch Sullivan nodded and made a note on his pad.

"Hal, find out about the ship, where it went, where it stopped, and whether we have any Company activity in those places. I want to know where the crates in that shipment ended up and who collected them. Also, were any of them opened for inspection at any time along the way. Penkowski, have you still got any strings with the Brits?"

"I got a few."

"Fine. Pull them and see what our friends in London can turn up. They're pretty close to the Indians and will certainly have people on the ground in theatre. Everyone feed your information to Mike who will co-ordinate and provide resources as necessary. Use my authority as you need to, Mike, and if that isn't enough use the Chief's. I will clear that with him. I want this thing wrapped up pronto so that we can all get back to what really matters in the world."

Green set the next session for three days time, then invited the whole team over for supper the next evening and the meeting broke up. As Mike was leaving Green called him back.

"Mike, you looked uncomfortable when the Senator's name came up. Like to tell me why?"

"Nothing solid, Malcolm, just an uneasy feeling. That's all," he said.

"You also looked thoughtful yesterday when I told you about that jerk staffer I fired. Hey! Swingate! They're not related are they?" Green's voice rose slightly with excitement.

"The Senator is his father," Mike said flatly.

"Come on. I know there's more. You'd better sit down and tell me the rest of it. Just what do you know about the Senator and that son of his?" Green's nose told him there was something here that he should know about.

"I wasn't sure yesterday," Mike said, "but made some calls earlier to check a few things. I know nothing about the Senator except what the public sees on TV and in the papers. But I have come across Connor Swingate before. He's one of the Company's microelectronic wizards. Been involved in several unsavory shows, and there was even talk that he was implicated in the Watergate business but nothing tangible was found."

"He's not old enough is he?" Green asked.

"He's thirty nine. All that happened before he was recruited and I have heard it whispered that it was his involvement that made the Company go for him. He has some pretty advanced talents that could be useful in covert activities. There have also been suggestions that he has a penchant for bugging his colleagues just for fun. Nobody has ever been able to hang anything definite on him so there's nothing on file, but he has been moved abruptly several times without any recorded explanation of why. Given all that, I didn't like the fact that he had been staffer to this team. I just found it an uncomfortable coincidence that his Daddy is the chairman of the Senate Committee that's looking into this arms question."

"You don't think...?" Green saw the doubt on Mike's face. "Shit. That's all we need."

Mike grinned. "I have some equipment arriving this afternoon, complete with specialist operator, to check out these offices. I've already looked in the most obvious places, but found nothing."

"I'm not sure I want a snoop in here," Green said. "Can't we do it ourselves?"

"Connor Swingate is very creative. I don't think any of us are even remotely in his league. The man who's coming is one of the Brits on secondment to the Company. He's no friend of Swingate's, and equally as good. He would just love to nail the bastard. He's a Hong Kong Chinese and about as talkative as a Trappist clam."

"You seem to have the matter well under control, Mike. I'll leave it in your hands and we can talk after your Brit had been through the place."

THE DEBUG SPECIALIST arrived at two thirty with a collection of black boxes. He was a small man with an expressionless face, wearing a sober blue suit and gleaming shoes. His handmade shirt was one of Hong Kong's finest, in cream silk. As he came in his eyes rapidly scanned the office, locating the telephone, power points, light fittings and the layout of the furniture.

"This is Hua Foo Yong," Mike introduced him. "His friends call him Egg."

"Do you know what you are looking for?" Green asked, coming round from behind his desk with his hand outstretched.

"Not yet, Mr Green," said Egg, putting his equipment down and shaking Green's hand with a steel grip, "but these boxes will find anything there is to find."

"Good. I just hope there is nothing here to find. You go right ahead. I'll get out of your way. How long do you need?"

"About half an hour," Egg replied, "but please stay. I shall need voices talking for some of the time, but have to concentrate on the instruments myself. It would speed things up."

"Sure," Green agreed, and watched with interest as the debug specialist, moving with feline grace, unpacked his boxes and proceeded to festoon the office with a Technicolor spaghetti of wires which he connected to one of the black boxes. He attached sensors to every cable in the room, with several on the telephone, and unpacked a strange glass globe, filled with circuitry. He mounted this on a photographer's tripod in the center of the room and wired it up to a control console. When everything was connected, Egg took a device like a television control from his pocket, turned it on, and began to scan the walls, window and door frames with it. The device was silent but several times Egg stopped and gave a section of the wall a second sweep. Green and Mike watched with interest.

When he had completed his scan Egg went to the mysterious globe and depressed a switch on the base.

"Now please talk, gentlemen," he told them.

Green and Mike looked at one another, not sure what to say. Mike recovered first and started talking about the Open Golf Championship. Green picked up the thread and the two men chatted while the expert fiddled with his instruments. After a few moments a ribbon of paper began to unwind from a slot in one of the smaller boxes in his network which lay scattered around the floor. Egg reached for the notepad on Green's desk and wrote in large letters "Keep talking, I got one," he held it up for Green and Mike to see before turning his attention back to his dials.

Several minutes went by and more paper emerged from the slot. Egg wrote on the pad again. He took three sets of ear defenders from a bag and passed them to others along with the pad. The message read: "Don't stop talking. Put headsets on with hands over". All three put their headsets on; Egg made an adjustment to his console, and then looked at the other two. He nodded and depressed a small black button. There was a short, very loud, high-pitched shriek, then silence.

Egg took off his headset and motioned Green and Mike to do the same.

"Someone is going to find a lot of very expensive equipment just caught fire," he announced with a grin. "And if anyone happened to be listening at the time he will have a nasty headache for several days."

"Is the place clean now?" Green asked.

"Yes. Now, do you want me to trace out the bugs? They are all dead, and cannot be used again, but it might be interesting to have a look at them."

"How many were there?" asked Mike.

"Just three," Egg said in an offhand way. "He did not really need that many. I could have done it with one."

"Who's to say you won't?" Green muttered to himself.

"Mr Green!" said Egg, sounding hurt. "I assure you I only have one paymaster."

"Sorry, Egg. No offence meant." Green grinned. "That was an impressive performance you just gave."

"Thank you, Mr Green. I've been wanting to fix that man for some time. I hope this time you'll put a full stop to his games. Now, let me show you how he did it."

"Yeah, but before that we got to take some action. Mike, I want that jerk on ice, in complete isolation, soonest. Get Penkowski to help you. He knows more tricks than Harry Houdini. Just you two; go find him."

"It'll be a pleasure." Mike was already on his way to the door and Green wondered what the jerk had done in the past to upset him.

"Now then, Machiavelli, let's see what devious devices you have to show me." Green said, turning his attention back to Egg, who was packing away his equipment.

Chapter 7

CHARLES BRADEN HAD BEEN with the Company longer than most of the office furniture. When asked what his position was he generally replied "Oh, about half way to the top, on the side of the shelf." The hierarchy of the Company is deliberately kept somewhat obscure, even to most of the employees. This has certain advantages for those in positions of power and makes the Company's already shady activities less identifiable. It is also intended to make infiltration difficult. Braden was, in reality, very close to the top and one of the Director's closest advisors. He was Chief of the department among whose special interests and activities were the People's Republic of China and its neighbors.

Braden had spent time in the field throughout the Orient and had participated in more than a few covert operations of dubious purpose. As he gained seniority he collected around him a close knit, highly specialized team. Many of the team were Asiatic Americans and all had spent several years active in theatre.

Braden was justifiably proud of his team's record and resisted all efforts to lure individuals away. His men, and more than a few women, for Braden was one of the least chauvinistic chiefs in the Company, were all loyal to a high degree. Only one person had ever requested a transfer off the team. Braden and the man concerned were the only two people who knew the reasons for this, but everyone else knew better than to ask.

After years of patient intelligence gathering and a few low-key covert operations the tide of things had only recently begun to flow in Braden's yard. With the British Royal Visit to China a couple of years ago, access had become much less restricted. Braden's team had recruited and trained a huge cadre of local informants and agents provocateurs. There were periodic hiccups when one of them overstepped the limits of tolerance shown by the local People's Revolutionary Committees, but so far there had been no major incidents that might have ended with spy trials or the expulsion of his agents. Now, with the approach of the date for the first official visit to China by a senior leader from the Soviet Union, things had really begun to move. Braden's years of patient groundwork began to pay off.

Then some self-important Senator raised a scare about illegal arms shipments to the Indian Ocean and the shit hit the fan.

SINCE WATERGATE AND the Iran-Contra scandals, people on Capitol Hill were getting jumpy. Following what was felt by the Democratic majority to have been an unsatisfactory election, somebody challenged the new President's choice for Defense Secretary. The Attorney General designate was challenged and rejected, and then the Speaker of the House was all but impeached for irregularities in his financial affairs. Scandal followed scandal as surely as agents follow foreign diplomats round the nation's capital. Everyone aspiring to or holding public office began to look over their shoulder. Some even started groundless scares just to divert attention from their own activities and to give them time to cover their tracks.

In Braden's opinion this was what Senator Jefferson Swingate from Idaho had done. There was prima facie evidence of a sort, but it left too much hanging in the air. At any normal time the matter would have been answered by a brisk letter from the Director and then dropped. Now, with the witch hunting mania rife, the whole affair could blow all sorts of things wide open that were better left hidden, and thereby set back some of the Company's work by decades. There was not even any guarantee that the affair could be limited to the one Section.

Braden had been annoyed when the Director asked him to second his best Senior Executive Officer to the Section to carry out the search. A request from the Director was effectively an order, but with things starting to get busy he did not want to lose his best man. He nominated Jim Burkitt, but the Director was on the line within minutes.

"What the hell did you nominate Burkitt for, Charles?" he demanded.

"He's very sharp and will do a good job," Braden told him. "Besides, with what's going on in China just now he's the only one I've got free."

"That's crap, Charles, and you know it. You put the Nose in there. He's the one with the ferreting instinct. I want this one cleaned up, sewn up, washed up and dried double quick, and he's the man to do it. No arguments please Charles. Just do this one for me and I'll get you some more fun in the bamboo garden."

Braden was more than reluctant to agree, but the Director had never sounded so earnest. They had been friends and colleagues for a lifetime. No sense in spoiling it now, especially when he knew that Dan was right about Green.

"OK Dan. You can have him this afternoon," he said with a heavy sigh, "But I want him back soonest."

"Thanks Charles." The phone went dead in Braden's ear.

GREEN WAS BITTERLY disappointed when Braden told him the score. He was itching to run one of his new plans on the ground in China, and it could well have meant another field trip for him as well. He loved Betty, the kids and his home, but he came alive in the field. The prospect had thrilled him for several weeks as he had seen the potential growing. Now some crummy Senator had screwed it up.

That had been three weeks ago. He had called several times to try to talk his way out of the assignment when sparks really began in China, but Charles Braden had had to close his ears to Green's entreaties and make the best of a bad deal. He could do with Green back here now, but…

NEWS OF THE STUDENTS' democracy demonstration in Tienanmen Square came in only a few days before Gorbachev was to arrive for his historic visit. An improvement in relations between the Panda and the Bear held many implications for the West. For years Western politicians had played every advantage the glacial relationship between the two great powers had offered, and Braden was determined that his team would keep abreast of developments. It hurt to have Green, with his uncanny nose, sidelined right at this time. His other SEOs could handle all the regular stuff, and one or two of them were quite enterprising, but they were in a different league to Green. He rang Dan again to plead for Green's return.

"You can move him back just as soon as he's cleaned the deck over there and put the Senator back in his cupboard where he belongs, Charles, and not before," Dan had said.

CROWDS OF STUDENTS and ordinary citizens poured into the square and assembled in front of the Great Hall of the People. Very soon there were more than a million gathered. Charles Braden had men on the ground, with minute by minute reports coming in. John Walker, his man at the embassy, was doing a superb job co-coordinating the reports and repositioning the members of his team.

The world was amazed by the tolerance shown by the Chinese leadership. Could it really be as simple as not wanting to act whilst the Soviet leader was in town? Certainly Gorbachev had commented on the demonstrations. He expressed approval of people being given the freedom to express their wishes, but questioned why they should feel that this sort of demonstration was necessary. He urged his hosts to learn from the Soviet experience, to take action as he had done, and make proactive reforms. He had been through this himself and knew all the benefits to be accrued from carefully managed change. He was the epitome of the new breed of Soviet leader. He had ousted the geriatric die-hards, whose entrenched attitudes had been as fossilized as themselves.

The old men in the Kremlin had been trapped by their own mendacity and fear. His hosts in Beijing were dinosaurs of the same breed, clinging to power, afraid to hand authority on to a younger generation with a new vision of the future. The end looked likely to be bitter indeed.

GORBACHEV LEFT THE Chinese capital for Shanghai. The world's press was expected to go with him, but few did. Within hours of his departure, John Walker was sending through reports of troop movements in the city. Seven regiments of the People's Army were moved from their garrisons around Beijing into the suburbs. Most of the soldiers were unarmed, and their attitude was friendly. International television reports showed the city's population talking and joking with the soldiers as they sat, waiting in their trucks. There was speculation that these simple soldiers would not want to act against their own people. There seemed, almost, to be a festival atmosphere in the banter between citizen and soldier. The crowd in the square was given extensive coverage on national television news broadcasts, and one of the inner circle members was even filmed debating with some of the demonstrators.

The People's Army waited.

The world watched.

The demonstrators were energetic in portraying their demands before their leaders and the world. Banners and flags were in constant motion, singing and chanting were incessant. Still the festival atmosphere persisted, with good humor among the demonstrators and watchfulness from the authorities.

AFTER ALMOST TWO WEEKS people began drifting away in tens and twenties to resume their normal lives. They had shown their support; now they had jobs to do, lives to lead. The slow exodus made no visible reduction to the size of the crowd in the square. They wanted an open debate, a hearing.

A group of university students made a ten meter high replica of the Statue of Liberty. They called it the Symbol of Democracy and carried it in triumphal procession above a million heads to be installed directly across the square from the Great Hall of the People. Democracy faced the massive portrait of Mao Tse Tung in mute challenge. Somebody splashed red paint across Mao's picture. The authorities' calls for the people to disperse, broadcast faintly and intermittently over the city's public address system, were drowned by the voice of the people and ignored.

Still the People's Army waited.

Still the world watched.

DURING SATURDAY THE TROOPS were withdrawn. Their replacements arrived armed. Gone was the jocularity and easy banter. These were cold-eyed men with closed ears and fathomless expressions. People began to cross the road to avoid the parked trucks. Voices stilled and heads turned apprehensively as convoys rumbled past.

An atmosphere of tension crept insidiously upon the city, but the singing, chanting and banner waving in the vast square never faltered. The tension reached the fringes of the crowd and it felt as though a carelessly struck match would set the very air ablaze. Rumors began circulating about a power struggle within the Inner Circle of the government. Some were said to be calling for hard action to end the demonstrations, other voices demanded change.

The People's Army waited.

The world continued to watch with fascination.

REPORTS POURED INTO Braden's office. He was too busy now to continue his regrets over Green's absence. Just as information flowed in, Braden and his staff were expected to provide briefings to the State Department, the men on the Hill, and even to the media. A news flash came in from Walker that troops had been moved into the diplomatic quarter of Beijing. Roadblocks were being set up. A net was being cast around the center of the Chinese capital. Some of the foreign embassies were sending their families and dependants out of the country.

Still the People's Army waited; silent, cold-eyed men in long lines of trucks.

Still the world watched, expectant, holding its breath.

AT TWO FIFTEEN ON Sunday morning the tanks rolled into Tienanmen Square and ground the nascent voice of democracy to bloody pulp beneath their tracks.

Chapter 8

IT TOOK MIKE AND Penkowski nine and a half hours to catch up with Connor Swingate. He had been given a week's furlough after Green sent him packing, while someone found a useful task for him. His neighbor told them she had seen the family packing their car with camping equipment and what looked like three aluminum ice boxes. Swingate's wife and kids had been with him when he left, but they had not told the neighbor where they were going. She called her own kids and asked them. Neither had seen the Swingates leave, but her eldest boy, a dumpy child of eleven with a marked Asian look to him, said they had gone fishing in Kentucky.

"Don't take too much notice of Damien," the mother had said, "he's Down's Syndrome and rather simple. He makes up tales."

Penkowski sat beside him on the wall and gave him his full attention.

"Kentucky is it, Damien? Now why would they want to go there?" he asked, making the child feel important.

"Cos they gone fishing," the boy said easily. "Henry and Luther went before and went in a big hole in the ground, in a boat. Their Dad took them fishing and got a big fish."

"That sounds great," encouraged Penkowski. "You think they went there again?"

"Their Dad promised them," said the smiling boy.

"Do you like fishing?" Penkowski's attention was now fixed on the boy.

"Don't know," Damien mumbled, "Mom won't let me."

"Doesn't your dad take you?" Penkowski asked.

"He's gone." The boy sounded disappointed.

An ice cream van was parked down the street and Damien's brother was dragging at his mother's skirt, demanding, as she chatted to Mike. Damien was absorbed with the big Pole. He thought Penkowski was like a huge teddy bear.

"Say, how about I buy you and your little brother an ice cream?" Penkowski asked, rising and lifting the boy easily to his shoulder. The boys' faces lit up. Their mother looked doubtful.

"He just can't resist kids," Mike told her, "it won't do any harm."

"Sure, if you want to," she accepted, and the Pole stalked off along the sidewalk with Damien perched majestically on his broad shoulders while his brother trotted along holding a huge paw.

Mike leaned against the wall and continued chatting with the woman as they watched.

"Don't take too much notice of Damien," she said. "He was real broke up when his dad left. He isn't usually so forward. In fact at times I have problems getting him to do anything at all. It's amazing how he responded to your friend."

"I've never heard of a kid yet that could resist Penkowski's charm." Mike laughed. "He has seven grandchildren of his own, and you'd think they were the center of the universe itself."

"He's very kind." The boys' mother relaxed.

"Yeah," Mike nodded.

Penkowski and the two boys came back. The boys had white rings round their mouths, like circus clowns. They all sat on the wall and Penkowski told them a funny story about a fat brown bear stealing honey from a bees' nest in the woods, and getting his nose stung. The boys giggled between mouthfuls of ice cream. When they had finished and Penkowski's story was told he got up.

"Well, since we're too late to see your neighbors, we'll just have to wait till they come back," he said.

The boys clamored for another story.

"Another day," Penkowski said gently.

"Promise?" demanded Damien.

"Sure thing."

"Promise properly," the boy insisted. His mother was about to rebuke him for his manners but a glance from the big Pole stilled her tongue. He knelt down and held the boy's gaze.

"I promise I'll come by and tell you another story some time real soon, Damien. But just now we have to go back to work. OK?"

He stood up when the boy nodded and Mike was thanking the mother for her help.

"Did you thank the man?" she asked her sons.

"Thank you Mister," they said in happy chorus.

Penkowski waved goodbye and he and Mike headed back to their car.

"Shit," said Penkowski as he slammed the car door. "Now we've got to go trailing all over the U.S. to find them. That guy's slippery like a Mississippi mudfish."

"Not necessarily," Mike said. "How much can we take the kid's word?"

"The voice of innocence. He's probably spot on," Penkowski said. "Only trouble is there must be thousands of camping places near good fishing in Kentucky, and we don't have time or the help to check them all."

"So?"

"So we go back to the office and ask the Nose."

"What the hell are you talking about?" Mike sounded frustrated.

"You'll learn, Mike. You'll learn," Penkowski said with the hint of mischief in his voice.

GREEN WAS PREPARING to leave the office when they arrived, but waved them to sit.

"So where is he?" he asked.

Mike explained.

"And now you want me to tell you where to look?

Mike nodded and looked glum. Green leaned back in his chair and closed his eyes. The others waited. After a few minutes Green opened his eyes, leaned forward with his arms on the desk and looked smugly at the other two.

"Elementary, Watson. You go into the biggest cave in the world by boat. It is in one of this great country's finest National Parks where the camping is good and the fishing is better. Several million happy tourists wander the lake shores and woods every year. What place could be better to lose yourself in for a while?"

The two agents waited for more.

Mammoth Cave, in the Brownsville National Park, is my guess." Green continued. "He'll probably want to get there as fast as he can, so he'll head out through Charleston, Huntington, and Lexington. Then round Louisville and down to Munfordville. Somewhere round there is where he'll find his campsite. All you guys have to do is figure out exactly where and then lift him."

The two agents looked at one another, and then back at Green, aware that he still had more to tell them.

"You've done well to pick up his trail so fast, and you can resume the chase in a moment. Meanwhile, I have done some work too. Firstly, Senator Swingate has been on the horn demanding that I go see him. I managed to stall that one but think we'd better find out what's burning his tail. You and the others are due at my place tomorrow evening, so I've invited the Senator as well. We will spend some time unraveling the spider's web, and see what we've got. I've also set up a deal that will help you put his boy on ice. You'll have to think up your own way of separating the jerk from his family, as they are definitely not included in this and must not know what we've done. When you've got him away, take him to the airfield at Louisville where a Company plane will be waiting. Sim Thornton will take over from there. Either of you know him?"

Penkowski nodded. "I worked with him a couple of times, back aways."

"Fine. All you may tell the jerk is that he's needed to make a surveillance plant. You have been diverted to find and deliver him on your way to the West Coast. Sim will tell him the rest. Once you've handed him over and seen the plane take off, get your asses back here soonest. Now call home and get your wives to pack overnight bags, and get moving."

The two men got up to leave.

"One last thing," Green said. "Did you say the neighbor had seen him loading metal boxes into his car?"

"Yes." Mike said. "Aluminum ice boxes, she called them. Three of them."

"Hmm." Green was looking out of the window at the fading light. "My nose tells me he has no intention of spending his time fishing while his wife takes the kids on trips. He's preparing to play another of his electronic games. Those boxes contain the makings of his toys. Make sure he brings them along when you collect him. Play it light, but make it an order if you need to Penkowski."

"Sure thing, Nose. We'll get him. See you tomorrow night."

"Fine." Green showed them out, then put through a call to Braden.

"I'm not calling just to beef, Maureen. I've got my hands full here. I could, however, use a few words with our master."

"Hold the line then, Nose. I'll try for you," she said. "As you can guess, it's all going on here. How's things your end?"

"I hardly know yet, but I have found a weevil in the peapod. That's what I wanted to talk to Chuck about."

"Don't call him that. You know how he hates that name." Maureen's voice carried her smile down the line, despite her admonition.

"What can I do for you, Nose?" Braden's voice asked a few moments later.

"Charles, I still have no idea what's going on, but I have turned up a problem. Or perhaps I should say that smart staffer you sent me has. I may need to take your name in vain, so I thought I'd just call and clear it with you," Green said.

"What have you found?" Braden asked.

"This is an open line, Charles."

"Oh." Braden paused. "I see. Like that. OK, go right ahead and keep me informed as you can."

"Thanks Charles. Now let me change the subject," Green said, and Braden knew that this was anything but a change of subject. More like one of Green's cryptic explanations. "Betty and I are having some friends over for supper tomorrow. Senator Jefferson Swingate has been pestering to see me, so I invited him along too. There will be some folks there that you know, so I wondered if you would care to join us?"

"I'd enjoy that, Nose. Thanks."

"About eight thirty then. Informal. And thanks Charles. Good night."

"Nose?"

"Yeah?"

"You didn't ask about China." Braden sounded almost hurt at his apparent lack of interest.

"Would it get me back any sooner if I did? Tell me tomorrow. I've got plenty to occupy me here just now. Bye."

"Bye."

Green picked up the phone again and dialed Sim Thornton.

"Come over, Sim. I'll brief you now," he said simply.

When Thornton arrived he spent forty minutes briefing him, and then went home.

Chapter 9

PENKOWSKI HAD NO need to go home for his bag; it lived in the trunk of his car. They stopped at Mike's place and Chevvy waddled down the path with a bag. Mike embraced her warmly and introduced Penkowski.

"Doesn't he have a first name?" she asked.

"Good to meet you, Chevvy. And no, I gave that up when I first left Poland. Nobody could say it properly, and it's so long ago that I hardly remember it myself now," he grinned broadly and stepped forward to peck her cheek.

"OK. Nice to meet you anyway. Mike, what about the Greens' tomorrow evening?"

"We'll be back by then. We are only hopping a couple of states to help a pal who's too weak to carry his own bags." He took the bag and nuzzled her neck.

"Get off, you big oaf." His wife laughed as she pushed him towards the car. "Have fun. I'll see you tomorrow."

On the way to the airport, Penkowski asked when the baby was due, and the two chatted easily about children and parenthood. They had to wait twenty minutes while the Company pilot got his clearance, and then took off direct for Louisville. The plane was old and noisy. Since talking was difficult and it looked like being a long night, the two agents dozed until the pilot began his descent.

After landing, Mike went to the Avis desk while Penkowski briefed the pilot. He was to go back and bring Sim Thornton, then wait here.

"I have no idea what time we will bring our man up, so you will have to be ready whenever. Sorry about that. Sim Thornton will give you the onward briefing when you collect him. The important thing is that you should be ready to go as soon as we bring your passenger."

"No trouble, Mr Penkowski. I'll be ready when you want me." The pilot was enthusiastic. He was very young and eager to please. A good pilot all the same, thought Penkowski, who had watched him with an experienced eye during their flight.

Mike came back with a set of car keys swinging on his finger.

"See you tomorrow," Penkowski told the pilot, and followed Mike to the car.

"I never realized that you came over from Poland. I thought you were born here," Mike said as they drove out of the parking lot.

"I was just seventeen when I left Poland," Penkowski said. "My father was shot by the Germans when they destroyed Warsaw. When the Russians came they took my mother off to a labor camp. She was a small woman in the early stages of TB, so she didn't last long. They had no feeling for the weak and infirm and probably beat her to death for not doing enough work. I got to England and trained to fly. Had to lie about my age, as they say in all the best war stories," he smiled at the memory. Mike listened in silence, wanting to know more but unwilling to pry.

"They put me on Lysanders, flying agents into Norway and Poland, then later on Mosquitoes. There were a lot of spare pilots at the end of the war and they didn't want me, so I worked my passage over here as a stoker on one of the ships bringing GIs home. One of the stewards on the ship was a Pole and he invited me to his home on Polish Hill in Pittsburgh when we landed. His family made me welcome like a son and I found a lot more Poles in the city. It was no problem to find a job. Jadzia lived in the next block. We started spending a lot of time together, and later we got married. Those people gave us such a feast. The only sad thing was my parents not being there to share it. They would have been so proud, and it was a real Polish wedding.

"After that I knew this was a good country to make my home and took out citizenship papers. I got a job flying mail planes for a couple of years, then joined the Company." He leaned back in his seat and stretched like a huge cat.

"That was a long time ago. Now I've got a good wife, who gives me hell if I step out of line, four great kids and seven grandchildren. The youngest is just seven months old. They all live down near Langley now, so we see a lot of them. It's a good thing to have a family round you. You've got all that to come, Mike, but you made a damned good start with Chevvy. Jadzia will love her. You must both come over to our place sometime soon."

"Thanks. We would like that," said Mike, overtaking a truck. "How did you come to join the Company?" he asked presently.

"I was flying out of a small field near Pittsburgh when the mail contract came to an end. A two bit charter operation that paid badly and maintained their planes worse. One day some guy came into the office wanting to hire a pilot for three days. He had a plane, but his pilot had got sick. He needed someone with short field experience. The boss said he only had one pilot available, but if the man wanted an ignorant Polack stick jockey he could have him. There was nobody else. I flew round the backwoods for that guy and his pals for three days, landing in some pretty tight corners. The man who hired me didn't like my boss and asked if I wanted to move. I said sure, if the pay was regular, and we shook hands. I didn't bother going back to the charter company; just kept right on with these guys. It was a week before I found out that I was working for the CIA. Never once regretted it. What about you, Mike, how'd they catch you? You got an even screwier name than me for an American."

Mike told him as the car ate up the miles to Munfordville.

TEN MILES SHORT OF the town they stopped at a diner for coffee and sandwiches and to fill the tank. It was a big, rambling place with two regular restaurants and a cafeteria beside a filling station. They were just pulling out of the parking lot with Penkowski driving, when Mike put a hand on his arm.

"Hold it. Look over there. The other side of the parking area. There's a woman putting a dog in the back of a red Chevrolet."

"I see her," Penkowski said, pulling up.

"See those metal boxes in the back?" asked Mike.

"Yup. They look like aluminum ice boxes to me. It looks like the angels smile on the righteous. We found our man," Penkowski agreed with a small whistle.

"We'll wait till he pulls out, then follow. Better to let him set up camp and then pull him out in the morning. If we go in just as they're having breakfast we won't have problems getting him away from the family."

"Sounds good," Mike agreed. He had been wondering how they were going to pull Swingate out and leave his family behind.

The woman finished putting the dog in the car and arranged bags and boxes around it. She closed the door and went round to the passenger side. Mike realized he had been holding his breath, and let it out slowly. They gave the Chevrolet half a mile start before following. Two miles along the highway their target turned right. Penkowski followed and fell back a bit more. Signs to a campsite appeared and Penkowski closed up until he had a full view of the Chevrolet's tail lights. The turn signal came on and the car made a left into the campsite gateway. Penkowski drove past and, as the road curved to the right, he slowed then stopped and doused the headlights. He got out of the car and listened for five minutes.

"We'll give 'em fifteen minutes, before following," he said, resuming his seat behind the wheel. The two men sat in silence in the gathering dusk.

After the quarter hour was up Penkowski turned the car and drove into the campsite. He stopped at the gatehouse and a young man came out to the car, yawning.

"Howdy," said a young Texan voice as Penkowski lowered his window.

"Sorry we got here s'late," the Pole said. "We wuz following my son-in-law, but lowst him when we gat a flat. I sure hope we came t' the right place. Never been up heeah befoah."

Mike was amazed to hear the sing-song Carolina twang, and almost burst out laughing.

"What car does he drive?" asked the gate man.

"Dark red Chevrolet with a rack on top."

"Yup. Y'all got the right place. Just follow the road and take the first two lefts. You should find him setting up camp by a grove of old oak trees down beside the lake. The fee is five per night, but we walk round and collect in the morning, sir. Have a pleasant visit." With that he stood back and waved Penkowski to drive on. He turned without another glance and went back into his cabin where the glow of a television screen beckoned.

Three minutes later Penkowski killed the engine and lights and pulled off the road.

"Take a look, Mike. See if you can find us a quiet spot to watch from."

Mike Reached up and flipped the cover off the interior light, removing the bulb before getting out of the car. Leaving the door open, he vanished silently into the darkness. Twenty minutes later a quiet voice just behind his left ear startled Penkowski.

"Just where the man said," Mike whispered. "About half a mile down from here. There is a thicket on the right where we can park. It's downhill all the way so you should be able to roll it."

Penkowski put the car in neutral and released the handbrake. As the car rolled slowly forward, Mike walked alongside and directed him into the cover he had chosen before coming round and climbing into the passenger seat.

Penkowski reclined his seat and leaned back. "Might as well get some sleep ourselves. They won't go anywhere before breakfast."

Mike looked towards the tent that had been erected and was illuminated from within by a gas lamp. Swingate's wife carried a bag from the car. Then the kids came out and carried boxes into the tent. Mike was just beginning to wonder if their quarry had somehow managed to give them the slip when Connor Swingate emerged from the tent. He stood there for a few moments, looking at the sky, then stretched and walked to a nearby bush and relieved himself. When he had finished, he closed up his car, went into the tent and closed the flap behind him.

Mike relaxed. Penkowski was already snoring gently.

Chapter 10

CHONG FIRST HEARD about the democracy demonstrations from one of the technicians. After his latest activities, both the radio and the television had disappeared from his quarters, and he lost touch with the news. Some of the other staff had radios, and there was also a television in the communal recreation room, but Chong had not previously been in the habit of going there. Now, after the most recent set of restrictions, he was not sure if it would be permitted. When he heard the news he decided to try.

When the next news bulletin was almost due Chong set most of the machines in his laboratory to an automatic mode, turned several others off, and headed for the door. His watchdog immediately demanded to know where he was going.

"To the recreation hall," Chong replied without breaking his stride.

The watchdog ran after him.

"Why are you going there?" he demanded.

"I am going there because I have reached a point in my work where the process must be left alone for a while. If I stay I shall be tempted to fiddle with the equipment, and that would upset the test. I am sure you do not want me to reduce the quality of the work. Also, my mind needs a change of direction before the next stage. I shall play chess." Chong kept walking rapidly.

The watchdog was forced to hop and skip around plant pots, seats, and other people in order to keep up. Chong wondered if the man realized how ridiculous his terpsichory looked. Certainly the faces of the people who passed showed their derision.

When they arrived at the recreation hall, Chong found there were only four people there. Two were playing chess and the others were patting a table tennis ball back and forth with little energy or enthusiasm. To his relief, someone had already turned on the television. Chong had been wondering how he would explain to the watchdog if he had had to turn it on himself.

Taking a board and pieces from a shelf, Chong sat down at a table close beside the television and began to set out the chessmen.

"Who are you going to play with, then?" demanded the watchdog.

Chong looked down at the board and then round the room.

"You play?" he asked.

"Of course," said the watchdog.

"Then sit down and play. You may begin," he turned the board so that the white pieces were in front of the man.

After the second move Chong knew what the man was going to do. He moved one of his pieces. The watchdog moved. Chong moved again. The watchdog appeared to consider carefully during the next three moves, then glanced at Chong with a sly look. Chong ignored him and shifted his rook. The watchdog's hand shot out and moved again. He had not been paying attention and had missed the trap. Now he would pay the price. Chong moved a bishop.

"Check mate."

The watchdog stared at the board in disbelief. He glared at Chong, hate filling his eyes at the humiliation. He reached out and knocked over his king, still glaring at Chong.

The news bulletin was about to start.

"If you are not on form today I shall be happy to work out problems on my own. Thank you," Chong said mildly, resetting the pieces.

"I will play again," the man said.

The next game went the same way. Chong glanced at the screen. The scenes being shown were startling and unprecedented. Something must have shown on his face for the watchdog turned to look as well. Chong watched, fascinated. He felt a tremendous urge to stand up and cheer. The openness of the demonstration was inspiring, beautiful.

The watchdog looked back at Chong. A scowl clouded his expression and he leapt up, switching off the set, and yelling that such counter revolutionary activity should not be watched. The room was suddenly silent and tense. The other players had stopped to look also, and five pairs of eyes stared at the party official.

Chong stood up and switched the set on again.

"You cannot watch that filth!" the watchdog yelled.

"That is a government broadcast. Loyal citizens should watch what our government wishes us to see," Chong replied calmly.

"You! You are nothing but a trouble maker!" the man shouted back and pulled the power cable from the wall. "Go back to your work, all of you. There will be no more of this disobedience!" He planted himself firmly in front of the dead set, challenging them.

He was still standing there, guarding the television, when Chong reached his quarters some minutes later.

"You should have seen it," Chong told San Kiu when they were alone later that evening. "I wish we could go and see it ourselves."

"That will make trouble again," his wife said. "The authorities will hardly permit this to go on for long. They are only waiting until the Russian has gone home."

"Yes. It will be hard for everyone afterwards. We should go immediately and see for ourselves."

"And when they find out?" San Kiu asked. "They will shoot people to stop this. They will send in the army. Tanks and live bullets to kill the demonstrators. I do not want us to be among those."

"Shoot to stop this?" Chong was incredulous. "They cannot massacre an idea. They cannot run tanks over hope. They cannot riddle people's yearning with bullets!"

San Kiu looked at him carefully and saw a new aspect of her husband. He was vibrant in his enthusiasm. His energy was infectious.

"We must go there! We have struggled for this!" He raised his eyes to heaven as he spoke.

"Then let us go. Now!" San Kiu said with decision.

"We may not be able to come back," Chong cautioned.

"So? We have faced that before. You more than I," she replied.

Chapter 11

IT WAS JUST GETTING LIGHT when Penkowski shook Mike awake. He stretched and yawned.

"Anything happening?

"Not yet. I think we should move back and drive down openly when they start moving about. Be easiest to peel him off before they get organized for the day. He may have plans for going off some place with the family."

"Good idea. We could go back to the Visitor Center and catch some breakfast ourselves."

Penkowski started the car, pulled out of the thicket and drove back up the track. The Center was just opening and the smell of coffee and food made both men's hunger acute. Half an hour later they went back to the car. Penkowski sat on the fender and lit a cigarette.

"I didn't know you smoked," remarked Mike.

"Only sometimes."

Mike walked round the car, kicking the tires.

Penkowski dropped his butt and crushed it with a heel.

"Let's catch our cat, then," he said, opening the driver's door.

Swingate and his sons were pulling fishing tackle out of their car. They planned to spend the day by the lake, and were going to try catching breakfast. The two boys were bubbling with excitement and took no notice of the blue sedan that pulled up just a few yards away.

"Hi there," called a voice from the sedan. "Are you Mr. Conner Swingate?"

"Yes. What can I do for you?" the boys' father answered.

"I'm sorry to intrude like this, sir, but your office asked us to locate you. Something urgent has come up and they need you back for a couple of days," the driver said, climbing out of his car.

Swingate turned sharply and banged his head on the tail hatch as he stood up. He faced a heavy-set man with a mass of loose black curls and a merry face. He ignored the offered right hand.

"What's that?" he demanded.

"Martin Pearson, Louisville office," said Penkowski, showing an identity card. "We got a call to say the Company needed you. Some rush job. They said you had come down here somewhere to do some fishing, so could we find you and let you know."

Swingate looked annoyed. He took the card and examined it, then looked at Penkowski and handed it back.

"OK, you have let me know. I will call in when we have had breakfast."

"They said it was urgent, sir. We have to take you to the airport. They have an aircraft waiting. The pilot will take you on, wait, and bring you right back. One of your own people will be there to brief you."

"What about my family? I can't just go like that."

"You should be back within thirty six hours, sir. The sooner we get going the sooner you get back."

"What's the job?" Swingate asked.

"I have no details, but I believe they need a listening watch on a bunch of foreign nationals. It seems you're some kind of specialist in that field. Just set it up and then get back to your fishing. Your man will give you the details."

At that moment Lois Swingate came out of the tent to see what was going on. Penkowski gave her his most disarming smile.

"What's going on, Conny?" she asked.

"Mr Pearson has been sent by the Company, Honey. They need me back for a day or so."

"But we only just got here!" she whined. "Why do they always have to screw up your time off?"

"I'm real sorry, Mrs. Swingate, but duty calls." Penkowski turned his charm on her. "You don't need to interrupt your holiday. We have an aircraft waiting and it will bring your husband straight back. He should be back with you tomorrow evening at the latest."

"Damn! They keep on doing this to us," she sounded aggrieved. "You tell them this is the last time, Conny. If they're going to go on doing this you tell them to go to hell and get a new job."

"I'm sure my wife would agree with you, Mrs. Swingate. They have done it to us all. That is what comes of being the best at what you do; they always keep needing you." Penkowski's charming smile defused and soothed her.

"Well, if you have to go I suppose you'd better eat first. You will give him time for breakfast?" she asked.

"Sure. A few minutes ain't going to matter none," the big Pole replied with a fatherly smile.

"Have you eaten? Would you care to join us?" Lois asked.

"That's mighty kind. Thank you, we'd appreciate that. Been up all night trying to find you. The office weren't able to tell us which campsite, so we've been driving round visiting 'em all. Been to six different sites before this one."

While Lois busied herself making food, Penkowski chatted with the two boys about the fish they hoped to catch. They were disappointed, but not too much when Penkowski assured them that their Dad would be able to claim a few days extra holiday because of this interruption. The prospect of extra fishing cheered them up.

Swingate pulled out a bag and stuffed a few clothes into it. He lifted three metal boxes out of his car and moved towards Penkowski's with them.

"Hey. You're only going for a day or so. You don't need much," Mike said.

"Pearson said they want me to bug some place, right? So I need the kit to do it with, right?"

"The kit will be provided."

"That junk!" Swingate was derisive. "I make my own. The Company stuff is just for amateurs. Since you can't tell me what the job is I'll just take this along. It's not heavy."

"Suit yourself. You're the expert." Mike helped him load the boxes into the trunk of the sedan.

"Mom will take you over to the caves today, and I'll be back to catch the fish rising tomorrow evening," Swingate told Henry and Luther. "Just you be good, and look after Mom till I get back."

He gave his wife a casual kiss on the cheek, ruffled the boys' hair and climbed into the back of the car behind Mike. The two boys stood with their mother, waving, as the three men drove off.

Swingate tried to question Mike and Penkowski about the job, but they could tell him no more. He seemed to accept that they were just messengers and sat quietly. Penkowski maintained a light chatter, keeping Swingate's mind diverted with amusing tales about the backwoods people in North Carolina. The drive back to Louisville was uneventful, and Swingate seemed quite cheerful when they handed him over to Sim Thornton.

Mike and Penkowski waited until the Company plane had taken off, then went looking for transport home for themselves.

Chapter 12

CONCEALING THEMSELVES behind a bamboo thicket, Chong and his wife changed into simple working clothes before reaching the city, and now went unremarked in the milling crowd. The atmosphere was electric and they felt almost light headed. After years of longing he was actually living one of his two great dreams. His and San Kiu's voices joined with a million others in front of the Great Hall of the People, chanting, singing, laughing, free.

He borrowed a banner and waved it energetically for a while before passing it on to someone else. Food was passed round and shared. Groups of people discussed their ideas about democracy and what reforms should be brought in. New chants started from time to time and were taken up by the crowds to swell like a tide and sweep through the masses.

They worked their way through the crowds and looked up at the huge statue erected a few days earlier by the university students. It was gaudy, new, and exciting. People said it had been copied from the American Statue of Liberty. San Kiu looked at it critically and observed that it had been made the wrong way round. Even so, it made a great impression on her.

As they worked their way through the crowd they came across several students who had attended Chong's lectures and some of the scientific meetings. Everywhere they were greeted with friendship and warmth. They heard their names being told to others in the crowd, some of whom cheered them.

A RIPPLE PASSED THROUGH the crowd. The word was passed that the soldiers, who had been sitting in their trucks along most of the nearby streets, had been pulled back. New banners appeared within minutes telling of the power struggle among the country's leaders. More proclaimed the new democracy. San Kiu led Chong towards the side of the great square. It was hot in the sun and she wanted to find some shade.

"This is the best day I can ever remember," Chong said as they sat down. "Nothing could make it better."

"Honored husband," San Kiu said, requesting his attention by her formality. "I hope that this is an auspicious moment to tell you that you will soon be Honored Father."

Chong looked at her for a long moment, trying hard to keep from his face the joy he felt. He failed completely and his mask gave way to a radiant smile of total pleasure that was soon returned by his wife.

"I was wrong. You have made this marvelous day ten times better, Honored Wife!" Still gazing deep into her dark eyes he reached for San Kiu's small hand and led her out of the square in search of food.

"Chong Tse Do, is that you?" a voice hailed them from behind, and they turned to find a tall foreigner weaving his way towards them through the crowd. It was the American CIA man who had been his English teacher.

"Mr Peach. We thought you had gone home to America. I have long wished to thank you for arranging publication of the paper that you took with you."

"My pleasure, sir. I'm here just as a tourist this time, to hear the great voice of the people."

"Ah, tourist, yes." Chong liked the euphemism. "We are going to find food. Will you come with us?"

"I would enjoy that very much," Peach said with a little bow.

"We shall celebrate for three good things, then," San Kiu said.

"Three?" queried the American.

"Democracy and free speech, meeting an old and valued friend, and the child my wife tells me we shall soon have," Chong explained with great dignity.

"That's great!" said Peach. "I am three times honored to join your celebration."

They had to go nearly a mile to find the sort of place Chong wanted. Over the meal they discussed all the dramatic events of recent days, and caught up on each other's news.

Talking in English attracted a few stares from other customers in the eating house, but, whereas previously these might have been hostile, there was a new tolerance abroad and the looks were mostly friendly and welcoming. They sat late into the evening, eating and talking. Peach particularly enjoyed the witty descriptions given by both his companions of recent events at the research center and the games they played with their watchdogs. He asked how they had managed to evade the watchdogs and get into Beijing.

"I told them to leave us alone as we were going to make love and start a baby. I did not know then that we had already done so." Chong giggled. "Then we locked the door and made suitable noises until we heard them go away. After that we climbed out of the window and stole their bicycles." All three laughed. Faces turned their way, smiling.

Peach got up and went through to the back of the building to relieve himself. He was just coming back when the room fell silent. He stopped and peered through the beaded curtain that hung across the doorway. Two policemen were standing in the street doorway.

"We are looking for Chong Tse Do and his wife, and a foreign devil," one of them announced to the proprietor, who had hurried forward. "We were told they had come here."

"Ah yes. They were here, but they went to the Square some time ago," he replied.

The policemen stared intently round the customers. Chong had looked round briefly, but turned back to the table and continued eating. San Kiu followed his lead and refilled her rice bowl. After a few minutes the policemen turned and went off towards the Square.

The proprietor scuttled through the crowded room and bowed to Chong and San Kiu, speaking rapidly in a low voice. He led them through the bead curtain and motioned for Peach to follow. Behind a log pile in the back courtyard there was a door. It led through into another building.

"Wait here. I will send someone, a young girl, who will take you to a place of safety," he said as he ushered them inside. Then he closed the door behind them and returned to his restaurant.

They waited in silence for ten minutes. A rumbling sound was just audible and there were slight tremors through the floor.

"An earthquake? Here?" asked San Kiu as the noise continued to grow.

"Tanks," said Peach.

"What do you mean?" San Kiu did not understand.

"The People's Liberation Army are moving their tanks into the city," the American explained.

"Why?"

"I believe they are going to use them to drive the demonstrators out of Tienanmen Square."

"No." Chong said, sadly. "They will not drive them out. The feeling is too strong. The people will not go. They will have to shoot."

"Have you anywhere safe to go?" Peach asked.

"If it has come to this, no."

"Then come with me to the US Embassy."

"They will not want us there."

"If you are with me they will give you safety until something else can be worked out."

Chong thought back to the day, so many years before, when the Jesuit priest had stood before his father and begged to be allowed to take Chong away to Macao. He had wanted to go then. Now he did not know what he wanted to do.

Chapter 13

IT WAS A FINE EVENING with the temperature still up in the mid seventies. Betty decided to barbecue for their guests. She had spent a happy day exploring the supermarket and several delicatessens she favored, and had made an assortment of salads, pies and desserts. Nose had come home a bit late, but soon got organized with drinks, glasses, ice, and a mountain of steaks and homemade hamburgers. He was particularly proud of his hamburgers, which were heavily laced with fresh herbs. The first thing he and Betty had done when they moved into their house, eight years ago, was to plant an extensive herb garden.

Most of the guests arrived promptly and were chatting comfortably when the Senator arrived in a chauffeur driven limousine, overdressed and trying to look important. Green met him at the gate.

"I'm delighted you were able to make it, Senator. If you are agreeable, perhaps we could just keep things social until we have eaten. Then we'll find a quiet corner and try to answer the questions you asked me on the phone."

"Fine, fine. Nice yard you have here. Got some good help?" His manner was lordly, and slightly patronizing.

"My wife and children do most of the work, Senator."

"Good, good." The man was like a stuffed peacock.

They walked round into the back garden, and Green made the introductions. He just used first names and left the Senator to sort out who was married to whom and what they did in life. It was easy to guess that Hal Johnson and Calpurnia were married, being the only black folks there, but Green thought the Senator might have trouble figuring out the others.

Penkowski and Mike were the last to arrive with their wives.

"How did you get on, fellas?" Green asked them immediately.

Mike and Penkowski looked at each other, sharing some private knowledge. "My lord, we rescued him; His Highness is in safety, fear you not. But on, my liege, for very little pains will bring this labor to a happy end," they said in chorus. Their wives burst out laughing at the look on Green's face.

"Hold it! Hold it! I got the monopoly on the Bard round here," Green responded and joined in the laughter.

"What's all this?" Betty asked, coming out of the house to join them. "Come on in."

"These two jokers just got one up on me with a very apt quotation," Green explained, still laughing.

"You mean Shakespeare met his match? Thank heaven for that. I get him all the time." Betty joined in the merriment.

The supper was excellent, and even the Senator commented favorably on Green's hamburgers. Earlier he had given everyone the instant impression that very little met with his approval, but they were generous and did not write him off untried. He was an undistinguished looking man, with brown hair, brown eyes and an expensive suit. His knowledge of agriculture was extensive and the others soon discovered that he was very well informed about foreign affairs and nuclear power as well. They wondered what other depths there were to be explored. Once he had shed his coat and tie, and been plied with plenty of food and drink, the Senator relaxed. He was easy enough company then, with a dry wit and strong sense of irony. After supper the women combined forces and removed all the dirty dishes and themselves to the kitchen. They chased out the first man who ventured near. This was women talk; get lost. It was part of the understanding shown by Company wives which allowed their men a few minutes privacy to talk work away from the office. It was part of their contribution to the team. The men would have an hour of privacy while the women talked babies.

"Senator, all these gentlemen are members of my investigative team," Green began as soon as the kitchen door closed. "I chose to invite you here, rather than coming to Capitol Hill, because we are very much a team, and what I know they know. If we could take a few minutes now, I think we may be able to get this thing running smoothly towards a speedy conclusion and not waste too much of your valuable committee time."

The Senator began with a splutter, "I … Mr Green, I only wanted a few words, really, to let my thinking take shape before the first hearing. I don't think it is necessary to involve the whole of your team."

"Senator, our task is to conduct an internal search for facts and to present them to your committee. All of us have been moved in from other sections to do this, and we must do so impartially. I wanted you to meet the whole team to assure you that you have our fullest co-operation."

"Humpf. It sounds irregular to me," the Senator said grumpily.

"Possible irregularities are what we have been assigned to check on, Senator," Green replied smoothly. "One thing that we don't know, and it would help if we did, is where the original disclosure about these arms came from. Perhaps you could help us there?"

"Well, er, yes. I suppose I can. General Rashkhar of the Indian Army informed us that advanced American weapons were being captured with Tamil Tiger rebels in Sri Lanka. He asked if we could do something to cut off the supply."

"Whom did he tell, and when?" asked Mitch.

"Well, er, me actually. While I was on a visit to Delhi with three other Senators," he looked embarrassed.

"Did he show you the weapons? Provide a list, with serial numbers, perhaps?"

"Er, no, he did not. He just told me about them and asked if something could be done. He did not want to make a major affair out of it."

"With respect, Senator, that sounds a mite thin to set off the kind of scare we now have on our hands. Wouldn't you agree?" Hal Johnson said from where he sat on the wall behind the Senator.

"I discussed it with our Defense Attaché at the Embassy, and also with the three Senators who were traveling with me. We agreed the matter should be looked into officially." The Senator was defensive. "We could hardly just ignore it."

Only the tinkling of the fountain in the fishpond broke the silence that followed.

"Senator, we have been looking into this for just over three weeks now. We have found nothing, so far, that suggests these alleged weapons have come from any official source in this country. We will also be enquiring of the less reputable arms dealers, but we must have hard evidence. We need to see those weapons, and have a complete listing of serial numbers. Do you still have contact with this General .....er Rashkhar? Could he provide this information? If not, we would appear to be chasing ghosts. This business is already costing Uncle Sam a bunch of dollars that could be better used." Green was firm.

"Well, er, I may be able to ask, unofficially. I have a meeting shortly with some Indian Government people who are visiting Washington. Maybe they could help." The Senator looked slightly uncomfortable as he tried to re-establish his position.

"Fine," said Green. "I can smell coffee and the ladies will join us soon, so I suggest we leave this now. We will continue our internal checks and keep you informed if anything turns up. Do you still intend to go ahead with the preliminary hearing next week?"

"Well, er, I'll have to take advice on that."

The wives came out with trays of cups and coffee. The evening returned to being a social event. Chevvy had received all sorts of advice and dire warnings from the other wives, with whom she had found instant rapport. Enough attention was paid to the Senator to make him feel his status had been duly appreciated, and after he had swallowed some coffee he pulled out a mobile phone and called his limousine to collect him. Within ten minutes he had gone.

"Jeez! That guy is something else!" Calpurnia Johnson voiced the opinion everyone else was feeling. "Are they all like that?" She raised her face to heaven, hands together in a gesture of prayer. "Sweet Lordy save us!"

They all laughed and spent a few minutes denigrating Senators, Congressmen and a variety of other public servants before conversation returned to more general topics and the group broke up into twos and threes.

Charles Braden, who had been noticeably quiet before, walked down to the fishpond with Green.

"Like to tell me about the worm?" he asked.

"He is Senator Swingate's son. After I told Mike who the former staffer was, he got suspicious and ran some checks. The son-of-a-bitch had bugged the office and was probably feeding everything straight back to Daddy. As soon as we found out, I had Mike and Penkowski collect him and we've put him on ice. It should be a couple of weeks before he surfaces, and by then I will have all the necessary evidence to hang his hide out to dry. I hate to think what he has passed on already."

"Did the Senator tell you anything useful?" Braden asked after a thoughtful moment.

"Nothing we didn't already know, except about the Indians visiting here."

"On that I can tell you a bit. They are coming at the Senator's personal invitation. He is due to take them to Idaho to meet with some nuclear power companies, and they will then spend a weekend up at his private hunting lodge in the Rockies."

Green began to laugh. He laughed so hard that he had to sit on the grass or fall over. Heads turned to look, people smiled, then turned back to their conversations.

"What's so funny about that, Nose?" Braden wanted to share the joke.

"I just … just sent his jerk son … off to bug that place!" Green squeezed the words out between fits of laughter. "I found out that the kid had never been there, so reckoned he wouldn't recognize the place. It seemed too god to resist, and I do think there is something not quite kosher about the Senator."

"Nose!" Braden tried to look shocked and failed utterly. "You mean to tell me that you sent a Company snoop to put an electronic surveillance device in a US Senator's private hunting lodge?"

"Device? Hell no! He's not just putting in a device, he's putting in a whole damned ring! Every last corner, even the outside john will be bugged so you can hear a roach fart."

"Well I'll be damned!" Braden was equally delighted. "The boy won't like it when he finds out."

"Don't be so sure, Charles. Wait till you hear the rest of it," Green said and called Mike and Penkowski over. "Tell the Chief how well the jerk gets on with his Daddy, will you?"

"He don't," Penkowski said flatly.

Mike was more forthcoming. "We got him talking in the car after we picked him up. Seems he blames his father for his mother's death about six years back. They were on a private cruise in the Maldive Islands and the lady died under abnormal circumstances. Daddy had a cast iron alibi, naturally, but Connor wouldn't accept it. He seems to have been very close to his mother, and the Senator had always been a rather old fashioned sort of parent. He and his son never got on well, and this nailed the lid on the coffin of domestic harmony. I got the impression Connor Swingate would be pleased to get even with his daddy."

"It gets better by the minute," Braden laughed. "But it won't take him that long to set up the wires. How are you going to keep him on ice for two weeks, Nose?"

"He was taken up to Idaho Falls by aircraft. From there by chopper to the hunting lodge. On the way back I have arranged for the aircraft to have a little engine trouble. Nothing serious, but enough for the pilot to have to put it down in some wild country where it'll take a while to walk out."

"Just so long as they don't get themselves busted up landing," Braden observed.

"The pilot is an old friend; used to be a Company man. He now does this sort of thing for a living in Hollywood." Green looked triumphant.

Braden whistled softly. "OK, you've told me your news. Let me fill you in on some of the stuff that's been going down in China." His briefing was comprehensive and built a vivid picture for those familiar with the background. They heard him out in silence, and when he had finished, Braden made his excuses and said goodnight.

Chapter 14

CHONG AND THE others waited for ten tense minutes before the girl came. Peach was alarmed to find that she was so young. She could not have been more than seven years old. His doubts diminished rapidly as the child explained how they would move. She spoke with assurance and authority, and he realized that there must be many similar children in this teeming city who had grown up ahead of their years because of the tensions that ruled their lives.

The noise of the tanks had increased to a steady roar. It became a crescendo as the girl opened the street door. This led into a narrow alley with an open drain running down the middle. The few windows in the blank walls were all heavily shuttered and in places the darkness became more intense where trees, growing in courtyards, overhung the walls.

Peach started as a cat, disturbed in its nocturnal patrol, brushed past his leg in its flight from the unexpected visitors to its hunting ground. Occasional scuffling sounds betraying the presence of rats, scuttling to the safety of the drain, and the rustling of leaves overhead, were the only noises apart from the heavy rumble that vibrated the air and now began to throb through the ground beneath their feet.

The girl led them rapidly along the alley, round corners, through archways and other narrow lanes. After some time she stopped by a door and listened. Apparently satisfied, she opened the door and ushered her charges inside. They entered a small courtyard with a low thatched lean-to along three sides. A fat pig grunted at them from its pen in the corner, as if expecting to be fed. White blobs in a line below the thatch resolved themselves into lines of roosting pigeons which took no notice as their silent visitors passed. Beneath the deep shadow of a large leafed tree another door gave access to a wider road. The girl looked out before turning to her followers.

"All talk now. We have just been visiting aged grandmother," she said. "You bend. Too tall. Shuffle feet like old Chinese man," she indicated the American, and then walked calmly out into the street.

"Grandmother is not getting any better." Chong began in a sing-song voice. "We will have to consult a better doctor. If only she would agree to go to the hospital," He continued to grumble about the foibles of an aged relative as they shuffled along the street. A vehicle with six soldiers in it was parked at the corner. Chong raised his voice and San Kiu joined him in his complaints. They continued towards the small truck, the girl leading, Peach in the rear, bent and shuffling.

"But she is old, Husband, and as stubborn as a peasant. She does not want to know what is good for her," San Kiu said.

"Maybe she is old. We all respect her for that. But she should listen to her son who is trying to keep her well to get even older," Chong wailed.

"She says that because she is the oldest she is the wisest and knows better what is good for her. How can we persuade her?" his wife replied.

The soldiers all turned to look as they passed. One made a comment and the others all laughed before they turned back to their own muttered discussion. Chong, San Kiu and the American wanted to run, but the girl continued her slow shuffling progress until they had turned another corner. Peach realized that he had been holding his breath and released it with a soft half-whistle. The girl's sharp glance silenced him.

More narrow alleys followed, and they crossed two larger roads. Peach hoped the girl knew where they were; he had lost his bearings completely.

Ten minutes later they came to a wide boulevard lined with trees and brighter lights. Two military trucks were parked some way along. The party crossed and the girl began to lead them towards the trucks. Peach wanted to scream as the tension gripped him. He became aware that they were approaching a large gateway, brightly lit, with two smartly uniformed soldiers standing by it watching their approach. It was only when they were ten yards away that he realized one of the soldiers was black and both were dressed in formal Marine blues. The bright crest on the gatepost was boldly illuminated. Embassy of the United States of America, read the polished brass letters underneath.

Peach produced his passport and a card. He talked rapidly to the Marine guards and gestured to Chong and San Kiu. He turned to the girl. She was nowhere to be seen.

The loud clatter of tank tracks and the roar of heavy engines brought every head round. Two tanks turned into the boulevard and began to rumble towards the Embassy gates. The parked trucks also started their engines and began to creep forwards. The streetlights reflected off weapons being readied in the backs of the trucks.

Chapter 15

SIM THORNTON HAD timed his operation to use the cover of darkness. The pilot put his Beechcraft down on a small farm strip just before midnight. At the end of the landing run he turned and taxied back along the runway, turning back into wind before he applied the handbrake and cut the power to idle.

"OK. You have six minutes to offload, gentlemen. Then I have to clear the field," he said, turning round in his seat.

"I'll have the copter pilot call you airborne for the return pick up," Thornton said, rising from his seat. "Thanks for a smooth ride."

"Yeah. I'll be waiting for you. Go easy guys," the pilot sketched a goodbye with his hand.

Thornton unlatched the door and began passing things out to waiting hands. He and Swingate unloaded the three metal ice boxes and tossed out their overnight bags. A red plastic box followed before the two men climbed down onto the short grass. Thornton pushed the steps back into their housing, latched the door, and slapped his hand on the rear fuselage, stepping back quickly. The plane's engines roared immediately and the Beechcraft began to roll. It gained speed rapidly and disappeared into the darkness.

Thornton took something from his bag and walked forward ten yards. He placed it on the ground and depressed a switch. A dim red light, barely visible to the other two men, glowed on top of the device. He walked back and accepted the cigarette offered by his partner, who had been awaiting their arrival at the strip.

"Two minutes," he said.

"What is that thing?" asked Swingate.

"Beacon to guide the copter in."

"Looks like you should have replaced the battery. He won't see that too well, even from above. I can hardly see it from here." Swingate sounded slightly derisive.

"It's infra-red. He'll ride in on the beam."

"Oh."

The two men smoked in silence while Swingate sat down on one of his boxes, feeling slightly left out. He hardly had time to straighten his back when the flop-flop of a rotor made all three men turn their heads and scan the black sky. Moments later the downwash reached them and a bright light came on, very close, illuminating the yellow box on the turf nearby. A matt black Jetranger settled lightly with the beacon directly beneath its nose, mid way between the skids.

"Very pretty," muttered Thornton's partner, picking up a box and moving forward. All three men carried gear towards the helicopter as the rotor pitch changed and the downwash eased. Thornton picked up his beacon before he latched the rear door and climbed up beside the pilot.

"Nice one, Jake. Any problems?"

"Nope." The pilot was resetting a dial on his instrument panel. "You want some coffee there's an Aladdin flask below your seat with some paper cups."

"Thanks pal. You want some?" Thornton asked, reaching under his seat.

"Later. I need both hands for the next bit," the pilot replied. His hands were moving over the controls and as soon as the torque indicator reached its mark he lifted the machine lightly into the air. The nose dipped as he moved the stick forward and swung the machine round into a wide arc.

Thornton passed beakers of steaming coffee to the others and stared into the blackness ahead. Jake reset the radio and pressed the transmit button.

"Leapfrog," he said to an unseen listener. The speaker in the cabin roof clicked twice in response. "Rightee. I'll take that coffee now please," he turned to Thornton. "We have about eighteen minutes to set-down."

The rest of the flight passed in silence. Jake flew with an economy of movement and their landing was as smooth and precise as before. A figure hurried forward through the darkness and opened the cabin door. Within two minutes the boxes were on the grass, the three agents had disembarked, and the helicopter had disappeared upwards into the night.

"Let's get moving," Thornton picked up a bag and one of the metal boxes as he spoke and moved off towards a stand of fir trees thirty yards away. The others collected the rest of the kit and followed.

Light showed through the trees. It came from the open doorway of a large log chalet, standing clear on a rise beyond the trees. The windows were dark and heavily shuttered from within. Thornton led the group inside.

"Stack the boxes over here," he said, putting his own load on the floor.

After depositing his load, Swingate turned to look round the room. The walls were planked with polished cedar, cluttered with hunting trophies and big stuffed fish in glass cases. A huge moose head, mounted on a dark wooden shield, hung above the stone hearth with an old flintlock musket across its antlers and a cavalry saber hung beneath. His gaze came to rest on Thornton's other helper who had been waiting at the lodge. She was small and dark, with long glossy hair and deep, dark eyes. She watched him openly, and the frankness of her appraisal made him blush. He felt a tightness in his pants and his color deepened as her smile told him that she had noticed. He turned away.

"How's supper, Ro?" Thornton asked.

"Ready when you are."

"Right. Let's eat, then get some sleep. You can get started in the morning," he turned to Swingate. "I'll walk you round and explain the details after we've eaten."

Swingate found his glance kept returning to the girl during the meal. Each time he found her watching him. Her presence and open assessment of him already had him feeling disturbed, but there was something about this girl that he found incredibly magnetic. His pants felt tight again and he was glad she could not see under the table.

He was relieved when the meal was finished and Thornton took him on a tour of the building. It turned out to be much larger than he had thought, and very luxurious. There were seven large bedrooms, each equipped with a king sized bed covered in thick furs, and with a shower room off to one side. The modern kitchen was fitted out in style with two large freezers, a microwave and a Bluestar gas range. Two store rooms held a variety of outdoor clothing, skis, and other sports equipment. One had a rack filled with choice wines and several cases of Scotch whiskey. There was a work-out room with top-notch exercise machines and a sauna. Outside, two outbuildings were set back some yards into the trees. The smaller one turned out to be a generator house, with a large yellow power plant. The machine was efficiently silenced and the inside of the building was lined with thick rockwool cladding to further deaden the noise. Swingate had wondered where the power came from as he had not been able to hear the generator before. Even standing next to the machine there was no need to raise his voice.

"Where's the fuel?" he asked.

"There's an underground tank behind the building, holding about three thousand gallons."

"How on earth do they get that amount of fuel up here?"

"I guess it's all flown in. There is no road for miles."

"Some place. It must have cost a pile of dollars. Who's the owner?"

"You know the rules, pal. Need to know." Thornton said.

"Yes. I suppose so." Swingate closed the door and they moved over to look at the other building. This was much larger than the power house, with wide double doors that opened onto the clearing where the Jetranger had landed earlier. Like the main house it was built of heavy logs and the walls inside were paneled with ply. Racks along one side held two large open canoes, while the rear and the other side were fitted with work benches over steel cabinets. Thornton opened one. It was stacked with tool trays and boxes of what looked like auto spare parts. An overhead hoist mounted on a steel rail ran the length of the building.

"What's this place for? It looks like an auto repair shop," observed Swingate.

"Hangar for a helicopter is my guess," Thornton said. "Plenty of spares too."

"This is some fancy hunting lodge," Swingate said. "My father used to have one up north some place, but I thought they were all shacks and bare boards."

"You ever go up there?" Thornton's enquiry sounded casual.

"No. Dad always said it was just for the big boys, and by the time I was old enough I was off to college. Never had much time for hunting anyhow."

"I thought you were on a fishing trip when they pulled you in for this job."

"Yeah. But I only took that up because Henry and Luther, my boys, got keen."

"Kids do that sort of thing." Thornton acknowledged. "Come on, let's get some coffee and then some sleep," he closed the heavy doors and led the way back to the main building.

"What's in there?" Swingate asked as they passed a door Thornton had not opened when showing him round.

"I don't know yet. It's locked and we haven't found the key. You any good at picking locks?"

"I never tried."

"One of the others can have a go at it in the morning, while you are rigging the rest of the joint."

The smell of coffee was rich and strong as they came back into the main room. Swingate's eyes went straight to the girl who was sitting on the edge of the table with one foot on a chair. She was already watching him and the corners of her mouth turned up slightly as their eyes met. His pants felt tight again and her smile broadened.

"You take the second room," Thornton said, passing him a beaker of coffee. "I'm for some shut eye. Goodnight."

"G' night," Swingate mumbled with a mouthful of coffee.

"Night, Sim. Breakfast at seven thirty?" Ro asked as Thornton headed for the door.

"Fine."

Swingate and the girl watched each other in silence for several minutes as they drank their coffee. He was gradually becoming accustomed to her frank stare, but could not be sure what was behind it. He was tired, but did not want to leave her.

"Ro. What's that short for?" he asked.

"Rowatahanee."

"Sounds unusual. Hawaiian?"

"Backwoods Indian from Canada. My grandmother insisted on keeping some of the old traditions."

"You're a full blooded Indian?" Swingate sounded surprised.

"No. My Pa was a Norwegian sailor. He somehow got lost ashore and fell for my mother's charms whilst on a hike through the mountains."

"Must be where you got your beautiful looks." Swingate blushed deeply as he said this. His pants tightened again and he saw the girl's eyes slide downwards.

"Looks like you've got something pretty good in there. Like to show it to me?"

Swingate almost choked on the mouthful of coffee he was taking to try and hide his embarrassment. Ro took the cup from his hand, slapped him on the back, and led him towards the doorway.

Chapter 16

GREEN HELD A BRISK review meeting and before sending the team off to pursue their individual tasks. After hearing Braden's briefing the previous evening, he was anxious to complete this assignment in jig time and get back to his normal patch. He intended to spend the rest of the morning running a check on the Indian delegation due to arrive that afternoon.

As the meeting broke up, he asked Mike when they were likely to hear from the Customs Department about the freight company.

"Not for a few days, unless there is a problem," Mike told him.

"Good. What about the jerk's wife and kids?"

"They won't go anywhere, and should not start asking questions until tomorrow night. We have prepared a contingency plan for that. Hal is going to take Cal and their kids down to the same campsite and drop them off right next door. Cal's southern motherliness will take care of the rest."

"Is that wise? Involving Hal's wife?"

"She used to work for the Company, before they had kids. She volunteered."

"I'd forgotten that," Green said, leaning back in his chair. "Say, Betty and the others were real taken with your Chevvy. You're a lucky man."

"Thanks." Mike collected the papers from their meeting table and took them into the next office. The telephone warbled as he was leaving and Green snatched it from its cradle. Why couldn't they have bells like they used to, he thought. I must see if we can get the damned thing changed.

"Green," he said, bringing the handset to his ear.

"Nose, I need to talk to you," Braden's voice said without preamble. "Are you free?"

"Is it urgent, Charles? I was about to start on a new lead, but it could hold for a while, I guess. Want me to come over?"

"Yes it is. But I'll come to you. I'll be there in five minutes." The phone went dead in Green's ear and he wondered what had fired the Chief up. He pressed the intercom button and called Mike.

"The Chief just called. He's on his way over and we need an hour without calls please."

"You got it."

"Good, he'll be here in five, and he likes his coffee ... "

"Decaf with Sweetex and plastic creamer," Mike finished for him.

"How in apple blossom time do you know that?" Green's voice registered his surprise.

"Asked Maureen. That lady is a fountain of good information."

"Seems like she's not the only one around here," Green said and heard Mike chuckle as he cradled the handset.

The coffee arrived twenty seconds before Braden.

"We just got a flash from Walker. I want to run it by you and see what the famous nose comes up with," Braden said, sitting down and reaching for the coffee Green pushed across the desk towards him. He raised his eyebrows slightly as he drank, but made no other comment. Green waited.

"You remember all that stuff we were getting from the biochemist a while back? There was some hot material there. It seems that he is a very bright boy, pretty original in his thinking, and not above making the occasional scene in public," Braden began. "Well, he's done it again. This time he appears to have got his whole local People's Revolutionary Committee slung in the hoosegow. It happened a couple of days ago. Now he's disappeared from the center where he works. His own people haven't taken him and there's a search on. With everything else going on in China just now he may be able to stay out of sight for a few days, but they'll get him in the end. Unless someone else does. If we can get to him first, do you think he would be willing to come over? His wife has disappeared with him."

Green thought for a while, pouring himself more coffee.

"He never showed any inclination to leave before. He was always a loyal Chinese, but he wanted to be free to share his ideas with other scientists. He always played things just below the ultimate threat level before, and managed to stay in his job. On the information we have I can't say if he would want to come. He might prefer to stay there and work for changes. With all that's going on now he may see that as more attainable. It's not, but he isn't to know that. How would you want to bring him out, supposing he did want to come?"

"I was wondering if that courier you used could bring them out through Korea to Seoul." Braden said.

"No way. After I had that last little dust up the route will be white hot for years. The gooks don't take kindly to people rubbing out their border guards, and they've been bitching to Beijing about trust between allies ever since. Last I heard they'd moved a couple of divisions each into the area. Now they bristle at each other across the wire. I'm afraid I screwed that one up good. You'll have to think of another way, if it's on at all." Green looked slightly sheepish.

"Come on, Nose. You've done more snatches than anyone I know. Surely you can come up with something for this. He's a big one, and our guys would love to have him on the team. They made that clear when his first paper was published and have repeated it with every subsequent disclosure." Braden stared moodily at his empty cup. Green reached over and refilled it, pushing across the mixers for Braden to help himself. "Can't you come up with something?"

"The others all wanted out, and none of them were such big fish. We need more information. Is Peach still there?"

I sent him back in on a four week tourist visa, ten days ago. He's probably wandering round Tienanmen Square at this moment. He checks in with Walker twice a day."

"Could he locate Chong and his wife? Find out if they are willing?" Green steepled his fingers and leaned forward, elbows on the desk, thumbs pressed against his chin.

"Walker is going to ask him next time he calls in. There are seven others in the city who also know Chong. The first one to get a sight of him … " Braden drifted into silence.

The two men sat for several minutes thinking and saying nothing.

"He came originally from Shanghai," Green said at last. "You'd better have someone in there keep watch as well. He may try to go back."

"It's been twenty something years. Do you really think he will?" Braden asked.

"It's possible. Not very likely, but we've never been able to rely on him doing the obvious. Chong has been very inventive over the years. It's one of the reasons our academics have been so interested in him. If you are serious we have to cover as many possibilities as we can. The present turmoil just makes doing that a mite more complicated."

"What do you think the old men will do about these demonstrations?" Braden asked, shifting the subject.

Green leaned back and stared out of the windows for several minutes before he answered. Neither man noticed Mike slip quietly into the office with fresh coffee and a large plate of sandwiches. He left as silently.

"When does the Russian go home?" Green asked, turning back to his Chief.
"His aircraft is due to take off in the next couple of hours."

"What about the People's Liberation Army, any more movements?" Green was working through a mental checklist, cross checking Braden's updated information with the news bulletin he had heard on the way to work.

"Walker reports that some units have been pulled back. Others are still just sitting in their trucks, as before. The people in the Square are still behaving themselves, but singing and chanting a lot. A few people have drifted away, back to work I guess, but it hasn't visibly diminished their numbers. There must be well over a million still there. Mao's portrait has been replaced with a clean one."

"Broadcasts from the leadership?" Green asked, reaching for a sandwich without really noticing.

"All quiet for the last sixteen hours. The power struggle appears to have gone indoors." Braden also took a sandwich.

"It is early morning, Saturday, over there," Green began. "My bet is that the Army will pull more troops out during the day. They are setting the scene for the big crunch now. I would expect them to bring in different regiments during the night. Tanks probably. By breakfast tomorrow they'll have the lid on the pot. The move will come twelve to eighteen hours later in the other cities. By Monday they'll have the whole country sealed tighter than a duck's ass. From then on they'll have squads picking up the ringleaders, and anyone else who's in the wrong place at the time. There'll probably be a denunciation campaign, just as in Mao's time, and when a few have been rounded up the summary executions will follow."

"You really think the old men will go that far, Nose?"

"Sure. It wouldn't be the first time. Afterwards they'll simply say it never happened. They will rewrite the records, again, to show that. George Orwell never knew what a good prophet he really was."

"Why use tanks?" Braden asked.

"The soldiers who have been there so far will be considered to have been contaminated. They have had plenty of time to sit and listen. The people have been joking with them. Would you want to shoot your own folks after that? No, they'll use tanks. They have to crack down hard or risk a rebellion in the Army."

"What if the Army won't do it, Nose?"

"They will. Most of the commanders are old guard men. They know which side of the patty has butter on it. If they let a civil war start they go. Clamp down hard now, and they stay in command. No soldier wants to fight his own army.

Other people, okay, but not their own. So shoot up a few hundred civilians, release the tension among the troops, and then screw the lid down. Clear out the rebellious element and carry on as before," he sighed and took another mouthful of coffee before continuing.

"So it sets China back a few years in the world's popularity stakes. They have no need to hurry; a few years won't make any difference in a hundred. They lose a few good people. So what? There are plenty more in a population that size. In a few months the whole population will be saying that their government was right and the dissenters were wrong. You'll see."

"How can you be sure it won't blow up completely like a fire storm?"

"Look, Charles, a couple of million people have a bit of a party. The mass of the people don't know anything about it. The Chinese people have long ago learned obedience to authority. They still revere old age. That, and the habit of mass conformity, will be enough to do it."

"And later?"

"Later? The whole pot will simmer along for a year or two, like a pressure cooker on a low flame, letting off spurts of steam now and then. Eventually some of the old guard will die, but they're already well prepared with like-minded followers who will take their places. They breed their own continuity and security of tenure. It'll take another Mao to create a successful revolution, and they have nobody even remotely of his stature or ability." Green sighed again as he leaned back in his chair.

"What about Hong Kong?" Braden asked.

"That's safe enough. The Chinese won't mess with that, at least until after ninety seven. Maybe not even then."

"What makes you so sure?"

"They may be old and rigid, but they are not fools. They need Hong Kong as a gateway, a talking ground, an access channel to the rest of the world. The people in Hong Kong understand and are practiced in the ways of the rest of the world. With somewhere like that as their doorway, it is feasible for the Mandarins to control what comes in. Shucks, even Hitler knew he needed somewhere like that. He could have had Switzerland for breakfast and nobody would have stopped him. But it was more use to him as a neutral place for talking. Beijing will keep their deal. They usually do, with outsiders, and have more to gain by doing so than by not."

Both men fell silent again, Braden looking blankly into space, Green staring into his coffee cup. Eventually Braden hauled himself to his feet.

"Thanks Nose. I wish you would get this sewn up fast and get back where you belong. I need you there."

"You sent me here, remember?" Green said without bitterness, but agreeing with his Chief's sentiment.

"Yeah. How's it going?"

"Not much to show. We've found a suspicious shipment, and the boys are chasing that one now. I was about to start a check on those Indians the Senator is hosting when you called. I'm convinced there's a connection there."

"The boy?"

"Still busy bugging Daddy's playpen."

"Shoot! I just don't know where you get these crazy notions. Keep at it pal. I'll keep you informed on anything from my side." Braden headed for the door.

After he had left Green buzzed the intercom and asked Mike to join him. He was excited by the idea of bringing the biochemist out. He wanted to take the idea a bit further, but not with Braden, until he had more information. Mike came in and took a seat, helping himself to the last of the sandwiches that was beginning to curl up on the plate.

"Mike," Green asked, "if you had to bring someone out of China today, how would you go about it?"

"Through the front door would be easiest. Got someone in mind?"

"Not exactly, but maybe. Why the front door?"

"I would expect all the windows and side doors to be firmly bolted and well guarded by this time, if the news reports on TV are even half true."

"And if they have a watch on the front door?"

"Put a Groucho mustache and spectacles on him and just walk boldly out."

"You may just have something there, Mike. Thanks." A saucy twinkle lit up Green's eyes.

Chapter 17

CONNOR SWINGATE CAME slowly to wakefulness as the aroma of fresh coffee reached his nostrils. He reached across the bed, but it was empty. With his eyes still closed he stretched beneath the heavy fur and pushed it off him. He opened his eyes as he felt a weight settle on the bed beside him. Ro put a mug of coffee on the bedside table and ran her hand down his chest. Her long black hair fell in a silken wave over her shoulders and reached down to the cleft of her buttocks.

"Hello sleepy head. Want some breakfast?"

He reached up and pulled her down on top of him.

"Yes!"

She felt him harden against her belly as his arms moved to enfold her. Ro wriggled, laughing, out of his embrace and stood up. Her skin was a rich golden color, without bikini marks, he noticed, as he reached for her again.

"No you don't!" she tried to say seriously, but the attempt was ruined by the laughter in her eyes. "I said breakfast. Playtime comes after work, so put your gun away, cowboy, and get dressed." She tossed his clothes at him, slipped into her tracksuit and danced lightly towards the door. "How do you like your eggs?"

"Spoil sport."

Connor climbed out of the huge bed, went into the shower and turned the icy stream on full blast.

Ro was piling food onto the table when he came into the main room of the lodge. Thornton and Al were already there, helping themselves to canned fruit and cereals.

"Sleep well?" asked Thornton.

"Marvelous! How long have we got for this job?" Connor's mind was already turning to the task he had been brought here to do.

"I want to get done today if possible. Pick-up is first light tomorrow. That should see us clear before anyone is likely to turn up," Thornton told him.

"Someone expected soon then?"

"Friday, I'm told, but they could get here before. I want time to clean up and be gone long before that."

Connor laughed. "It could take a bit of explaining if we were still here with wires spread all over."

"Right. Al, can you make a full search for the key to that locked room? If you don't find it in an hour, pick the lock." Thornton's mind was now focused entirely on the job.

Al and Ro cleared the table when they had eaten while Connor started unpacking his boxes. Thornton opened the red plastic crate and laid out its contents.

"Any of this useful to you?" he asked Connor.

"Nicmar cells if you have any," he said, and came over to look at the selection. He picked up several small items and carried them to the main table with his own equipment. "I can group the power packs. How long do you want them to last?"

"We will not have access again for at least three weeks," Thornton said, "how long can you manage?"

"With these toys of mine that's no problem. I can give you three months, with a range of fifteen miles. More if the listening post is on a hill top in line of sight."

"It's not, unfortunately," Thornton said, "but it's only few miles in a straight line."

Connor laid out a series of shallow plastic trays and began distributing parts among them. When he was satisfied he sat down, pulled the first tray towards him and began rapidly to assemble the components, finally attaching three very fine wires. The whole assembly was then wrapped in thin plastic film from a large roll. The completed assembly was laid back in its tray and he began on the next. In an hour he had seventeen complete devices assembled in numbered trays. Running a lead from a wall socket, Connor plugged in a small hair dryer with which he warmed each device and shrunk the plastic film tight. When he had finished none of them was bigger than a golf ball, and each carried a number.

Ro appeared with a tray of coffee.

"Al's trying to pick the lock," she told Thornton as she handed the coffee round.

For the next six hours Connor was busy locating and installing his devices. Once the bulky part of the device was hidden behind the wall or ceiling panels, one of the protruding wires was fed through a small hole in the panel. Connor soldered the end to a tiny disc, no more than a millimeter thick and less than five across. A spot of adhesive was applied to the back of the disc before the wire was drawn back through the panel and the disc pressed firmly into place over the hole. The tiny spots were difficult enough to see when you knew where to look, but Connor left nothing to chance. He produced a packet of colored marker pens from one of his boxes and carefully colored each disc to match its surrounding panel. They were so skillfully placed that it was hard to find them, even on close inspection. The other two wires from each device were extended and linked to a carefully hidden network of filaments that came together below the apex of the roof.

Connor returned to the main room and rummaged in one of his metal boxes. Again he sat at the table and began to assemble another unit from a collection of chips and circuit cards. He packed the whole assembly into a black neoprene container no bigger than a cigarette packet, and sealed it with adhesive tape. Back in the roof space he spent a long time connecting the wires he had laid earlier, testing each circuit several times with another black box. At last he was satisfied and came down.

"All done in here. That leaves just the two outbuildings and the locked room," He told Thornton. "Has Al got in there yet?"

"Yes. While you were up in the roof. Come and look," he led the way.

The room was fitted out like a command post. Two computers occupied a table, and a very powerful radio telephone was built into one wall above a bank of metal filing cabinets. An antique roll top desk stood beneath the blind-covered window. Connor stared at it then turned away when Thornton asked if there was anything wrong.

"No, just looking at the desk. You don't see many like that around. Nice piece of furniture," he said, almost too hastily. "This will be easy. Want me to tap the computers as well?"

"I think not. You would need to turn them on and there may be a security device. We don't want to advertise. It's a pity, but we'll have to pass on them." Thornton sounded disappointed.

Connor was about to disagree but held his tongue. A suspicion had formed in his mind and he wanted to check it out before saying anything else. He looked closely at the radio instead and pulled a small manual from his pocket, thumbed through until he found the page he wanted, and then compared figures on the equipment's data plate with tables in the manual.

"This baby," he said, patting the radio, "and the room, will take about an hour. I'll do this before the outhouses because Al will have to relock the door. That may take time."

"Right. I am going for a scout round outside before it gets dark." Thornton left him to get on with the job.

As soon as he was gone Connor went back to the desk and looked carefully at the right hand end. He smiled at what he saw, and went to collect the equipment needed for this room. When he came back he jammed the heavy chair against the inside of the door and went to work. Bugging the computers only took him fifteen minutes. After that, he reached behind the desk and ran his fingers along until he felt a slight rough patch. He pressed this and was rewarded with a faint click. The roll-top slid silently up its runners. A quick look through the pigeon holes and small drawers produced no surprises except for a fat bundle of hundred dollar bills. Connor ruffled them in his hand. There must have been more than a thousand bills. He put them back and closed the drawer. Reaching up under the roll-top his fingers went unerringly to the tip of a small metal lever and he pressed downwards. With another faint click the right hand section of pigeon holes swung forwards revealing a secret compartment behind. At first he thought the space was empty, but as he pushed his fingers deeper they encountered a paper packet in the furthest corner. It was a large Air Mail envelope. Connor hardly bothered to examine the package, but laid it in the bottom of his tool tray beneath the manual. It took a few seconds to replace the moving section and reset the locking lever. He was about to pull down the roll-top when Ro tried the door.

"Hold it!" he called, "I've got the radio in pieces all over the floor. I'm almost finished."

"Good. I was going to ask if you wanted a beer." Ro's voice was muffled behind the heavy door.

"Yeah. Give me five minutes to finish putting this thing back together."

"Right," came the muffled response.

Connor waited a full minute before he pulled the heavy roll-top down and the lock clunked. He lifted the radio down and placed it beside the computers, swiftly removing the backplate. He pulled the chair away from the door and opened it.

"Floor's clear now, Ro," he called into the passage.

She appeared almost immediately carrying two cans of cold Coors, handed him one and accepted the kiss he planted on her forehead. She leaned against the door frame to watch him finish. In less than ten minutes everything was back in place. Connor collected his tool tray and they took their empty beer cans along to the main room.

Al was seated at the big table filing a piece of brass and looked up as they came in. The lock was spread out in front of him.

"All finished?"

"Just the outhouses to do," Connor said. "I thought you picked the lock."

"That's right, but there's no guarantee it can be closed the same way. It's much easier to take the lock out and make a key. After that we can always open it easily on another occasion." Al grinned as he held up his handiwork.

"Smart," Connor laughed.

Thornton came in at that moment and asked Connor how it had gone. Connor explained some of what he had done then took his tools and more of his gold ball sized modules and went out to rig the outhouses. He was back inside half an hour, the job completed.

Al cooked steaks that evening and after the meal there was a relaxed atmosphere round the table as Connor completed the assembly of the listening station and demonstrated the performance of his electronic wizardry. He had provided a separate recording device for each room, and where there was more than one sensor in the room an automatic selector would record the most powerful signal coming in at any moment. A green light came on whenever a tape had been activated. The completed console was housed neatly inside a plastic attaché case which could easily be hidden in a suitable location.

Connor took a strip of adhesive labels and stuck one next to each indicator light. Then he went round the whole place checking the system and writing on the labels.

"All systems Go," he announced when he finally came back to the main room. "Who is going to operate this set up?"

"Al," said Thornton, "but you'd better show us all, just in case."

The lesson took only a few minutes and they were all surprised at how simple the equipment was to operate.

"Jeez, Connor. They said you were good, but not that good. That is one dandy of a set up," Thornton complimented him. "Well, I'm for some shuteye. We have an early start. Pick-up at first light," he stood up and stretched. "Good night."

"Good night." Al got up as well.

"Night. I'll just pack my kit away now in case I'm still asleep when we leave," Connor said. Going over to the open boxes he began packing all the unused components. Ro went into the kitchen to wash up. When he had finished packing his equipment Connor went into the kitchen and came up behind Ro as she was drying dishes. He put his arms round her and cupped a breast in each hand, nuzzling her neck through her thick hair.

"Just hold it right there, cowboy. Let me finish this first," Ro said, leaning back into his embrace. Connor released her, picked up a cloth and began to dry dishes, smiling to himself. He never helped in the kitchen at home.

Chapter 18

PREGNANCY HAD BEEN remarkably easy for Chevvy. In the early months she suffered very little morning sickness and, being what her mother would have called 'a sensible girl', she made light of her few discomforts. Now, as she neared her time, the baby was very active and she was frequently woken during the night by its movements. Not wanting to wake Mike for something he could do nothing about, she often slipped out of bed, made a pot of tea, and walked quietly round the apartment until the baby eased itself into a comfortable position and settled down. Sometimes she would lie on the living room floor and practice the exercises she learned at the prenatal clinic. Later she would slip back into bed and sleep.

This morning she had woken but the baby was still. It had wriggled so much the night before that it must be tired, she thought. Even so, she eased out of bed and padded through to the kitchen to boil the kettle. She was just pouring the boiling water into the teapot when the phone rang. Chevvy looked at the clock as she lifted the receiver.

"Hello?"

"Sorry to disturb you at four thirty, Ma'am. Duty Officer Evans calling. May I speak with Mike please?"

"Who did you say was calling?"

"Dwight Evans, Duty Officer. It is urgent Mrs. Ah..."

Chevvy smiled to herself as the man sounded embarrassed over his difficulty with her name. "Just call me Chevvy, Mr Evans, everyone else does. Hold on a minute while I go and call Mike." She laid the receiver beside the kettle and went through to the bedroom. A sleepy Mike met her at the door and wrapped his arms around her.

"Oh. There you are Chevvy. I thought I heard the phone."

"You did. It's the Duty Officer and he says it's urgent."

"What time is it?" Mike asked, leading her back to the kitchen.

"Four thirty."

"The baby playing you up?" He asked, picking up the phone.

"No. I just woke up, that's all. Answer the phone, Darling." Chevvy pushed him away and went to the refrigerator in search of milk for her tea. Mike turned his attention to the phone.

"Morning Dwight. What's up?"

"We've found your ship. Better than that, the cargo is still on board," the disembodied voice said in Mike's ear as a smile spread over his face. They talked on for several minutes, Mike listening for most of the time as the Duty Officer told him the details.

"Fine," Mike said at last. "That's good news, Dwight. Now please call Hal Johnson on the bleeper and give him all the details. He's out of town, somewhere near Munfordville, Kentucky. When you've filled him in have him call me here. If you can't find him in thirty minutes call me back yourself."

Chevvy came back into the kitchen as Dwight Evans was apologizing for waking her.

"Problems?" she asked as he put the phone down.

"Nope. We've just found a needle in a haystack," he said stroking her bulging stomach. "Now, go and put a robe on. You'll get cold."

"I'm not cold. Mike?"

"Yes?"

"Will you take some pictures of me?"

"But you don't like having your picture taken, Chevvy."

"It's this," she said, smoothing her hands over the bulge. "It's so big and I'm such a funny shape. In a few weeks it will all be gone. I'd just like to have a picture of it. That's all."

"Sure. That's a nice idea. Now?"

"Yes please." Chevvy led him back into the living room.

They were sitting on the carpet, giggling like two teenagers, when Hal Johnson called twenty minutes later.

"Dwight Evans gave me the news, Mike. I'm going over there right away. There's nothing doing down here. Lois Swingate and her kids have gone. The man in the campsite office said one of the boys got sick or something. He didn't know where they went," Hal said.

"What about Cal and your bunch?"

"She'll get them home. I will get a flight from Louisville to Chicago and see if I can pick up an early flight to Europe and onwards. I'll call the office and let you know the schedule."

"Hold on a minute, Hal. That could take you thirty-six hours or more. Get a flight to JFK and fly the Arrow to London. There are direct flights from there. I will wake up the movements desk and fix it. Just get yourself to JFK as fast as possible. The tickets will be waiting for you there."

"Concorde don't come cheap, pal. Think the boss will wear that?" Hal sounded doubtful.

"Don't worry, Hal. He gave me the authority. I'll fix it. Ring me from Louisville."

"You got it. Love to Chevvy," Hal said cheerily, and rang off.

Mike replaced the handset and went through to the kitchen where Chevvy, still naked, was busy cooking.

"What are you doing, Chevvy?"

"Making you breakfast, of course. You don't think I'm going to let you go off to the office hungry, not knowing when you'll next eat?"

He wrapped his arms round her and nuzzled her ear.

"You're a wonderful wife. I love you," he mumbled into her neck.

"You're a pretty good husband too, and I love you. Now go and get showered. This will be ready in a couple of minutes, and I'm not having it spoiled because you're feeling randy. Shower." She threatened him with an egg-covered wooden spoon.

"Yes Ma'am!" Mike laughed, dodging out of range.

Chapter 19

IT TOOK MIKE LESS than thirty minutes to make Hal's travel arrangements when he got to the office. The movements people were busy when he arrived, but he chatted up a drab looking spinster from Sacramento, who was probably more accustomed to being ignored. Within a few moments Mike had made her feel important and valued and she swung into action.

June Connaught was highly efficient, with an encyclopedic knowledge of the world's airline schedules, customs rules, visa requirements, and all the minutiae of moving people around the world by every form of transport from airliner to bullock cart.

The early Concorde flight was full. June scratched her dull brown hair with a pencil as she watched the screen. Soon she began to type rapidly at her console. A complex mass of figures and symbols began to scroll across the screen. It stopped at a list of names.

"What's that?" asked Mike, looking over her shoulder.

"Passenger list. I'm just trying to figure out who to shunt off."

"You can do that?"

"Sure. Happens all the time on regular flights. This one is not so easy, but choose the right person and it can be done. Just one seat?"

"Yes." Mike was fascinated. June scrolled through the list to the end, then began again more slowly.

"That one." She stopped the scroll. "See here, Jack Boot. Sounds like a rock singer." She turned to another computer and typed rapidly. The machine buzzed for a while and the screen went blank.

"What's wrong?" Mike asked.

"Nothing. It's just tapping into the Immigration Department's database. Give it a minute and we'll have Mr Jack Boot's file, with everything down to the size of his mother's knickers."

"Jeez!"

June smiled at him. "They're great tools when you know what to ask them."

"What are?"

"Computers. Ask the wrong question and you get zilch. Ask the right questions and… jackpot!" As she spoke the machine bleeped and the screen displayed the file on Jack Boot. "There you are: rock musician. Been on tour over here. He'll do just fine to shunt off." June rubbed her hands together with glee.

"What if he objects?"

"He'll love it. All these creeps want is a bit of publicity, so let's make sure he gets some."

"But how can you … ?" Mike began.

"Just be patient for a few moments," June cut him short, "and watch. You might learn something useful. First I book Mr H. Johnson, US Government Officer, on the flight. Add a 'Priority One' flag to his standby rating. There." She was typing rapidly on the first console as she spoke. "Then we come back to this baby here. Now we insert an official request for our pop idol to be detained, searched, and questioned concerning his possible involvement in the handling of something nasty. What shall we say: Crack cocaine or meth-amphetamine?" June voiced her thoughts as she worked. "Then we put in a call-back reference. I'll put in my own number. If they bother to check I can spin a suitable tale for them. There, done. Your man will go on the flight. Easy." She turned to Mike with a smug look. "Now, where else do you want him to go?"

"Dakar."

"Bangladesh or West Africa?"

"Senegal," Mike said.

June Connaught turned her attention to her keyboard and screen again. Within three minutes it was done. All flights confirmed with open returns and tickets ready for Hal to collect when he reached JFK. All he had to do was get there in time for the flight. June turned to Mike with a look of triumph.

"Miz Connaught, you are a marvel!" Mike said with genuine enthusiasm. He planted a smacking kiss on her cheek and hurried back to his own office leaving the startled woman holding her face and staring at the swinging door.

The telephone was ringing as Mike reached his office. It was Hal calling from Louisville. Mike gave him the details, said good luck and hung up as a messenger came in from the communications center with a pile of incoming signals.

"Somebody loves ya today," he said with a smile as he dumped most of the pile on the desk and left to deliver the others elsewhere. Mike skimmed through the first few sheets and settled down to go through them in detail, highlighting parts of the text with a fluorescent pen. The log jam in this investigation was now well and truly broken and information had started to flow.

By the time Green arrived, just before eight, Mike had received another pile of telexes and compiled a synopsis of the key facts. A report had come in from the Bureau on their investigation of Shandar Freighting Company, and there were transcripts of their interviews with the bank clerk. An artist's impression of the customer was being prepared and would arrive by fax within the hour.

Mike wondered how Green had got on with his check on the Indian delegation. If the information on his desk was correct there should be some interesting revelations there.

Chapter 20

THORNTON'S SURVEILLANCE team was waiting under the trees when the black Jetranger's skids kissed the grass at first light. Connor had had a long whispered conversation with Ro when they went to bed. He had told her what he had found in the locked study, but not about tapping the computers. At first she had not believed him, so he fetched the envelope from beneath his tools and together they had read the bundle of letters it contained. Ro was shocked. For a while she lay beside Connor, beneath the heavy bearskin, in silence until he climbed out of bed and began dressing.

"Where are you going?" Ro asked.

"I'm going to make another bug. This one is for myself, not the Company," Connor said with a grim look.

"Can I help?"

"Sure, but stay here. I'll bring the parts in here," he went to collect what he needed. Two minutes later he was back with one of his ice boxes, and began to unpack electronic components and spread them out on the bed. Ro pushed the fur aside and pulled on a tracksuit

An hour later the job was done. Connor packed the unused components away and returned the box to the main room. He had a number of questions when they climbed back into bed.

"Ro, why wasn't I told who this place belongs to?"

"We did not know how you might feel about bugging your own father. Nobody knew anything about what you've just found, and the surveillance is for a different reason. You might have screwed up the job or refused altogether."

"You could have brought in someone else to rig the system."

"Sure, but you're supposed to be the best and someone in Langley wanted you on ice. This was an ideal way."

"Why?" Connor was puzzled.

"Why what?"

"Why did someone want me on ice? Who was it? Green?"

"Yes. He found out that you had bugged the office and thought you were feeding information to someone. The Senator, possibly. We are supposed to keep you busy for two weeks while he investigates."

"And you? Was that planned too?" he sounded bitter.

"I guess you have the right to ask that, but it hurts," her dark eyes held his. "No. I will do a lot for my country, but not whore to order. This was for me. The others have no idea. I just wanted to do it 'cause I find you very attractive. Now I'm glad it happened."

"So am I," he pulled her to him and held her close.

"What will you do now?" she asked.

"I don't know. Nothing till I've had time to think everything through carefully. This job has only taken two days, how were you supposed to hang on to me for the rest of the time?"

"You're going for a long walk. The plane taking you back will put down in some isolated place where you'll have to walk out. The pilot has done it before. He'll have survival gear on the plane. Green reckoned that two weeks would give him time to nail you."

"He won't do that. I only did the one office, and that was before Green was appointed. I got suspicious that Mason, who used that office before, was feeding information to an unauthorized person. I was going to remove the bug after Green arrived but he moved me out too soon. Now that we've found this he may be interested in what I recorded before. It all ties together and Mason made frequent calls to my father."

"I'd better talk to Sim Thornton and stop the stunt," Ro said.

"No. It'll give me thinking time. If anything good comes in from this rig in the meantime it will all add weight to what I already have for Green. Don't tell Thornton anything just yet."

"OK. Can I come with you?" Ro asked.

"What were you supposed to do?"

"I was just support on this one. Nothing briefed after pick-up this morning."

"Good. I'd like you to come, but only if we can arrange it without Thornton guessing there is anything between us," he ran a hand down the curve of her hip and felt her respond. Eventually they slept.

As it turned out Thornton had already planned to send someone with Connor Swingate. He had chosen Al, but as they were carrying their gear out to the Jetranger Al tripped and twisted his ankle. Thornton looked bleak.

"Shit! That screws things up. I was going to send Al back with Connor, but

I'd better take him and get that leg checked first. Ro, you take Al's place and go on in the plane when we rendezvous. OK?"

"Sure," Ro said with a neutral tone that hid the excitement she felt.

Connor heaved a big silent sigh of relief. The way Thornton had talked showed that he had no knowledge of what was between himself and Ro and that the stunt was still on. Chance had just granted him twelve whole days of Ro's company with no possibility of outside interference. God bless all rabbit holes, he thought.

Chapter 21

THE NEWS OF THE Mathilde K's discovery in Dakar, delayed by engine trouble, and the FBI's telex reports gave the morning review meeting a very different flavor from previous mornings. With information coming in Green could now see his way forward, although the precise direction was still unclear. The sooner all this was wrapped up, the sooner he could get back to things that really interested him. During the meeting the communications messenger brought in the facsimile picture of the bank customer from the FBI. Green grinned broadly when he saw it and passed it round for the others to see.

"It looks as if there is more to our good Senator than we had thought."

"He was laying on the lordy bit kinda heavy the other night," observed Mitch. "I thought it had just gone to his head. You really think he's mixed up with these guns, Nose?"

"No. My enquiries about the Indians he's hosting show that one is a nuclear scientist who's spent most of his time in the military field, although officially he's something in their Ministry of Energy Resources. Since Idaho is the focus of nuclear research in these United States, it does not take Sherlock Holmes to deduce that there is a link. The Senator has had a high profile in nuclear debates of all sorts and, Idaho being his home state, he probably has his fingers in many poi pots. This thing is getting more complicated by the minute. When is he taking those guys up to the hunting lodge, Mike?"

"Friday, according to the published schedule. There are two businessmen joining them."

"Any word from Thornton?" Green asked.

"Only 'Leapfrog' at first light this morning," Mike said.

"What's that mean?"

"The system is rigged and operational and the team have airlifted out. Pick-up was at first light. Swingate should have transferred to the other aircraft by now and will soon be walking." Mike smiled at the thought. "Sim was going to send Al with him to make sure that he doesn't walk too fast."

"Good. Where's Thornton?"

"He's setting up the listening watch at that dude ranch up by Orofino. It's run by an ex-Company man and is sometimes used as a field training base, so cover is no problem. It's also nice and close so signal reception from the target should be good."

"Have you checked on Swingate's wife yet?" Green asked.

"Hal reported that she and the children had left the campsite yesterday morning saying something about one of the boys being sick. She has not returned home as of this time, and we do not yet know where she has gone. I'll take that one over from Hal while he chases the ship," Penkowski told him.

"Fine. Inform me as soon as you locate her," Green said. "Now, Joe, you come from Idaho don't you?"

"Sure thing. Twin Falls."

"Find some suitable cover – freelance country news-hound researching a piece on the work of the Senator for his hometown paper, or something like that. Get me a detailed run down on all the Senator's declared interests. Also get a list of every Senate debate in which he has spoken since he was elected, with transcripts. See what you can find out about his informal activities, especially things like business lunches back home, meetings with people who have contracts and information to share, and who visits him at home and how often."

Joe nodded, thinking of the magnitude of the task ahead of him and knowing that Green would expect the information to start flowing in within hours.

"What about the guns, Malcolm?" Mike asked.

"Malcolm? Hell! that's just for casual friends, Mike. You've proved yourself now and earned your place on the team. Just insult me, like everyone else, and call me Nose. I never did like my given name much." Green grinned at him and the others all laughed. "My guess is there never were any guns. Hal will get a looksee in those crates later today and prove it. No, I think our Senator is into something a lot darker, and the guns were just a blind to tie up our manpower and divert attention from something else. The man is arrogant enough to think we're suckers, and if he can keep us busy chasing our tails he'll have time to complete whatever play he's making. We'll just let the Bureau follow the trails. It is rightfully their territory anyhow. For the time being we won't tell them about this other aspect to the game. They all have big feet and we don't want them stamping out the trail. Let's meet at eight thirty tomorrow."

After the team had left Green leaned back in his chair. Twiddling a pencil between his stubby fingers, he considered the new developments. It always excited him when he found a new lead. This one had the potential to shake some big stones. He was still smiling to himself fifteen minutes later when the telephone rang. It was Maureen.

"Nose? The Chief is on his way over to see you."

"Any idea why?"

"He didn't say, but he's like a cat that just stole a whole pot of cream." Maureen sounded amused.

"Thanks. I'll open a can of sardines and make his meal complete," Green replied.

"You've made some progress then?"

"You might say that, but this can's got bigger worms in it than we thought," Green replied cryptically.

"That doesn't sound nice, Nose."

"It ain't, but it's a good thing we've got the lid open."

Braden came in just as Green cradled the phone, with excitement in his eyes.

"Hi Charles. So you found your man?"

"How in the … " Braden looked incredulous. "Oh, I see, you've been sniffing the nose again," the Chief laughed.

"Nope. Maureen just called to say you were on your way over wearing your Cheshire Cat face, so I guessed."

"Yes? Well, you only guessed half of it. Chong and his wife just walked into the Embassy in Beijing along with Peach, and they want out. They made it just before the tanks arrived and closed up the Diplomatic Quarter of the city. At this moment we believe the Chinese authorities are unaware that they're in the Embassy, but it won't take 'em long to find out. I reckon we have a week, maximum, before they start putting heavy pressure on us to hand them over. So, we have that long to get Chong and his wife out. Or I should say: you have a week."

"Me? You're reassigning me to this?" Green's excitement rose.

"Yes and no." Braden looked slightly sheepish. "I'm giving you the job, but we're very thin on the ground just at this moment so you'll have to continue with the current job as well. Come over at three thirty and I will have a full briefing for you. After that you can have thirty six hours to come up with a plan. I know it's asking a lot, but that's the way it is." His tone was sympathetic.

"Shit! You don't want much, do you? And just when we've made a breakthrough on this one."

"Tell me about it?" Braden asked, settling himself comfortably into Green's armchair.

After Braden had left, Green called Mike in and spent half an hour bouncing ideas off him. The young man had plenty of imagination and Green found the discussion fruitful. He asked Mike to bring in everyone in the team who was available for Braden's briefing.

That afternoon the Chief gave them a clear overview of the situation in China followed by comprehensive detail with copies of all the reports filed by the forty or so field men currently in Beijing and the other main cities. The predictions Green had given two days ago were proving to be disturbingly accurate, but Braden was far from confident that things would continue as he had outlined. Reports from those on the ground suggested the whole affair would get out of hand and explode into a full civil war. Several thousand people were already said to have been mowed down by the tanks. Penkowski commented glumly that the brutality and callousness made Stalin's pogroms look amateur.

Several foreign missions were already sending all their dependants and non-essential staff out of the country. Consular offices throughout the world were being besieged by Chinese nationals asking to extend their visas or demanding asylum. So far Chong Tse Do and San Kiu had not actually asked for asylum but had made it clear that they wanted American assistance to leave China.

Several foreign television crews had been beaten up and had their equipment confiscated. Two radio journalists had been expelled, and there had been frequent denunciations of foreign correspondents on Chinese television accusing them of spreading imperialist propaganda in order to encourage rebellion.

Whether this was true or not seemed unimportant since rebellion appeared already to be well under way. A train had been stopped by students in Shanghai. They had killed the engineer and a number of soldiers and set fire to the train. Mass arrests had begun all across the country, with the People's Liberation Army preparing internment camps for the thousands of ordinary citizens being rounded up like cattle by the security forces.

Within the last hour the American Ambassador had issued a bulletin advising all United States citizens in the country to contact their Embassy and to leave as soon as possible. He was in constant contact with the Chinese authorities, trying to arrange safe passage for them. American Airlines had been asked to hold six 747s at Hong Kong, ready to evacuate American nationals from Beijing and Shanghai.

Returning to their own offices two hours, later Green and his team were subdued. They spent a few minutes discussing what they'd heard, before Green chased them off to get on with the tasks he had assigned that morning. He asked Mike to stay behind for a moment.

"You said 'through the front door', yesterday, Mike," Green said as the door closed behind the last man. "Got any ideas just how to do that?"

"That was just hypothetical. I'll have to think about this one now we have some facts to work with."

"It's a bold idea, Mike. More likely than most to succeed. The real problem is how to distract the watchers while our birds walk out. Since they were already looking for Chong they won't take long to find out he's in our Embassy. After that we cannot legally deny them access to him unless he actually asks for asylum. I wonder why he hasn't."

"Maybe he still thinks the whole thing will blow over and he can just go back to work as he always has before," Mike offered.

"I doubt it," Green said. "Chong's had a lot of experience in twisting the dragon's tail, but he's always stayed put before and played the offended innocent. This time he's run for cover and he's brought his wife along too." He wandered over to the windows and stared out at the manicured lawns. "There has to be some reason why he has behaved differently."

Chapter 22

"THE SENEGAL CUSTOMS Department was very helpful," Mike reported to the morning review meeting. "Hal went on board the Mathilde K with them during the night and was allowed to inspect all the crates and their contents. All but two contained pumps, gate valves and fittings as declared in the documentation. The last two were much more interesting. They contain all sorts of boxes with papers that range from scientific and technical documents, including pages of complex formulae, to what appear to be assembly instructions, wiring diagrams and some engineering drawings, none of which have anything to do with pumps or irrigation equipment. There is also a substantial quantity of carefully packed electronic components. Hal said he can't understand much of it but is certain that it is all nuclear stuff. The local Customs Chief has impounded it all and will inform the US Ambassador today that the cargo does not conform to the manifest. The ship's captain has been arrested, a guard had been put on the ship and the crew are confined ashore. The Mathilde K is currently tied up to the Dakar Customs wharf and a seal has been placed on the engine room hatch. Hal said they were reluctant to hold the ship at first but were persuaded to do a full rummage search and turned up a couple of kilos of drugs in the purser's safe. Hal is staying on for a couple of days to make sure nothing goes astray."

"Thanks Mike," Green said. "Joe, what have you got?"

"I have the lists of all Senator Swingate's known and declared interests. All the detail is in here," he tossed a thick file onto the table. "The most interesting parts are his involvement with three nuclear companies. He has also been involved with the Shandar Freighting Company – the one that shipped those pumps – but passed his holding over just before he was elected to the Senate. Now ask me who to," he said, looking smug.

"Who to, Joe?" Green asked expectantly.

"Senator Swingate passed the whole of his holding – over seventy percent – to Lois Ellen Mason, better known to the rest of us as Mrs. Lois Swingate, his daughter-in-law. I have started looking into what part she plays in the company's operations, but my enquiries so far suggest that the company is more or less dormant most of the time."

"You mean it only comes to life after dark," Green laughed. "My guess is that its only transactions will turn out to be of a highly dubious nature. Where is the lady now? Has she been found yet?"

"Not yet," Penkowski said. "She dropped her two boys off with her mother yesterday, with some tale about going to join Connor. The old lady loves having her grandchildren and agreed they could stay for a few days. She says her daughter often leaves them with her like this, so did not ask exactly where her daughter was going. I thought she looked familiar, but cannot quite place her," he explained.

"I think I can," Green said with a sardonic smile. "Joe, didn't you say that Mrs. Swingate Junior was born Lois Ellen Mason?"

"Yep."

"And her Daddy is Gerry H. Mason, who, until a few weeks ago was running the section we are now investigating. He used to … Hey! Mike, when did that jerk rig this office? Was your tame Chinaman able to say? I wonder if it was before we moved in here. Maybe he doesn't know what's been going on," he continued, thinking aloud. "Maybe I did him an injustice. What if he got suspicious of his pa-in-law, and just decided to do a little bitty private snooping on his own account?"

"There was no way to tell when the rig was put in, but you've raised some interesting possibilities, Nose," Mike replied. "Pity he's gone for a long walk. It could be useful to bring him in and ask."

"Any word on that operation?"

"Only the ATC report that the plane had made a forced landing with engine failure. The pilot failed to give a final position, but we have no reason to think there is anything wrong. Thornton's backup flight will fly the same route this morning as a safeguard."

"Right. Let's wrap this up for now. If anyone has any further ideas, let me know immediately. I want that woman found, top priority, and let's have Hal back here as soon as possible."

Chapter 23

WITHIN AN HOUR of the helicopter dropping him at the dude ranch near Orofino, Thornton had the listening monitor installed and working. Carlo Rosario, the owner, was an old friend who had worked with Thornton on a number of operations in Latin America some years before. He had left the Company after getting a bullet in the hip during an unsavory little show with the Contras, and had retired to the Idaho hills. The Company had him repaired in a private clinic and paid him a handsome sum in compensation for his injury. Once he was set up on the ranch, they hired his facilities and expertise to train their field men. The arrangement worked well, and Rosario's skills in developing people's talents turned out to be an unexpected bonus.

With an artificial hip Rosario was unable to indulge in many of the energetic activities he had enjoyed before, but this bothered him little. He had four sons, aged between twenty four and twenty eight and two daughters-in-law who, between them, now did the donkey work. Rosario himself managed the ranch and did the cooking whenever they had guests, which was most of the time. He also had a thirst for beer that would make a storm drain look parched, and sank prodigious quantities of Moose Head Lager. As a result Rosario had earned himself the nickname Moose, had a belly like a Sumo wrestler and the easy going good humor that his corpulent frame implied.

Lisetta, his wife, who kept the books and made the reservations, was a complete contrast. Pretty and petite, she spoke heavily accented English, having refused absolutely to abandon her Mediterranean origins. She was quiet and reserved where the guests were concerned, but warm and welcoming with her family and friends. She doted on her sons and would sit on the porch in the evenings, work-box at her side, and mend their jeans and shirts and socks with immaculate stitches. When one of her daughters-in-law complained that she was never allowed to tend her husband's clothes, Lisetta was heard in the furthest corners of the ranch.

"When you canna sew lika me an' keepa five big men fed, clean, an' happy you canna do the sewing. Now you go off an' look after my son who isa you husband an' make me a Grandma. Then you canna sew an' I willa play with the bambino!" With this Lisetta burst into guffaws of laughter. Nobody could take offence, and all present soon had tears of delight streaming down their faces.

Carlo Rosario had built twenty small log chalets, with two rooms each and a bathroom between. They formed a semicircle round the main ranch house on the side away from the stables and the service buildings, and he had grown a large lawn in the center. This he tended with loving care and a ride-on mower. On the side of the main house he had built a small extension. This was his quiet room, where nobody would disturb him, and it was here that Thornton set up his monitoring station.

He showed Rosario how the equipment worked and spent a few minutes discussing the watch with him. By nine thirty that morning the two friends were reclining in old padded chairs, with their feet on the desk and a crate of chilled beer between them, talking about the past. The monitor console in its attaché case was on the desk, and Rosario had just pulled the ring on his eighth can when a green light came to life.

"Hello. You got a fly in your web, Sim," the big man said.

Thornton leaned over and turned up the volume on the built in speaker. A woman's voice, singing, came from the small grille in the lid of the attaché case.

"Someone sounds happy. Must be the local help, come to open up for visitors," he said.

The two men listened for a while and continued sipping their beer. The singing stopped and the green light winked out leaving a small red indicator glowing above one of the recording units to show that it had been activated. Thornton reached for another beer and the two men resumed their reminiscences.

A few minutes later another green light came on and there was a loud click from the speaker. Rosario stopped what he was saying and the two men looked at the console. The woman seemed to be talking to herself, and there was a background hum followed by a rattling noise.

"What's that?" Rosario asked.

"Don't know," Thornton leaned over and read the label below the recording light. "She's in the locked study, according to the bug."

"Now, what's the access code?" the woman's disembodied voice asked, then answered herself: "Six one seven ought two return l-e-t space m-e space i-n space star return. That's it," her voice spelled out the letters and there were more rattling sounds.

"Goddam!" Thornton swore. "I should have let Connor bug those dammed machines. She's using one of the computers. Now what in the name of little green apples would the help be doing messing about with computers?"

"Search me," Rosario said, tossing his empty can with deadly accuracy into the waste basket by the door and reaching for a refill.

The rattling of the keyboard continued for several minutes, then paused.

"Oh, nice! Big J gonna be pleased with you, Lo," the woman said. She pressed a few more keys and there was a declining whine as she turned the machine off. There were thumps and clicks as she closed and locked the study door, then the green light winked out, leaving a second red tell-tale glowing.

"What do you suppose that was all about and what does Lo mean?" Rosario asked his friend.

"I wish I knew. One thing's for sure, she is not just hired help come in to clean the place. I guess Lo could be a name," Thornton said. "Dammit, I wish I'd let him bug those machines."

"Can't be right every time, old buddy. Have another beer. Maybe when someone else shows up she'll tell what that was all about. You gotta be patient to be a good ear hole," Rosario chuckled, and tossed him a can.

Thornton caught it, pulled the ring, and leaned back. The two men sat sipping in silence for a while.

"Want to call Nose?" the big man asked at last.

"Can't do any harm. At least he'll be happy to know that the system works and Connor didn't spook it."

"Any reason why he should?"

"No reason. I was just thinking. He didn't know whose place it was anyway. I didn't tell you he laid a bug in Nose's office, did I?"

"He did what?" the big man spluttered with amazement. "No wonder Nose wanted him sidelined. Why'd he do that?"

"We still have to find that out," Thornton said. "Right now he's off taking his little hike in the backwoods of Montana so we'll have to wait a few days before we can talk to him about it." Thornton pulled the monitoring console onto his lap. He copied the access code onto a scratch pad, pressed the erase button and rewound both tapes.

"Nose is going to be mad about the computers. I know we have an access code now, but the trouble is there are two computers and I have no idea which one she was using. I wouldn't let Connor turn them on in case there was a security device installed."

"Too late to worry about it now," Rosario said.

"Yeah. Let's call Nose." Thornton pushed the attaché case back onto the desk and reached for the phone. In a few seconds Green was on the line.

"Hello Sim. How's it going?"

"There's a woman in there," Thornton said. "We thought she was there to clean up, but she's been working one of the computers we found in a locked study. I hate to tell you this, Nose, but I wouldn't let Connor tap the machines in case they were security coded."

"Never mind, Sim. As long as we get all the talk. How do you know it was a woman?" Green's voice crackled through a burst of static on the line.

"She was singing."

"Singing?"

"Yes. She talked to herself as well. I got the access code to one computer when she spelled it out. Trouble is I don't know which one. Does Lo mean anything to you Nose? Moose thought it might be a name."

"Lo? No, I don't think it does," Green replied. "She say anything else that might … Lo, did you say? Wait a moment, Lo.... Lois! Sim, you just keep close to that machine. That could be Lois Swingate, Connor's wife. We've lost contact with her. She dropped her boys with her mother saying something about having to go and join Connor. Only thing is she didn't know where her husband had gone. Then we found another link between her and the man who owns that hunting lodge. Keep your ears wide open Sim. I want a round the clock live listening watch until we know if that's her. Call me as soon as you get a definite make on her. The man and his five guests are scheduled to arrive about five, local time today."

"Will do."

"How's the Moose? Still pouring beer down his gullet?"

"He's in fine shape," Thornton laughed. "Just opened his fifteenth can."

Green laughed too. "Say Hi for me. I'll talk to you later." The line clicked off.

Chapter 24

MIKE WAS NOT SURE what had woken him. He lay close to Chevvy, one arm draped across her, with his hand resting on her swollen belly. The baby moved under his hand and he felt a surge of excitement. For some minutes he lay there, thinking about the marvel of pregnancy and Chevvy's unflappable approach to this and all other things in life. The baby gave a violent kick and Chevvy stirred. Rolling over onto her back, she opened her eyes.

"Can't you sleep either, Mike?"

"No. The pressures of being an incipient father finally got to me," he chuckled. "Would you like some tea?"

"That would be nice. What time is it?"

"Almost four fifteen," Mike said, climbing out of bed and heading for the kitchen.

Chevvy listened to the noises he made as he boiled the kettle, set out mugs, and made tea. She had an idea what was on Mike's mind and eased herself into a more comfortable position as he came back.

"Mike," she said as he climbed back into bed, "Nose Green is planning to bring that Chinaman out, isn't he? The biochemist?"

"How did you … have I been talking in my sleep? What did I say Chevvy?"

"Nothing, my love. Just put it down to my Celtic sixth sense. I read the papers and watch television, like everyone else. It's obvious really, and since they have the whole place surrounded and watched now, someone would be sure to notice if he tried to creep out through the scullery window and over the garden wall." She watched his face, and his eyes were distant.

"Yes. The trouble is they're watching the front door just as carefully," he said eventually, half to himself, and lapsed into silence again.

"Fortuna favente," Chevvy announced some minutes later with a large grin on her face.

"Wassat mean when it's in English?" Mike asked, breaking his reverie.

"Latin. My old school motto," Chevvy said with a twinkle in her eye. "Fortune favors the bold. You know, kind of 'who dares wins'. That sort of thing. You've got to be so obvious that nobody will think you'd try that way. Then they won't notice."

"It sounds good, but how? My brain has been going round and round in circles and come up with nothing better than a pair of heavy framed spectacles with a false nose and mustache."

"Groucho Marx?" Chevvy grinned.

"Yes."

"Why not try the diplomatic bag? Wrap him up like a parcel, drop him in the sack and toss him over your shoulder. They do it in all the best spy novels." She was being mischievous.

"He's got his wife with him."

"Toss her in as well. It might make the sack a bit heavy but who would dare look?" Chevvy was laughing now. Mike laughed too. It was a nice image, but no better than his answer.

Chevvy got up and went to the bathroom. When she came back she stood by the bed, running her hands over her bulging abdomen.

"Look, he's moved down. I think he's getting ready to make his entry into the world. Mike, you won't have to go off before he's born will you?"

"How do you know it's going to be a he?"

"It's obvious," Chevvy snorted. "My Dad had four brothers, I have four, and you have three. I'm the only girl. Both the Thomases and the Ashkenaharovs breed a strong line in sons. I aim to carry on an old family tradition." The light in her eyes danced like fireflies. "Anyway, the way he's already started playing rugby he couldn't possibly be a girl."

"Tell it to the Marines, Chevvy. You can't possibly know, unless the clinic have told you something you've been keeping secret from me." Mike pulled his wife down beside him on the bed, but she sprang up again immediately.

"That's it, Mike! Send in the Marines and rescue your brave scientist."

"You can't do that sort of thing in the modern world, Chevvy, especially in a country like China. You're crazy. It must be the effect of advanced pregnancy, sending you daft. At least you haven't had weird cravings for egg and apricot sandwiches or something similar, like some women do," he pulled his wife back onto the bed.

Eventually they both drifted back into sleep, to be woken only an hour or so later by the shrill tones of the alarm clock.

Later Chevvy was preparing breakfast, singing to herself. The baby had settled into a comfortable position and she felt a warm glow of wellbeing. Mike rushed in from the shower, covered from head to foot in soap bubbles, dripping water all over the floor with a cake of soap still clutched in his hand.

"I've got it, Chevvy! You gave me the answer!" He enfolded her in his arms and danced her round the kitchen.

"Put me down! You're covering me in soap and spreading water everywhere." Chevvy managed to pull herself free. "Just look at the mess you're making, you great clown. Go and finish your shower, then you can tell me about it."

"I must ring Green," Mike said, heading for the phone. Chevvy got there first.

"Not like that, you don't. He won't mind waiting while you get clean. No go and finish your shower."

Chevvy managed to make her excited husband eat breakfast before calling Green and it gave him time to put the idea into more coherent form. Green listened without interruption, and there was a long pause after Mike had explained the outline of his plan.

"You know, Mike," Green said at last, "that has got to be the craziest idea I have ever heard. It's so crazy it could even work. Our problem is going to be in getting official approval and the co-operation of the key players. I'll meet you in the office in fifteen minutes and we can put some flesh on the bones. How's Chevvy?"

"Great. Getting ready to hatch."

"Give her our best. See you in the office," Green said and hung up.

They met in the office a quarter of an hour later. Green rescheduled the daily team review for three thirty, and the two men spent the next three hours developing the plan in detail and working out how to gain the sanction of those with the authority to make it happen. They were composing the projected timetable when the phone on Green's desk warbled. Green leapt across the room to silence the insistent noise.

"I wish these damned things still had bells, like real phones," he complained, snatching up the receiver. "Green," he said into the mouthpiece.

"Hello Nose, Carlo Rosario here. Long time no see. How ya doing?"

Hello Moose. I'm fine. How's things with you? Got any good news for me?"

"Yes. We just got a make on your dame. She's here with her hubby's pa and his visitors. Plenty of other good stuff on the tape as well. Your man is up to some dirty little games, old buddy. About the only thing he hasn't tried yet is blackmail, but with what we collected off last night's tapes even that would be in character."

"Tell me more," Green said.

"This is an open line, Nose. I'm going to squirt it down the fast wire. There's a lot of listening to do so we've bleep marked the hot bits."

"Thanks Moose. That's good work. You're sure about the lady?"

"As good as got her driver's license. I can even tell you the color of her panties."

"Fine. Is Sim there?"

"Yes, he's just setting up the tape shoot. Hold on."

Green waited .

"Morning, Nose." Sim Thornton sounded bright.

"Sim, we've got to find Connor Swingate. Can your back-up fly the route immediately, and have a helo pick him up as soon as they locate him? I need him back here double quick."

"I'll fix that right away and call you back with an ETA as soon as we locate him."

"Make it fast, Sim. Talk to you later." Green cut the connection and turned back to Mike. "They have found Lois Swingate. She is up at the hunting lodge making whoopee with her pa-in-law and his Indian pals. It sounds like the bastard is also selling nuclear secrets. Sim is sending the tapes down the fast wire now. We'll call Penkowski and Mitch off that hunt and let them check the recordings. You had better come with me to tell the Chief about this plan."

"What do you want Connor for?" Mike asked.

"We need to find out what he knows, and why he bugged this office. I now have the feeling that it had nothing to do with us. I think he got wind of something Mason was doing and decided to run a private check. I was wrong about Connor and should have talked to him first instead of just blasting him out of here. Now, where did we get to?"

Mike called Penkowski and briefed him, then called Maureen and warned her they needed to see Braden.

He and Green spent another half hour refining their timetable before going over to talk to the Chief.

BRADEN LISTENED IN SILENCE as Green explained the plan. He made occasional notes on a pad, but offered no comments. After Green had finished he studied the timetable for several minutes. When he finally looked up neither Green nor Mike could read anything from his expression as he looked from one to the other.

"That has got to be the craziest plan I ever heard of. In fact it is so darned crazy it could even work. Whose idea was it?"

Green jerked his thumb in Mike's direction but said nothing.

Braden stared at him for a moment then leaned across the table with his hand outstretched.

"You're a daring thinker, Mike," Braden said, shaking his hand. "I hope you are as resourceful in the field, because I'm going to back this plan and I shall insist that you take personal command of the active part of the operation. Nose, you'll head up at this end. Now, I shall obviously have to get approval from the top. With some of the players you're proposing this has to go to the President. Leave it with me, and I'll get back to you as soon as I can."

"I'm sorry we couldn't come up with something more conventional," Green said, "but there are so few options in this thing."

"Don't be sorry, Nose. This is the most exciting idea I've seen since Moose Rosario snatched Nguyen Ho from that place outside Tanh Hoa. You get on with the detailed planning, while I sell this to the big men."

Chapter 25

ART WESTON LIFTED the Piper Navajo off eight minutes after Thornton's call alerted him. Eager to impress, he had done his pre-flight checks at sunrise that morning, and then hung around the airfield office chatting to the manager and a couple of club pilots. That day there had only been two movements from the field, which was mainly used by club fliers at weekends. The Company kept a small hangar on the far side of the field, with a workshop and their own fuel supply. Art had only flown in there twice before, bringing agents in training en route to Rosario's ranch. He had slept the previous night on a camp cot in the back of the hangar, where he could be within earshot of the telephone in case Thornton called.

Cruising at seven and a half thousand feet he called the Area Controller. "Six one zero X-ray overhead Lewiston."

"Roger six one zero." The controller's disembodied voice crackled in his ear. "Steer one zero zero true, one eighty knots, for twelve minutes."

"One zero zero true, one eighty, twelve minutes, Roger," Art responded, turning onto the new heading and resetting his direction finder.

Beside him Al sat staring out of the right hand window at the landscape unrolling below them. His right foot had been strapped up by a local doctor the previous morning and he was given a walking stick, but there was nothing wrong with his eyesight so Thornton had sent him along to help with the search.

"It looks a rough sort of place to put down. Do you think they made it in one piece?" he asked, without turning from the window.

"It gets flatter as you go along. They flew about thirty five minutes beyond Lewiston, as far as we can estimate. They should have found somewhere a bit easier than this," Art told him. "Six one zero X-ray two minutes to the time point," he said into the radio.

"Roger six one zero. Make that three minutes, then turn one zero five true for another ten," the voice crackled in his headphones.

"Six one zero Roger." Art watched the sweep hand on the dashboard clock, and made the course correction as the hills below began to give way to open rolling grassland.

The two men continued to look downwards in silence, their eyes constantly roving over the shimmering green gold sea.

"What color was the aircraft?" Al asked.

"Bright yellow. It should show up well against the grass. The pilot should have headed for an open flat landing area. The plan was to be further north, but the plot showed him drifting southwards. He never confirmed his final position. Must have been too busy."

"Didn't they carry a beacon?"

"Nah. That kite was one of the Wright Brothers' cast offs. It only had the basics. No point in throwing away a good machine." The pilot sounded sad that any aircraft should be deliberately dumped. "Six one zero X-ray two minutes to the time point," he informed the Area Controller.

"Roger six one zero. He must have gone asymmetric about here. Speed would have pulled back to about one forty. He was at nine thousand, but may have started to descend immediately. We don't know. You are entering the probability zone now. I have you bright and clear on the radar."

"Six one zero on search." Art made an adjustment to his instruments, reset the clock and adjusted the controls to bring his speed back. "We'll fly this heading for twenty minutes, Al; then we turn round. If we don't see him we'll start a ten minute sliding box pattern at one fifty knots."

The two men continued to stare out over the passing grassland. At the end of the allotted time Art called the controller and turned onto a reciprocal heading.

"This sure is empty country," Al observed as Art turned again at the end of the run.

"Six one zero X-ray, we have completed two runs on your track. Going back to the midpoint to start a sliding box pattern now," Art told the controller, as he turned again onto the original heading. "Roger six one zero. We think he was trying to make for the field at Miles City."

Six one zero, thanks. We'll expand our box that way."

The headphones clicked twice in response.

They flew six times round the box pattern, moving it a few miles towards Miles City each time. Coming to the end of the last leg Art was thinking of his fuel state.

"We'll make one more box, Al, then go and get some more gas," he said as he started the turn.

"Yeah. Hold it! There is something down there reflecting sunlight. Can we take a look?" Al almost shouted.

Art rolled the aircraft smartly over and stood it on its wing tip.

"Where?" he asked.

"Close below us. I can't see it now, but I caught the flash," Al said, craning his neck to see past the pilot's head.

Art widened the turn slightly, scanning the green sea for the elusive reflection.

"There!" Al's arm shot out, pointing.

"Got it." Art turned towards the reflection. "There's a swathe of flattened grass. Let's go down and take a close look," he completed his turn and lowered the Navajo's nose. "Six one zero X-ray, we have a possible. Mark my position, I'm going down for a look," Art told the distant controller. He eased the throttles back and settled the aircraft into a wide spiral descent pattern, keeping the target constantly in view below and to his left.

"Roger six one zero. We have your position," the controller's voice crackled in his headphones.

Chapter 26

"CAN YOU HEAR THAT, Connor?" Ro began to scramble out from under the wing. "It sounds like an aircraft."

"What? Oh!" Connor rolled over and followed her into the brilliant sunlight. Ro was scanning the sky, screwing up her eyes against the glare.

"Where is it, Ro?"

"Somewhere above us, I think. Where are the flares?"

Connor picked up the packet and tore at the wrapping. He pulled out one flare and ran a few yards clear of the downed plane, trying to read the instruction as he ran and wishing he had thought to do so earlier. He pulled off the gray plastic cap and, holding the flare upright at arm's length, pulled sharply down on the brass ring protruding from the base. Nothing happened. He pulled again. Still nothing.

"Shit!" He flung the flare down and ran to get another. Again he pulled on the brass ring. Again nothing happened. He flung the second flare down and was reaching for a third when the first one exploded. Clouds of orange smoke began to billow from the grass where it lay. Connor leapt back in surprise, and had to move further away as the choking cloud enveloped him.

"There it is! Connor! They've seen us. They're coming down. There. Can you see?" Ro was yelling and pointing up towards the circling aircraft.

The vagrant breeze shifted slightly and the orange cloud smothered them, obscuring their rescuers from view.

"Move further out, so they can see us," Connor shouted. At that moment there was a loud pop as the second flare exploded into life, and a shower of sparks rained down on the wing of their crashed plane. There was a smell of burning paint, and the smoke took on a gray color. They both ran clear of the acrid, colored fog.

Ro looked back.

"Connor! The pilot! The wing has caught fire!"

He dived back into the smoke, groping his way towards the spot where the still unconscious man lay. He blundered into the wing, feeling the lick of flames on his face. Dropping to his knees he felt his way forward until his hand encountered a sleeping bag. It was empty. He pushed it aside and moved further under the wing. A shift of wind cleared the air for a moment and he saw the pilot. Grabbing the man by the collar of his flying jacket, he dragged him clear of the wreck. Ro came to help as he emerged from the smoke, and together they pulled the inert form to safety in the long grass.

With a roar of engines the search plane passed close overhead, pulling up into a steep climbing turn. Connor and Ro could see the pilot's face turned towards them. They stood and waved. The pilot waved back.

A loud woomph behind them had Connor and Ro spinning round to see a billowing red and black mushroom thrusting skywards from the remains of their wrecked aircraft, where a fuel tank had exploded. The Navajo above them made another low pass, disappearing behind the pall of smoke and flames. The pilot made a wide turn and came back slowly, with his wheels and flaps down.

"He's trying to land," Ro said.

"No, he can't land here. He's just trying to go as slow as possible to get a good look," Connor corrected her.

As the machine passed over them the engines roared with increased power and the plane pulled up sharply. The two on the ground could see something fall from the back of the cabin as the plane climbed steeply.

"He's dropped something," Connor shouted above the noise, and they both started to run towards the tumbling object.

It landed close by, but it still took them fifteen minutes to locate the package in the long grass. It turned out to be a metal cylinder with a heavy rubber cap on each end. When one of these was pulled off they found a compact radio beacon inside, packed in styrofoam. As Connor pulled the beacon out a coiled spring antenna sprung out of the top and the unit emitted a loud shriek. Connor almost dropped it with surprise before he heard the voice crackling from a small speaker on the side.

"Press the green button to speak, and release it to listen. Do you read me? Over," said the voice.

"We read you loud and clear," Connor replied, grinning at the device. "It's good to see you. We thought you might not come. Over."

"Well, we didn't know exactly where you were, and you took a bit of finding," said their rescuer. "There will be a copter here to collect you soon. What is wrong with the third man? Over."

"He's the pilot. He got his head cracked in the crash. He's still breathing, but no more. He hasn't moved since we got him out of the wreck. He has no open wounds. We tried to get some water into him but he doesn't swallow. Can they bring a doctor with the helo? Over."

"Will do. Any other injuries? Over."

"One dislocated shoulder and a lot of very big bruises. Nothing else. Tell them to bring some water as well. We only had one small bottle," Connor told him.

"Will do. We have to go and find some gas now. Can't stay here much longer. Keep that beacon turned on and listen out for the copter. It will come from the direction we go in and should be along in about two hours. Good luck. Out." With that the pilot swooped one more time over the site and climbed away towards the south east.

As they stood beneath the column of smoke, watching the plane get smaller, Ro reached out for Connor's hand and pulled it to her breast. Together they sat down to wait for the helicopter.

Chapter 27

AFTER THE DAILY TEAM meeting Green and Mike called their wives to say they would be working late, and got down to the detailed planning on the big table in Green's office.

The table was covered in maps and charts, the floor was stacked with rows of files, and the wall board was covered in Mike's neat writing, with lists of equipment, personnel and, on the right hand side, the beginnings of an operational timetable. This was now being filled in as the two men worked out the minutiae of their plan.

Braden had insisted that the minimum number of people should be involved, to reduce the chance of any leaks. There would be enough people in the know later. Once the President had given his approval the State Department would have to be consulted, then the Pentagon, the Secret Service and certain other bodies would be informed since they would be required to contribute either key personnel or other resources.

By eleven that night they had made good progress, and Mike had transferred the plan from the wall board to his computer. He and Green were going through the timetable print-out looking for flaws.

"Mike, I think we should leave this for a few hours and get home." Green said, after a time. "Maybe a bit of sleep will help. Let's start again at six tomorrow morning. Maybe by then we'll have a response from the White House."

"Do you think the President will buy this?" Mike asked.

"I guess that depends on how much the men at the top want this scientist out. In a few days time it's likely to get mighty awkward having him hiding in the Embassy, so they'll have to do something, and you can imagine the outcry if he were simply handed back. That is not an option. The President has taken a few daring risks in the past. He may go for it."

Mike saved the plan to a disk, cleared the computer and shut it down. He stacked all the loose files with the computer disk in the steel wall cabinet while Green cleaned the board and shredded the waste paper. Then they went home.

Chevvy was on the phone when Mike arrived. She laid the receiver down as he kissed her hello, and told him that Braden had called.

"What did he want?"

"Ask him yourself. He's on the line now," she said with a cheeky grin.

Mike picked up the phone. "Good evening, sir."

"Hello, Mike. I have just come from the White House. The President wants to see you and Nose right away. I've just called Nose, and he'll collect you in about ten minutes."

"I'll be ready, sir."

"Good. I will meet you both at Nose's office and we'll go over to the White House together," Braden said, and cut the connection.

"Sorry lover," Mike said, replacing the phone, "I have to go back to the office. Green is coming to collect me. We have to go see someone in Washington."

Chevvy made him wash, and change his shirt, and fed him a quick omelet before Green arrived. Green spent a couple of minutes apologizing and making a fuss of Chevvy before the two men departed.

"We may be late," Green told her. "Don't wait up for him."

Braden was waiting outside the office when they arrived, and he helped them carry the heavy rolls of maps and piles of papers down to the helicopter waiting on the lawn with its engine running. A blank faced security man held the door open and climbed in after them. The pilot lifted into the night without delay and headed for the lawn behind the White House.

Five armed Secret Service men ringed the helicopter as it landed. The senior man, pistol in hand, approached the door as the rotor slowed. He ran a flashlight over the passengers, checked their ID, and led them towards a doorway where another guard also inspected their cards. The roll of maps and papers was passed through an X-ray scanner and each had to walk through a metal detector. Satisfied, the guard led them along corridors and round corners to a waiting room where a third stone faced man stood guard inside the door.

The corridor door had just closed behind them when a second door, on the other side of the room, opened and an aide ushered the three men into the Oval Office. The President was standing by the window, talking to the Secretary of State and the CIA Director.

"Good evening, gentlemen." The President came forward and shook hands. "Let's get straight down to business. Mr Braden has explained the basis of your plan, so now I want to hear the details please. Mr Green, I understand you are responsible for this?"

"Yes, Mr President. My team has prepared the plan. I asked Mike here how he would get the man out. He believed, as I do, that the only way was to walk boldly out of the front door. He and I have taken that principle and made some refinements," Green answered, and went on to explain the details.

After talking for twenty minutes, Green looked round at his audience to see how the idea had been received. "The Secretary of State is due in England next Thursday," he continued. "We propose that Beijing should be contacted immediately to request that he makes a brief visit and that he should go there first. There are plenty of burning issues that he can discuss there, but we believe the old men will be flattered to receive him. After a few hours he can fly on, over the pole, to England. We will arrange for his aircraft to land at a US air base and he will proceed to Chequers by road or helicopter from there.

"That is the plan we have worked out, Mr President. Here is the detailed timetable, to meet the constraints I have described," Green said, handing over a computer print-out. "We feel that the sooner we move the better will be the chance of success," he stepped back from the table to allow the President and the Secretary of State to discuss the matter in private.

The President had some questions and called Green back.

"How sure are you this will work?" he asked.

"We believe it will be successful if we move fast, sir."

"What will you do if the Chinese refuse to let the helicopter in?"

"We divert Air Force Two to Seoul with some minor technical problem. Since the time schedule will be tight Mr Secretary will fly on to Beijing in the long range helicopter. The USS Callistoga is currently 300 miles off South Korea. She carries two helicopters that have the range and capacity we need. Air Force Two will follow on to Beijing three hours later. The helicopter will return to the carrier as Air Force Two takes off for the flight to England," Green explained.

"Are you sure this scientist wants to come out?" The Secretary of State asked.

"Yes, sir. He has asked to be brought out. He has not yet asked for political asylum, but we believe he will do so," Green told him.

The President and the Secretary of State exchanged glances. There was a slight smile in the President's eyes as he looked at Green.

"This has got to be the most audacious plan I have ever been asked to approve. We need to be sure that it can't backfire. The United States has been embarrassed enough over operations of this sort in the past. Nothing, repeat nothing, must be allowed to go wrong with this. Given the players you are asking for it would cause a scandal we could never live down in a hundred years if there were any mistakes," the President said. "There is coffee in the ante-room, gentlemen. I want half an hour to consult and consider this."

The three CIA men were ushered out.

Twenty minutes later the door opened and they were called back into the Oval Office.

"OK. Do it," the President said, without preamble. "Keep me informed of the details – unofficially. Good luck."

Green, Braden and Mike looked at each other and began to grin. They gathered all their papers together and left.

Chapter 28

IN THE MIDDLE OF THE vast sea of summer grass Connor Swingate and Ro sat beside the unconscious pilot. He had still shown no signs of recovery and they were now worried there might be something seriously wrong. From time to time one of them checked his pulse. This remained steady, but his face now had a sickly gray pallor. Even wrapped in a thermal sleeping bag and lying in the hot sun he was cold.

The pall of smoke from the burned wreck had gone now. All that remained was a tangle of torn, blackened metal. Many of the thin covering panels had been consumed in the fire, leaving an obscene skeleton like a new-age fossil, lying in a patch of scorched grass. The air was still heavy with the smell of the fire. Because everything had happened so fast, their survival kit had been destroyed, but Connor's bag with the listening device had escaped. It was some yards away when the fire erupted and he'd been able to reach it and drag it to safety.

They sat with the pilot stretched out beside them and Connor's bag with the beacon at their feet. The beacon hissed gently as they listened for the first signal from the rescue helicopter.

An hour and a half after the Navajo had disappeared into the haze the radio came to life with a tinny voice breaking through the static hiss, and they both jumped.

"This is rescue forty four. Do you read me? Over."

Connor picked up the small radio, stood, and scanned the horizon to the south east.

"We read you loud and clear, forty four," he said, holding the instrument to his mouth.

"Fine. We have you clear as well," the voice responded. "We have about thirty miles to run. What is the pilot's condition? Over."

"No change. He has not moved. Breathing and pulse steady. He has gone a dirty gray color, otherwise the same. Over."

"Has he moved at all since you landed? Over."

"Negative. He's been like this since we pulled him from the wreck. The plane ended up on its back and we were all knocked senseless. I don't know how long he was hanging in his straps before we got him out. Maybe ten minutes. Over." Connor tried to be informative.

"OK. Just hang in there. ETA nineteen minutes. Out."

Connor and Ro sat down again and waited. After a while they heard the beat of rotors, and Connor called up to tell the rescue pilot they were near.

"Good. Just hold down your transmit button for twenty seconds so we can get an accurate bearing," the pilot told him.

The helicopter came in high and made a steep descent straight towards them. Charred bits were blown off the wreck by the downwash as the big machine settled onto the grass nearby. A doctor and two paramedics dropped from the open door and ran to the prostrate casualty. After a brief examination the doctor came over and made a quick examination of Ro's shoulder while the paramedics put the injured pilot onto a stretcher and strapped him down.

Within minutes they were airborne again, heading back the way they had come. The crew had brought plenty of water and high energy rations. Connor and Ro tucked into these while the medical team got to work on the pilot.

An ambulance was waiting for them when they landed, and all three were whisked off to the local hospital. After a thorough check, some brisk manipulation of Ro's shoulder and the application of a few Band-Aids, Connor and Ro were taken back to the airfield. The Piper Navajo was waiting with its engines running and Art Weston sitting at the controls. He took off at once and headed east.

"Where are we going?" Ro asked him.

"Langley. Mr Green wants him in the office." Art jerked his thumb in Connor's direction.

Chapter 29

THERE WAS A LONG TELEX from Hal Johnson waiting when Mike arrived at the office the following morning. He spent a few minutes going through it with a highlight pen before Green arrived. The Bureau had also sent word that they intended to interview the Senator and Lois Swingate about the activities of the Shandar Freighting Company, as soon as they could be found. Mike picked up the phone, called the local Bureau office, and told their duty officer that their two suspects were at a hunting lodge in Idaho. Explaining that both were the subjects of a separate investigation that would suffer if the Bureau intervened at this point, he mentioned that the Company had placed a listening watch on the place and was asked to pass on any relevant parts of the tape. Mike agreed and rang off.

Joe was in early as well, with reams of paper from the Senate. He had a complete record of the Senator's official activities for the last six months. He had been chatting up one of the Senator's secretarial staff and would collect details of his private meetings later in the morning. He sat down to compile a précis for Green.

The phone was ringing when Green came into his office. He was about to answer it but stopped and listened to the pealing tone of the bell. Mike heard the bell and, not realizing Green had arrived, came in to answer it. He found Green standing there, looking at the ringing phone, with a wide smile on his face.

"Anything wrong, Nose?"

"Nope! You hear that?"

"The telephone? Sure."

"A real bell. No more of that irksome warbling. Your doing Mike?"

"You said you wanted one like this, Nose."

"And never expected to get one. I thought these things were gone forever. Thanks Mike."

"No problem. You want something, you ask. That's what I'm here for." Mike went back to his own office as Green picked up the phone.

"Green," he said.

"Morning, Nose." Braden's voice was rich and clear. This instrument has a good tone, Green noted.

"Good morning Charles. How did it go?"

"Fine. I've been busy. General Harrison Elworth will be here at ten thirty. He has agreed in principle, but wants to hear the details direct from you. He already knows the sort of guys you want and will bring some details with him. The same goes for Admiral Denver. He'll be over at the same time, so you can brief them together," Braden told him.

"That should save time. Did they sound keen?"

"Elworth would do the job himself, given a chance. Denver says it is entirely a Company and Marine Corps show, but he'll be happy to provide the carrier and helicopter. See you at ten thirty." Braden was gone, the line dead, before Green could ask anything else.

Green called Mike in, told him the news, and asked him to assemble the rest of the team.

Mitch and Penkowski had done a good job extracting relevant material from the hunting lodge tapes. They thought they could now prove that the Senator and Chester P. Howard, the COE of an Idaho based nuclear company, were selling nuclear technology to the Indians under the counter. What they were selling related to the preparation and handling of weapons grade volatiles, along with fusing components and control circuitry.

"If they go ahead with this they'll make real dirty bombs," Mitch commented after presenting his report. "I'm surprised the Indians want that sort of thing, their scientists were thought to be more advanced than that."

"Maybe they have a hidden agenda that we have yet to uncover," Penkowski said.

"Like what?" Green asked.

"I don't know, but Hal has been asking why they shipped the technical manuals to Sri Lanka. He said there was no way of identifying the two crates from the others, and they were all clearly marked with a Colombo destination. The Indians have had a 'Peace Keeping Force' on the island for some time now, but do you think that's all they want? Didn't they lay claim to Ceylon years back? Could this be a gambit to justify revival of that claim, or simply a means of letting them overrun the place with apparent cause?"

"It sounds somewhat unlikely, given the amount they have committed as expenditure on this project. And the Indians have played the honest broker on the world stage for years now. However, just because it is unlikely that makes it worth thinking about. Keep looking, and see if Sim and Moose have any other juicy bits on their overnight tapes. Those should be coming down the fast wire any time now." Green started to wrap up the review meeting.

"Joe, you take over liaison with the Bureau. Mike got a yard of paper from them this morning. Keep after the Senator. Everything he does, and anything that involves that Lois woman, we want to know about it. When's Connor Swingate due here?" He looked at Mike.

"They've been picked up, and are on their way here now," Mike said. "I'm waiting for an ETA."

"OK, guys. That's it for now. Mike and I have to get on with this Beijing thing. We'll be busy until at least half past four. See you later." Green closed the session.

As the others left Mike brought out the plans from the filing cabinet, and he and Green spent the time reviewing possible problems and devising contingencies until the two military men arrived.

General Harrison Elworth was the epitome of a marine. Tall and fair haired, with a strong jaw, he had penetrating blue eyes and a direct gaze. He was the youngest of the Chiefs of Staff by almost ten years, his career littered with spectacular successes. He had played baseball and football at college and been vigorously sought after by NFL head-hunters. Whilst he enjoyed sport, Harrison Elworth had never had any intention of being anything but a marine. His father had been a Colonel in the service during the Pacific War, serving with distinction. Harrison, in his turn, had led a series of successful operations in the waning days of the Viet Nam conflict, and his subsequent promotion was meteoric and very popular with the Marine Corps. His one frustration, now that he had reached the top, was being confined to a desk in Washington when he would have preferred to be out with the men he commanded so well.

From the moment Charles Braden had first outlined the plan Elworth had supported it with enthusiasm and energy, and had personally burned plenty of midnight oil searching out likely participants. He was in high good humor when he walked into Green's office.

In contrast, Admiral Milton Denver was a dapper little man with a shock of steel gray hair and shaggy eyebrows that overhung his eyes like unruly hedges. He was quietly spoken, thoughtful, and the best naval strategist since the Second World War. Milton Denver had intended to become a lawyer when his studies were interrupted by the Korean War. The draft had taken him into the Navy and, on a whim, he had volunteered for submarine service. His cold, logical mind had soon brought him to the notice of his superiors and resulted in a permanent appointment and later command of the first operational flotilla of nuclear powered boats. Now he was the oldest of the nation's military commanders and was due for retirement next year. He disliked and distrusted the Chinese and saw this operation as a way of having one last dig at them to sign off a distinguished career.

Green and Mike spent two hours briefing the Chiefs of Staff in detail and answering their questions. When they finished General Elworth brought out the personnel list he had compiled and scrubbed two names. He handed it over and Green, Braden and Mike bent their heads over it.

"Who is going to fly the helo?" Braden asked.

"There is a pilot listed at the bottom," Elworth said with a grin. "I thought we should keep this thing in the family. The Captain of the Callistoga says he's the best man for the job."

All eyes went to the bottom of the page. "Captain Peter Ash," Braden read aloud as Green looked at Mike, raising a questioning eyebrow.

"He changed it when he joined up. The Marines couldn't say his own name." Mike said, and he and Green began to laugh.

"Share the joke?" Braden demanded.

"The pilot's real name is Piotr Ashkenaharov," Green said, but Braden looked blank. "He is Mike's brother."

Braden joined in the laughter.

After further discussion Elworth and Denver pressed for the alternate flight plan to be used as it gave less opportunity for the Chinese to refuse the presence of the helicopter. This was agreed and the meeting broke up just before one fifteen. The two commanders went off to give instructions to their staff. A military outfitter would arrive later with a selection of uniforms for Mike to try on, and a Marine instructor would be sent over to prepare Mike for his role as the commander of a Marine Guard of Honor. Meanwhile Elworth was having the chosen Marines collected from bases across the country and Denver was diverting the USS Callistoga from its present task.

Air Force Two would depart for Seoul in three days.

The next three days were hectic with preparations. Mike spent a whole day with the drill instructor learning to look and behave like a Marine Captain, whilst the rest of the team was assembled and briefed by Green.

They went through the operation again and again until everyone was perfect on both the main action and the alternates.

Mike came back to the office on the evening of the second day looking tired, but still enthusiastic. The telephone rang as he came in and Green waved him to a chair as he answered the call.

"Green," he said, and listened for a few moments. "Right, I'll make sure he comes right over," he cradled the instrument and looked at Mike.

"All ready to go, Nose," Mike said.

"No, you're not," Green said, "There is one very important thing that you have to do before you go anywhere. That was Chevvy. She's in the clinic and asking for you. Go and help her give you a healthy … " He faded into silence. Mike was already pounding down the corridor.

Mike broke every speed limit in town and arrived at the clinic in twelve minutes.

Forty minutes later he was cradling his new son in his arms while the baby yelled lustily.

"He's got a good voice," Chevvy said, "Maybe he'll be a good singer like my Da."

"It's a shame he won't see his grandson," Mike said. "What was his name? Shall we call this little one after him?"

"Thomas he was, but shouldn't we give him one of your family names?"

"Thomas Ashkenaharov. Welcome to the family." Mike kissed his son, laid him beside his mother and kissed her too. "Thank you, Darling, for a beautiful son." His eyes filled with tears of joy.

"I'm glad you were here, Mike. I didn't want you to go off without seeing him."

"No chance. I would have come right round the world to share this moment with you Chevvy. I'm so proud of you both," he kissed her again.

"Good. Now go and ring your father and tell him he's a grandpa. I'm tired after all that exertion."

Two hours later Nose arrived with Betty. They were soon followed by the other members of the team with their wives. Chevvy was showered with prettily knitted and sewn gifts for her new son. Braden came too with Maureen on his arm and a magnum of vintage Champagne in his hand. Chevvy's room took on a party atmosphere.

Young Thomas slept through it all.

Chapter 30

MIKE HAD A CAR WAITING at the airport when the Navajo landed from Miles City. Connor Swingate and Ro were swiftly transferred and driven to the office. They had managed some sleep on the flight, and Ro's shoulder felt much better after the doctor had manipulated it and given her some pain killers.

"Come in and sit down," Green said briskly, when they appeared in his office doorway. He pushed the file he had been reading to one side and leaned back in his chair. "It seems I should have asked some questions before sending you off, young Swingate. Suppose you start by telling me why you rigged this office and when you did it."

"Well, sir, I did it five weeks before you moved in. Before you were even appointed, in fact. I overheard a phone conversation between Mason and my father that did not make sense. It concerned an Indian military scientist called Hari Prasaad. I already had reason to think my father was involved in commercial activities incompatible with his status as a United States Senator, and this made me suspicious. When a second call came in I wondered why he had so much business with the Company. Mason was evasive when I asked if the caller had been my father, so I thought I'd just do a little discreet listening, and laid a couple of small bugs."

"Quite apart from the fact that one of the parties was your father, and a Senator besides, don't you think it was somewhat unethical?

"Well, sir, had it been anyone other than my father it might not have caught my attention. You are probably aware that there is no love lost between me and my father. I believe that he has abused his position before, and that to ignore this would be falling down in my own duty."

"What is the substance of your disagreement?" Green asked.

"I believe my father was responsible for my mother's death some years ago. I have been trying to find out the truth, but so far he's been very clever in keeping the whole thing clouded. The only other person who was known to have been present at the time died last year in a motor accident," Connor explained.

"Who was that?"

"Philip Howard. He was the President and sole owner of the Howard Power Corporation back in Idaho. They were cruising on Howard's yacht, in the Indian Ocean, at the time my mother is supposed to have died."

"Was there another woman? Howard's wife, perhaps?" Green asked.

"I thought at the time there must have been, but Howard's wife died from kidney failure five years previously and he never remarried. I have never been able to identify anyone else, or prove that there was another woman there at the time. He seems to have led a celibate life after his wife died."

"OK. Let's leave that for a moment. Did you catch anything with your bugs? That was a pretty smart system by all accounts, and well hidden," Green said.

Connor nodded his acceptance of the compliment. "There was nothing solid enough to use as evidence, but a lot of veiled references that continued to fuel my suspicion. I'm sure there is, or was, some business tie-in between Mason and my father. I still have the tapes if you want them, Mr Green."

"Yes. I shall want them later. Tell me about these links between your father and Mason."

"Well, apart from the obvious, the Indian scientist, Prasaad, was mentioned a number of times. There was also something about a shipment, but neither one ever said precisely what it was or where it was going. Mason made several references to 'your lady' and 'the girl', but they never gave her a name. I might have made more progress if they had." Swingate looked thoughtful.

The hell you would, Green thought, the shit would really have hit the fan if you had found that out then. He scratched his nose for a moment and asked "What else did you pick up?"

"There was a reference to a payment of some sort. My father said the freight outfit would handle all that."

"Any idea which outfit?"

"No, they didn't use any name. Just called it the 'freighting company'. There was also mention of a pump manufacturer in Chicago. I never had time to check that one out. At the time you sent me off on furlough I was about to build a set of devices and rig them in my father's house. I had taken a lot of parts and equipment with me to do the assembly during the evenings in camp. Then you sent me off to do that hunting lodge and I used the equipment there. Mr Green, why was I asked to bug my father's hunting lodge?"

"Who told you that?" Green tried to cover his surprise.

"Nobody. No need to know, Sim said, but I found out while rigging the place.

There was a locked room, and when it was eventually opened I recognized the roll-top desk. It used to be in our house when I was a kid and I had carved my initials on one end. They're still there. I looked inside when I was left alone to plant the bugs."

"Did you just! Find anything?" Green sat forward and leaned his elbows on the desk.

"Nothing to do with what I thought I was looking for. There were two small computers there. I imagine they might contain something interesting."

"Sim told me about them. He said he had instructed you not tap them." Green said.

"He told me not to turn them on, yes. But I laid a couple of bugs anyway. Ones that would only operate when the machine was turned on. Someone has been using one of them since we left." Connor reached into his bag and pulled out the monitoring unit. "This box has a download recorder in it. As soon as the machine is switched on the dingus I fitted pumps the whole memory into here. It won't show up on the computer, which will continue to operate normally. Everything done before shut down will also be pumped into here," he held up the box. "I fitted a high power booster to give it range by bouncing off a communications satellite, so it should work even here."

"That was neat work," Green said. "What do you do with it now?"

"Feed it into a compatible machine here, and just dial up the menu. Then you can access the complete memory that was in the other machine. Do you want me to show you?"

"Later," Green said. "We have some very clear tapes from your system. I shall want you to listen to some of them in due course. In the light of what you have told me this may be useful. You can do this at the same time. Tell me about yourself. Are you married?"

"Yes." Connor paled. The response was not missed on Green.

"Tell me about your wife, then."

"Lois? She was the second reason I bugged Mason's office. He's her daddy, and I didn't want her to find out he was doing something irregular. I thought I might be able to stop it before it became an issue."

"Do you get along well, you and Lois?"

"We used to, at first. Then she got kind of distant. Mostly now we get by without too much friction, but you wouldn't call it an exciting marriage. Without the kids it would have died long ago."

"How does your wife get along with her own father?"

"She dotes on him. That was why I thought she would be so hurt if it ever came out that he had been doing deals on the side."

"What about the Senator, how does she get along with him?"

"Real good. They made friends when Lois and I were engaged to be married and have been ever since. There is something I ought to tell you here, Mr Green." Connor reached into his bag again, and withdrew a large Air Mail envelope. "When I was looking through the desk I found this. It was hidden in a secret compartment," he tossed the envelope onto Green's desk.

"What is it?"

"I would prefer you just read it first, sir, before I talk about it."

Green picked up the packet. It contained seven letters, each in its own envelope, numbered sequentially. He opened the first and began to read. At the bottom of the first page a low whistle escaped from his lips. He read all seven letters before he looked up and spoke. "You had no idea?"

"Of that? No. I told you that I felt certain my father had been responsible for my mother's death, but this was something I had never suspected. They've been at it for years. The man is a monster."

"She know about this?" Green indicated Ro, who had said nothing so far.

"Yes. I showed them to her. I had to talk to someone. I don't know what it will do to my boys when they find out he's their father, not me."

"Do you think Mason knows about this?" Green asked gently.

"I guess so. There are enough references in there, and with what I already have on tape, to suggest they are all in this together. After all that it would not surprise me to find she had been bedding with him as well."

"What about her mother?"

"She died when Lois was four. Mason married again, a woman called Karen Sibfield, but she and Lois never really became close. I doubt if she knows anything about any of this," Connor said.

Green buried his face in his stubby hands and thought for a minute. Looking up, he asked, "What are you going to do now?"

"Nail all of them. Right down the line, right by the book."

"Good," Green said with a smile. "As of now you are back on this team. There are a lot of things about this affair you still don't know. To start with, Lois has spent the last three days at the hunting lodge with your father and a party of Indian nuclear people. I want you to work with Penkowski and go through all the tapes that have come off your system. While you are at it, get that computer stuff on a stand-alone machine and go through that as well. You are to take no further independent action unless so instructed by me, but I promise you, action will be taken." He leaned back in his chair for a moment, scratching the back of his head before continuing.

"We may have to hand it all over to the Bureau in the end, but I want to find out what the heck has been going on before we do. You can rest assured that you will have the full backing of the Company in this, and they will not get away this time. I suggest you talk to one of the welfare people about your boys."

He turned his attention to Ro. "You go with him and make sure he doesn't do anything stupid. As soon as they clear out of the hunting lodge we'll have someone in there to heist those computers. Then we'll take the place apart, stick by stick, and see what else comes out with the beetles. Don't let Connor go home in the meantime. Both book in to a local motel or use the overnight rooms here. I have another operation in hand at the moment, and have to spend a few hours on that. We'll talk again in the morning." Green pulled himself out of his chair and came round the desk. "I'm real sorry about all this, Connor, but let's do it right. No side plays."

"Yes sir. And thanks." They shook hands, and Ro followed Connor to the door.

When they had gone Green called Penkowski and briefed him on what had happened. They spent some minutes talking about the information that had come in during the day from Thornton and Rosario before Green hung up and turned his attention back to the forthcoming operation in China.

Chapter 31

AT 1105 ON A WARM summer morning, Air Force Two thundered down the runway and lumbered into the air. On board, the Secretary of State and his staff occupied the executive suite in the forward section. In the rear, twenty Marines in civilian clothes and one CIA Special Agent stretched in their seats, and settled down to get what sleep they could.

On the ground, Braden and Green stood with General Harrison Elworth and Admiral Milton Denver and watched in silence until the aircraft disappeared in the azure haze.

"Well, all we can do now is bite our finger nails and pray," Braden said.

"Don't worry, Chuck," the Admiral said. "The plans have been gone over time and again in the minutest detail, and that's a fine young man you have in charge. It's all going to work out real dandy."

"I bet he's been like this every time he's seen me off before," Green muttered. "I know how he feels. I wish I were going too, but you're right, Admiral, Mike is bright, quick and will do a good job."

Braden turned back. "After some of the crazy stunts you pulled off, Nose, is it any wonder I wanted to go in your place?" He laughed. "It's like a mother eagle watching her chick learn to fly and hoping it won't end up with its beak buried in the mud."

The three others laughed with him, but each felt the twist of excitement and the tremor of fear in his guts.

"I have to get back," Green said. "I have another operation running alongside at this time, and someone has to mind the store. Will you ride with me Charles? I need to talk over a few things. I will keep you two gentlemen informed as soon as anything comes in until this show is over."

"We would appreciate that," the two military men said shaking hands before heading for their own cars.

"What's on your mind, Nose?" Braden asked as he seated himself and closed the door of Green's car.

Green told him in detail about his interview that morning with Connor Swingate.

"The jeezly bastard!" Braden exclaimed. "So that's the game that sonofabitch Senator is playing. When does Hal Johnson get back?"

"He should be back tomorrow. He's been making arrangements for the return of those two crates from Dakar. We thought about loading them with seeded information and letting them proceed to their destination, but we have enough evidence off the hunting lodge tapes now. The pumping equipment will continue normally, and our people are providing a new set of documents to cover the reduced number of crates. They will be watched all the way, and it could be interesting when the recipient opens the boxes and cannot find what he expects."

"What are you going to do about Connor Swingate?" Braden asked.

"I have told him he's back on the team. There is an agent with him at all times. He'll play it by the book as long as his Daddy doesn't get away. The kid's OK."

"Fine. Just keep me informed, ahead of everyone else, on both these operations."

"Sure thing, Charles." Green pulled out into the traffic stream and gave his full attention to driving in the early lunch-time rush.

Maureen had the television tuned to the midday news as Braden came back into the office. The title sequence was already running as he perched on the edge of her desk to watch.

"This is Martin Hallett with the midday news from Washington across the nation," the announcer said as Hallett's face filled the screen.

"The Secretary of State flew out this morning on a four day visit to Great Britain, where he is to have talks with the Foreign Secretary. It is expected that he will also meet the Prime Minister, the Home Secretary and the Secretary of State for Defense. The meetings will focus on the American proposal to reduce land forces in Europe in response to recent Soviet reductions. The Secretary of State is also expected to discuss the case of Joseph Patrick O'Rourke, a member of the outlawed Irish Republican Army, who escaped from the Crumlin Road Jail in Belfast, Northern Ireland, two years ago whilst serving a fifteen year sentence for terrorist offenses. O'Rourke has been held in New York for the last seven months, pending the outcome of extradition hearings." The announcer turned the page of his notes.

"In a last minute change to his schedule the Secretary of State is first flying to Beijing to hold urgent talks with the Chinese leaders. Since the events of last weekend, there has been concern for the safety of American citizens visiting and working in China. The Secretary will be asking the Chinese authorities to guarantee safe conduct for all US citizens, who have been advised by our Embassy they should quit the country as soon as possible. No decision has yet been taken as to whether non-essential staff will be evacuated from the Embassy, but our contact there informs us that the Consulate in Shanghai has already been withdrawn to the Chinese capital." He turned another page.

"In the long running trial of Cicero Brognola, accused of conspiracy to..." Maureen switched the set off.

"So they're on their way. When do we expect results?" she asked the Chief.

"Tomorrow night, if all goes well," he said gloomily.

"Don't be such a pessimist," she chided him with a smile. "Now, Mr Anderson will be here in forty minutes. Do you want some lunch before he comes?"

He asked for a sandwich and went through into his own office as Maureen called the canteen.

IN HER HOSPITAL ROOM seven miles away, Chevvy was watching the same news bulletin. Mike's parents had arrived and were cooing with delight over their newest grandson. Neither noticed the tear that trickled down Chevvy's cheek, nor the surge of pride she felt as the screen showed Air Force Two lifting into the sky.

Chapter 32

AS THE DAILY MEETING broke up, Green called Braden to advise him of the team's intended strategy for the Senate hearing. The Chief had another bit of interesting news for him.

"Apparently this Indian, General Rashkhar, does not exist. I have been in contact with the Embassy in Delhi and they've given me a copy of the guest list for each of the functions that the Senator and his colleagues attended. I've also talked with our people at the Embassy and none of them saw the Senator talking with any of the Indian military people who were present. In any case, it would have been normal for the Indians to approach our own military attaché first on something like the arms question," Braden told him. "I'm sending those lists over to you now."

Green was leafing through the details of Senator Swingate's activities which Joe had obtained when Braden's messenger arrived. He took a quick glance at the lists and went back to his search. Three minutes later he had found what he was looking for. Joe had managed to obtain copies of the same list from one of the Senator's secretaries. There were pencil marks against two of the names on one list, with 'guns?' written faintly against a third name. The other marks looked like radiation symbols.

Green pulled a message pad towards him and began composing a signal to the Company's man in Delhi. Reading it through, he added a footnote requesting a reply within the hour. He took it along to the communications room himself, and asked for it to be sent at once. The clerk gave him a dazzling white smile, pushed aside the romantic novel she had been reading, and began typing the message into the encoding machine at great speed.

"Do you want the footnote encoded as well, Mr Green?" she asked.

"No. Leave that in clear. It may just attract their attention like that."

It did. Watson's reply came back in twenty five minutes, and Green smiled as he read it. It may have been written in a hurry, but there were three concise bio sketches under the names Green had asked about. In addition, Watson had confirmed that there was no General Rashkhar, either currently serving in the Indian Army, or on the retired list. Green read with growing relish and felt the tingle of excitement in his stomach that a hunter feels when his quarry comes into full view for the first time.

Connor and Penkowski spent that day transcribing and analyzing the hunting lodge tapes that Thornton and Moose Rosario had squirted down the wire from Orofino. Some of the tapes had already been bleep marked, and they made rapid progress.

With the preliminary Senate Committee Hearing starting the following day, Green called the whole team together at six that evening to review progress. Penkowski talked through the taped evidence. Joe presented the details uncovered by the Bureau, and Mitch took the team through Hal Johnson's contributions from Dakar. They went over some parts several times, discussing other implications and projecting what further evidence might remain to be unearthed. By eight thirty a clear picture had emerged, supported by solid facts.

"I think we should leave this now," Green said. "I will take the file home and read through. Let's meet again at eight tomorrow and finalize the details. You have done a good job with this."

"I see that nose twitching again. He's hatching some plot," Penkowski observed to no one in particular.

Green just smiled and waved his hand towards the door to indicate that the meeting was finished.

"What was that about?" Connor asked Mitch as they left.

"Search me."

Green stayed late. He went through all the summary sheets again, twice, and periodically delved into one or other of the files for more detail. After a while he extracted some sections and listed them in a different order. By ten he had made a series of long distance calls which produced five more closely written sheets of notes. Just before midnight he locked everything in the secure cabinet and went home.

AT SEVEN THE FOLLOWING morning Green was back at his desk. Sleep had brought him several new ideas, which he wanted to verify before the team assembled. He called communications to see if there was any further information from Hal. There was nothing, but the messenger came in a few minutes later with several messages from the Bureau. Green's eyes lit up when he saw these, and the angle he had been searching for crystallized in his mind. He was just completing his draft for presentation to the Senate Committee when the team arrived. He called them in immediately and spent fifteen minutes briefing them.

"There it is then," he concluded. "That should be enough to get us a few weeks adjournment. We have enough to get the whole thing thrown out now, but keeping it going a little while longer gives us the opportunity to sew up the whole bag of tricks, not just squash this gun running ploy. We need time to drain the computers at the hunting lodge while the parties involved remain unaware that we are onto them. Do you have the key to that room, Joe?"

"Sim has it."

"Good. I want you and Connor on standby to fly back to Orofino. The minute Sim Thornton is sure the place is empty I want the three of you back in there. Take the place apart. Bring every piece of paper you can find, and you had better recover the snoop system, Connor. Now, does the Senator have any staff at his house in DC?"

"A maid," Connor said. "She goes out to the shops, dry cleaner and so on each day from around ten till eleven thirty. There is also a cook, but she is only there to prepare evening meals on days when he is not dining out. When she is needed she arrives about five thirty and leaves at about ten."

"Right. You'll have to identify the maid to Mitch," Green told Connor. "He can then follow her and delay her by a couple of hours. During that time you and Penkowski will bug that house. You must be out before the maid comes back. I want that place so well wired we can hear the cockroaches fart, and I want it done today."

"It'll be a pleasure, sir." Connor grinned.

"Just one more thing," Green said. "Where did you sleep last night? It would be better if you did not go anywhere near your own home for a while."

"Don't worry; I'm not going back there while Lois is around. I would only want to strangle her. I said I'd do it by the book, and I will. I stayed in a motel down the road last night, and Mitch has offered me a room for a few days, so I'll put up with him."

"He means I'll put up with him!" Mitch said, punching Connor's shoulder. They all laughed.

"Good. Now get moving." Green said. "I want tapes coming in from that house by this afternoon."

As he gathered his papers together Green suddenly remembered that he had forgotten to arrange transport to get him to the Senate. He lifted the telephone and called Movements.

"This is Malcolm Green. I have to get to the Senate Committee. Can you help?"

Yes, Mr. Green. Mike told me you would need to go. Everything is organized." June Connaught forestalled his question. "If you would care to go down to the pad, we have a helicopter waiting for you. Clearance for the flight just came through. There will be ground transport waiting at the other end to take you to the Hill."

"Why, thank you. That sounds very efficient." Green was impressed.

"Our pleasure, Mr Green. Any movements you need, just call me on 2616 and I'll be delighted to oblige."

"I'll remember that. Thanks." Green smiled to himself, thinking of Mike. He was now ten thousand miles away and had still remembered a detail like that. That young man will do very well, he thought. His confidence in the success of the Beijing operation rose several notches, knowing it was in capable hands.

On the way out of the office he met Hal, just returning from Dakar. He asked Hal to accompany him to the Senate so that he could get a first hand update from him. Hal chattered away as they climbed into the helicopter. Green interrupted occasionally with questions, but mostly he just listened and made neat notes on his pad. When Hal finished, Green brought him up to date with what the rest of the team had found out during his absence.

Although traffic was heavy in the capital the Company driver dropped the two men at the side door of the Capitol with twenty minutes to spare. They went in search of coffee before the proceedings began. It was the first time Hal had been inside the great building that housed the nation's policy makers, and his head kept turning like a radar scanner.

After coffee they found the appointed room and were shown to seats in the front row by an usher. A printed notice lying on each chair stated that the purpose of the hearing was to examine prima facie evidence to determine whether weapons of United States origin had been illegally supplied to a terrorist organization in Sri Lanka by an individual or by individuals as yet unknown in contravention of the laws and constitution of the United States of America for the purpose of supporting, encouraging, or maintaining a rebellion by the aforementioned terrorists against the legally constituted and recognized government of Sri Lanka and or its neighbors.

"Jesus!" said Hal. "Do they all talk in this sort of gobbledygook?"

"Pompous crap," said Green, folding the notice into his file and sitting down. He turned to look round the room and found there were about fifteen people in the public seating area, most of them sporting Press badges. Those who were not from the Press had the well scrubbed, innocent look of graduate students doing summer research projects for their theses on the workings of government.

Green noticed a little old lady sitting to one side. She was about seventy years old, dressed in a smart, if dated, gray suit and a straw hat with wax cherries round the crown. She sat upright, with her back very straight and her white gloved hands neatly folded over her purse. She was staring intently at the flag draped behind the curved desk where the committee members would be seated. He was wondering who she was when the thought was driven from his mind as the five members of the Senate Committee began to file in and take their seats.

Everyone rose while the Senators sat down. An official rose from his seat in front of the dais and banged a gavel. "This Committee is now in session, Senator Jefferson Stanley Swingate in the chair. All be seated," he announced in well rehearsed stentorian tones.

They all sat down.

Senator Swingate shuffled his papers for a moment and pulled the microphone in front of him closer. He cleared his throat noisily and looked slowly round the room, scrutinizing every face. People seemed to be holding their breath, waiting for him to begin. Green wished he would just get on with it.

Two hours later the hearing was adjourned.

Chapter 33

THIRTY-NINE THOUSAND FEET above the island of Ullung-do in the Sea of Japan, the Captain of Air Force Two called Seoul and told the controller that he was entering South Korean air space. The controller responded with a list of figures, which the co-pilot noted and made some adjustments to the instruments. The autopilot made minute course corrections. Apart from a forty five minute refueling stop in San Francisco they had been airborne for fourteen and a half hours, and both men were starting to yawn. They had taken turns earlier to stretch out on the crew bunk, but neither man felt rested.

"Charlie, go back and tell the leader of that bunch of hoodlums that we've entered Korean air space, will you. Ask him if he'd care to come up to the flight deck and we'll let him in on a few secrets."

"OK. I could do with a walk," the co-pilot said, heaving himself out of his seat.

"And see if they've got any fresh coffee in the galley as you go by," the skipper added.

"Will do." Charlie opened the cockpit door to find Mike, coffee pot in one hand, reaching for the door handle with the other. "Say! Do you read minds or something?"

"No," said Mike. "I just thought you guys might like some fresh coffee, and I'd appreciate a word with the Captain as well."

"Good. He wants to talk to you. I was just coming to get you. Gimme that," he lifted the pot from Mike's hand and gestured forward. "Take my seat."

"Hi, Mike." The skipper turned round as he climbed into the right hand seat. "We've been in Korean air space for about five minutes. Everything is right on time. Are your men all ready?"

"Yes. They are just getting dressed up now. Have you decided how you are going to play it?"

"I'm going to overfly and then call up just before we leave Korean air space. That will be in about nineteen minutes time. There is a commercial flight due off any minute, heading south to Hong Kong. We'll give them time to get clear first. The helicopter has been on the ground for half an hour, and is all ready to go. As soon as I've made the call and started our descent we'll get the comms officer in the back to squirt a signal to the Embassy in Seoul and they can contact Beijing with the change of plan. We should be on the ground in twenty eight minutes from now. Normal landing procedures." He took a mouthful of coffee. "Ah, nectar!"

"I'm glad you like it. I made it myself, to an old Russian recipe," Mike laughed. "Hey! What's that?" He pointed out of the window beyond the pilot.

"It looks like Uncle Sam sent an Eagle to keep us safe. There'll be another one around somewhere," the pilot responded craning his neck to look behind. "Look out your side, ahead and below."

"There he is," Mike said as the second fighter rose into formation alongside, no more than a hundred feet away to his right. He waved to the pilot and received a smart salute in return.

When the coastline passed beneath them, Charlie tapped Mike on the shoulder and jerked a thumb as he turned. Mike relinquished the seat and stood behind and between the two pilots.

"OK. Here we go," the skipper said, and pressed the transmit button. "Seoul Control, this is US Air Force Two. Do you read?"

"Air Force Two, Seoul Control, I have you loud and clear," came the reply over the ceiling speaker.

"Seoul, I have indications of a hydraulic leak. I wish to divert and make a precautionary landing. Can you take me?"

"Stand by Air Force Two," the speaker crackled.

The Captain looked at Mike and lifted an eyebrow. They waited. Ten seconds seemed like an hour. Mike's hands were beginning to sweat when the speaker crackled again.

"Air Force Two that is affirmative. Turn zero seven five and commence your descent."

"Zero seven five," the pilot said. The two men moved as a well practiced team and the huge plane banked and began to lose height. The skipper turned to Mike with a grin. "OK, Mike, will you tell the man we are on our way?"

"I think he will have guessed by now. See you on the ground," he turned to go back to the main cabin.

"Yeah. Thanks for the coffee. Please tell the comms officer as you go by that he can transmit his signals in precisely seven minutes."

Mike nodded and was gone.

"Cabin crew, landing in nine minutes," the Captain said over the cabin intercom. "OK, Charlie, let's get those checks done."

The co-pilot pulled a flip-card from the pocket beside his seat and began the litany of pre-landing checks as Air Force Two sank rapidly towards the waiting runway.

Chapter 34

CONNOR AND JOE had flown direct to Idaho after planting the listening devices in Senator Swingate's Washington home. Thornton was waiting with the helicopter when they landed, and airlifted them direct to the hunting lodge. He had brought along several empty cartons, and it didn't take Connor long to start filling them. He left the bugs in the radio and the computers, and removed all the rest. Since the bugs in the study had their own transmitter, he went into the main roof space and removed the main transmitter from the apex of the rafters, disconnected and gathered all the tiny microphones, then began reeling in the hundreds of feet of fine wire which had connected everything. Where the sensors had been removed, a smear of dirt soon disguised any evidence that they had ever been there.

In the study Connor showed Thornton how to open the desk, and where the secret compartment was, then he sat down in front of the computers and turned them both on. He had previously dumped the first recording from his electronic sponge into the office computer back in Langley, and had brought the device with him. It took very little time to copy the complete memory from both machines so that he could start to explore the programs. Much of the data was tabular, or in machine language, but he found occasional sections of text. This was gibberish. Thornton, looking over his shoulder, thought he had tripped a security device.

"No. This has been put into some sort of code. I think we'll find that the other machine has an encrypting program in it," Connor said calmly. He turned to the other keyboard and tapped out a sequence of commands. The screen scrolled for a moment and then stopped. "There you are, 'Code-it'. That is an off-the-shelf commercial program. Eighty dollars from your neighborhood software store. It first came out about four years ago and is mainly used by companies handling commercially sensitive material through an electronic mail system and wanting to preserve basic confidentiality. It won't stop a good hacker, but prevents the casual snooper from reading your letters."

"Why have it in another computer, then?" Thornton asked.

"It takes up a fairly large slice of memory. This is only a small computer. Cheaper to get a second unit, and run them linked, than to buy a bigger one. Also, he uses the same model back home. I would bet that you'll find Chester P. Howard also uses one of these. The machine is old enough to be exempt from the regulations governing the export of computer technology. That means his Indian friends could have got one too. They hook them all together via the normal telephone system and talk to each other. Data transfer is almost instant and more or less undetectable."

"You mean he could be sending out nuclear secrets through this? Hell's bells! He could have shipped out God knows what by now," Thornton said in exasperation.

"He could, but he hasn't. At least not from here." Connor pressed some more keys and columns of figures scrolled down the screen. "This list here keeps a record of all outgoing transmissions. See this column of numbers here?" He pointed at the screen with a pencil he had been sucking. "These are destination index codes. They correspond to telephone area codes, and they are all within the continental United States. Most of them will probably turn out to be fairly local, and I'd hazard a guess at the Howard Nuclear Power Corporation. There are one or two strays that we will have to check out, here, and here," he tapped the screen again with his pencil. "When we examine the memory in detail we may be able to identify what he sent where. With this set up he has to go through the radiophone net for his calls. They will have records also, for billing purposes, unless he used a direct radio link. I don't think he has done that often as there are only a few without any code at all."

"What will the telephone records show?" Thornton asked.

"Not much. Only the date, time, destination and duration of each link up. We'll have to cross reference all that with the computer's memory to identify what was being handled at the time. Do you want to take these machines with us?"

"Not at this time. Nose still wants to lay out rope. Let the Senator believe we're not yet onto him. If this thing keeps records of all activity, won't it record you looking around now?"

"It would, normally," Connor said, "but I entered through a trapdoor and shall erase that from the program before I turn off. I'm going to make a second copy of everything on disks, as a back-up. Takes about twenty minutes, OK?"

"You're the expert." Thornton grinned. "I'm going to help Joe collect paper from the rest of the place," he left Connor to copy disks, and went in search of Joe.

In the main room, Joe had a portable copier set up on the table. He was busy feeding sheets of paper into one end when Thornton joined him.

"Found anything interesting, Joe?"

"Bank records, and I'll bet they are not declared. I found them inside a false book cover in the bedroom drawer. He's been stashing away loot by the bucket load. Mostly deposited in cash."

"This place is becoming more of a gold mine by the minute," Thornton said. "Connor has found some goodies in those computers that should be enough to put him in Sing-Sing for a hundred years."

"Let's just hope it does," Joe said. "Here, Sim, could you feed the next bunch through, I have to go to the john."

"Sure." Thornton gave the moose head on the wall a friendly pat, and came over to the table. He opened the next file and let out a low whistle. It was full of bearer bonds, each worth a hundred thousand dollars. There were thirty-one of them.

Thornton started feeding them into the copier. The government is going to get rich when we finally nail this bastard, he thought.

Joe came back and started returning the papers that had already been copied to where he had found them. Connor came in as Thornton was feeding the last of the bonds into the copier.

"What have you found here?" he asked, picking up one of the bonds. "These belonged to my mother. They disappeared after she died. My father said he had never seen them."

"Are you sure about that Connor?"

"Sure I am. The argument went on for months. They were supposed to have come to me, but could never be found. The old man must have hidden them before they went away on that last trip, and brought them up here. They were specifically mentioned in my mother's will. In the end the lawyers decided that she must have disposed of them some time beforehand."

"Wouldn't that have shown in her accounts?"

"It should have, but her papers were in such a mess they couldn't prove anything. It was strange, because she had always been such a tidy, well organized person," Connor said, replacing the bond in the pile. "I have finished in there, Sim. I'll load my gear into the 'copter, unless you have anything else for me to do first."

"No, we're about done here too. Let's clear up and get out. We'll take these bonds with us," he turned off the copier and coiled the lead.

The pilot was lounging on the grass, enjoying a cigarette. He stubbed it out and got to his feet when Connor appeared with the first carton. Opening the baggage hatch, he took the box from Connor and pushed it to the back of the compartment. Joe came out carrying the copier with Connor's second box on top.

"Sim is just having a final check round. There is a carton of copies on the table. That's the last," he said, handing his load to the pilot. He was just turning away when he stopped and cocked his head at the sky. "Sounds like we have company," he called.

The pilot stood up from the baggage hatch and listened as well. The rhythmic throb of a rotor grew louder behind the trees.

"Tell Sim," the pilot shouted, slapping the hatch closed. He ducked under the tail boom and climbed up onto the engine housing, pulling at the clamps to remove the cover. Thornton came out of the lodge, locked the door and pocketed the key. He turned and casually strolled along to the window and was peering inside as a bright green Jetranger appeared over the trees.

All four men turned to look at the new arrival. The pilot waved from his perch on top of the engine housing, Joe leaned against the cabin door, hands in his pockets, while Connor just stood and watched.

The new arrival settled on the grass beside the black helicopter and a man in a gray uniform leapt from the open door with a pump action shotgun in his hand.

"What the hell are you doing here?" he shouted.

"Howdy," said their pilot from his high perch. "We got a malfunction and had to put down. Saw this place and thought we might get some help. Are you the Park Ranger?"

"This is private property. You'll have to leave," the man replied, holding his weapon loosely but ready.

"I just told you, we had to put down in a hurry. Are you the owner? I could use the loan of some tools," The pilot seemed unperturbed.

Thornton walked over from where he had been peering in the lodge window. "There don't seem to be anyone here, Rich," he said to the pilot. Turning to the newcomer he said, "Hi. Do you happen to know where we might find the owner of this place? Maybe he could help us."

"I just told your pilot, this is private property. You will have to leave. The owner is not here, and he don't like people coming here uninvited. Get in that thing and get outa here."

"Hold on, friend," Thornton said, smiling and raising his hands in a settle down gesture. "Our bird is broken. We can't go anyplace until we get some tools or a mechanic. Maybe you can help us. Have you got a tool kit?"

"No. Where are you headed, anyway?"

"We were on our way back to a ranch near Orofino. Our mechanic's over there," Thornton told him.

The man appeared to hesitate. He was young, and heavily built. His chin was pockmarked from acne, and he had a small piece missing from his left ear. He looked from face to face with suspicion. "Orofino's only a few miles over there," he jerked a thumb over his shoulder. "Why didn't you go on?"

"Our pilot said it wasn't safe, and seeing there was a place here where we could put down and maybe get some help, we landed. Sorry if it's private. We don't mean to intrude." Thornton kept his manner friendly.

The man continued to eye the group suspiciously.

"You said you got a mechanic in Orofino?" he asked.

"Yeah. At a ranch just north of town. We came up for a bit of fishing. We were just looking round the area, getting to know the lakes, when this happened. Say, could you fly one of us over and bring our man back? That would be real helpful."

The man seemed undecided for a moment, then shrugged. "Wait here," he turned back to the green Jetranger and talked briefly to the pilot. "You, come here," he pointed the gun at Thornton. "You go with him. Show him where to go," he indicated that Thornton should get into the Jetranger, and held the door open for him.

"Thanks friend. That's real nice of you," Thornton said and climbed up beside the gray uniformed pilot.

"You three get in that thing, and wait there," the heavy man said, moving back towards the others.

Joe and Connor climbed into their seats. Rich clambered down to the grass as the green bird lifted and scooted away over the trees. Ignoring the guard, he strolled off and, taking out a packet of cigarettes, sat on the grass twenty feet away.

"Where are you going?" demanded the guard. "I told you to get in there."

"Smoking ain't allowed in the aircraft," Rich told him, flicking open his Zippo. He lit his cigarette and inhaled deeply, saying no more.

The guard eyed him suspiciously, but decided not to insist, and moved back to where he could see both Rich and the two men in the helicopter.

Inside the helicopter Connor asked Joe quietly, "What are we going to do about that box of copies still in the lodge?"

"Where is it?" Joe asked.

"Still on the table, I guess. Sim didn't bring it out, and I didn't have time to get it before that peapod dropped in."

"Shit! I just hope they can't see it from the window. We'll have to come back for it later."

They sat in silence for fifteen minutes until they heard the Jetranger returning. It settled on the grass and Thornton jumped down with one of the Rosario boys carrying a toolbox. He and Rich climbed up on top of the black helicopter and buried their heads inside the engine compartment. Their muttered conversation could not be heard from the ground, and was covered by the clanking and clinking of a selection of tools. After a while they replaced the cowling and climbed down.

"That will do to get the bird back to the ranch. I'll have to replace some parts once we get there," Hank Rosario said, loud enough for the guard to hear. The man appeared to have relaxed and was no longer so suspicious, but it would pay to be convincing. "Just don't use any of the auxiliaries for the hop, and lift her gently. That's the best I can do without a workshop."

Joe was talking quietly to Thornton as the two men took their places, and Rich made a show of doing his start-up checks. Once his engine was running, Rich waited for the rotor of the green Jetranger to start turning before he lifted gently from the ground. He climbed in a wide arc, keeping the other machine in view all the time. Well before the other could lift he turned onto his heading and flew off over the trees. As soon as they were out of sight he lost height rapidly towards another clearing.

Rich came to the hover five feet off the ground as Connor slid back the rear door. Joe and Hank tumbled out and ran for the trees. Connor closed the door again as Rich lifted slightly and resumed his course at treetop height.

Within seconds the peapod jumped, like a jack-in-the-box, from the clearing half a mile behind, and came racing after them. It continued to follow until they landed on Rosario's front lawn, where all the ranch guests ran out and surrounded the black helicopter as the rotor slowed. On the edge of the crowd, Moose raised his beer can to the pilot of the Jetranger hovering above them, and it turned and flew off southwards.

"I thought the crowd would add a bit of color," Moose told Thornton. "How'd it go?"

"Close, but we managed to get them out before the other bird appeared. They are going to have a long walk back with that heavy box."

"No problem. Hank knows all the trails, and they'll be back in a couple of hours. Bobby has taken a couple of horses with saddle bags out to meet them," Moose said. "Come in and have a beer. Nose is on the horn, and wants to talk to you." He led the way to the house.

Green was delighted with Thornton's news, but slightly uneasy when he heard about the watch being kept by Howard's goons and the box of copies that had been left behind. He gave instructions for Thornton, Joe and Connor to return to Langley as soon as possible, and cut the connection.

Joe, Hank and Bobby turned up two hours later in high spirits. There had been no problem recovering the box of copies. They had been in and out within three minutes of Rich dropping them off, and the peapod had not returned. Bobby had met them before they had walked half a mile.

Connor spent five minutes showing Moose how to empty his electronic sponge down the fast wire, in case anyone should go back and use the computers or the radio. Thornton called the airfield at Orofino and warned their young pilot to have the Navajo ready.

Moose pressed a can of cold beer on each of them as they again took their places in the black helicopter to begin the long trip back east.

Chapter 35

ON THE DAY THE People's Liberation Army drove its tanks into Tienanmen Square and crushed the demonstrations, they also moved troops into the rest of the city. There had been a constant military presence in the diplomatic quarter since that fateful Sunday afternoon. There were also civilian observers, posted to watch the foreign Embassies in case any ringleaders of the insurrection, who were now on a wanted list, should try to seek sanctuary. These observers were also part of the network of loyal citizens whose duty was to watch the activities of any foreign devils still at large in the city. There had been little for them to do in recent days but wait and chat idly with the troops. Many of the legations had sent home the families of their staff, and some had gone so far as to evacuate their non-essential personnel as well. Most of the consular offices were shut for an indefinite period, and many of the Embassies had closed their compound gates.

A crowd began to gather outside the gates of the American Embassy. One or two of the watchers mingled with the crowd, and found that it was almost entirely composed of foreign journalists. More arrived by the minute, all hoping for a briefing from the Embassy Press Officer. The milling crowd was noisy, but the watching Chinese kept back as if sensing that this was not a repetition of the demonstrations that they were there to prevent, but something that might even embarrass the Western Imperialists.

A French television crew arrived in a van, parked across the street, and set up their camera on the vehicle's roof. They were careful to keep the camera directed towards the US Embassy gates, and not to point it at the watching soldiers. Earlier in the week several crews had their equipment confiscated for such actions, and had undergone long hours of interrogation and faced accusations of illegal filming and trying to discredit the Chinese people.

Chapter 36

AIR FORCE TWO taxied to a maintenance area away from the main passenger terminal at Seoul's international airport. A huge, long range helicopter had arrived an hour before from the USS Callistoga, and was parked nearby. The crew had finished refueling and were ready to go.

As the boarding ramps were driven up to the huge blue and white aircraft, a convoy of cars drove onto the apron. A hastily assembled deputation from the South Korean Foreign Ministry, accompanied by the American Ambassador, disembarked from a small fleet of gleaming black limousines. Protocol demanded that the Secretary of State spend a few minutes in discussion with his country's allies during this unscheduled visit before continuing his mission. The Secretary of State and a couple of aides descended the steps and greetings were exchanged. The whole party walked a few yards to a hastily erected marquee, while the flight engineer and three co-opted Pan Am ground crew made an inspection of part of the big jet's hydraulic system.

On hearing the reason for the unexpected visit, the Koreans had immediately offered a Boeing 747 from their national airline's fleet, but the offer had been skillfully and diplomatically parried by the Ambassador. A signal received from Beijing just a few minutes previously had, due to the unusual circumstances and importance of the visit, reluctantly agreed to permit the Secretary of State to proceed to Beijing in the Marine Corps helicopter. Air Force Two would follow as soon as repairs had been completed.

No mention had been made to the Chinese that an escort of Marines was accompanying the visitor, and therefore their inclusion in his entourage was not disputed. While the Secretary of State was doing his diplomatic duty in the marquee, the marines discreetly transferred themselves from the Boeing to the helicopter.

Forty minutes after Air Force Two had rolled to a standstill, the diplomatic niceties had been observed. The American party took leave of their bemused hosts and boarded the helicopter. A few minutes later the clattering leviathan lifted from the concrete on the first leg of the six hundred mile flight to the Chinese capital. It would touch down briefly, to refuel, on the flight deck of its parent ship, which was now steaming northwest past the Shantung Peninsula towards the Po Hai Strait.

The new American President had been in office for only six months. Having had several false starts with the appointment of key members of his administration, those who had taken office were still attracting a good deal of attention from the world's press. So many reporters had applied to accompany the Secretary of State on his visit to London that a special aircraft had been laid on to convey them there from Washington. Their flight had taken off half an hour ahead of Air Force Two. The announcement of the Secretary of State's revised itinerary had not been made until his own plane was airborne, so they flew across the Atlantic in happy ignorance, soaking up prodigious quantities of free alcohol and dreaming up suitable clichés to describe the opening of a new era in Anglo-American relations.

When the press plane landed at Heathrow, its passengers were outraged to discover that the subject of their attentions had gone elsewhere. Some tried, in vain, to catch flights to the Far East, thinking that they could catch up and still get a story. Most besieged the ranks of pay phones, trying to contact their agencies or to warn colleagues and stringers already in Beijing. The US Embassy switchboard in Grosvenor Square was jammed in minutes.

The Chinese authorities, already smarting from the lashing that the world's press had given them over the past few weeks, were quietly grateful that their American visitor had managed to leave the pack of news-hounds behind. They sent a New China News Agency television crew to the airport, but said nothing to the Chinese people.

The troops sat in their trucks and watched. The noisy crowd, by now some two hundred strong, continued to mill around outside the gate.

The sun had already sunk into the smog close to the western horizon and the light was fading when a ripple ran through the crowd of reporters. Many had sat down and were chatting in patient groups. Some were even playing cards to pass the time, unwilling to leave in case something did happen and they missed it.

Within moments everyone was on their feet, and the previous clamor resumed. An official came out of the front door of the Embassy and approached the gate. There followed several minutes of intense discussion with those nearest, and there was some reshuffling of people around the gate. At last a side gate was opened and five of the correspondents were taken inside. Shouted comments and questions followed them as the official led the way across the wide, empty forecourt. They went inside the building, the heavy front door closed with a solid thunk, and the noise subsided to a low murmur. Two more television crews arrived and set up their equipment where they could get a view of the Embassy doorway, over the heads of the expectant crowd.

Everyone waited.

Fifteen minutes later the big door opened and the five correspondents emerged. Ignoring the broad sweep of the driveway, they hurried across the lawn to rejoin their colleagues at the gate and share the news. The Marine guard let them out and they were swallowed by the mass of jostling bodies. A hush descended as everyone listened to the news from the five. Another ripple flowed through the crowd, and a ragged cheer went up.

To the watching Chinese this was strange behavior, but then they found most of the foreign devils' behavior strange and uncouth. They wondered what those who had been taken inside could have been told that made the others assume a festive mood. They did not have long to wait to find out.

THE CROWD WERE still milling round the five journalists, asking questions and demanding explanations, when a heavy rhythmic pulse began to fill the air, accompanied by a deep droning noise. Within a minute the sound had resolved itself into the steady growl of heavy aero engines and the throbbing beat of a huge five bladed rotor.

Every face turned skyward to look for the approaching helicopter. They soon saw it, coming in high, directly towards them.

Everyone was on their feet again. Cameras focused and clicked. The television crews zoomed in for close-ups of the approaching machine. Microphones and tape recorders appeared, as if by magic, as the hours of patience began to reap their reward.

The soldiers, still seated in stiff rows in the back of their trucks, were alert now. Some stood up, and the rest followed suit. Every weapon was pointed at the sky. The radio operator in a command car, just along the street from the Embassy gates, was yelling into his set, demanding instructions. His troop commander snatched the handset from him and snapped off several short, sharp commands. Behind the approaching machine two more helicopters came into view. These were more familiar. They were gunships and belonged to the People's Liberation Army. Their presence reassured the soldiers that if this strange machine were an invader of the imperialist forces it would not escape.

As it came closer the markings on the sides of the big helicopter became clear, showing it belonged to the US Marines. The crowd at the gate began waving and cheering. The noise they made was completely drowned by the intense roar of the huge machine. It slowed and came to the hover a hundred and fifty feet above the Embassy. Slowly it began to descend and drift sideways to position itself above the open front lawn. The downwash reached the ground, blasting the leaves from several small trees and flattening the grass. Reporters lost their hats; whipped up into the air they flew tumbling and spinning across the street.

The front door of the Embassy opened as the heavy machine settled onto the grass, and the Ambassador with two of his staff stood waiting on the top step. The noise dropped abruptly as the pilot throttled back and then shut down his engines. The rotor slowed; the artificial wind subsided and stilled.

Overhead the two Chinese gunships circled, their open doors bristling with heavy machine guns, trained on the scene below.

Before the heavy rotor had stopped turning a door in the side of the helicopter slid back. Two Marines, in full dress uniform, jumped onto the grass and hauled a set of steps from the open doorway. These were hardly in place before sixteen more Marines poured out of the helicopter's doorway and formed two lines, one either side of the direct path between the helicopter and the front steps of the Embassy.

The Ambassador walked slowly down the steps and stopped at the bottom. An officer beside the helicopter doorway barked an order and the two lines of Marines sprang smartly to attention. Another command echoed across the now silent garden. In perfect unison the escort presented their arms in salute as the Secretary of State stepped down onto the grass and walked towards the Ambassador.

The two men shook hands and exchanged a few words before turning to face the helicopter. The Secretary of State threw a quick salute to the honor guard, and the two men turned, mounted the steps and went into the Embassy.

Another crisp command returned the escort's weapons to their shoulders and, as one, they turned towards the building, marched up the steps and in through the door.

The silent Press Corps at the gate broke into excited cheers as the heavy door swung closed again. The watching Chinese soldiers stood, silent and amazed, in the backs of their trucks, unsure what they had just witnessed. The two gunships continued to circle five hundred feet above, their noise puny and unnoticed after the mighty roar of the giant American machine.

The two American pilots climbed down from their cockpit and were greeted by calls from the reporters at the gate. They waved, but turned and walked slowly towards the small side door of the Embassy.

Daylight was almost gone now, and arc lights came on all round the Embassy compound bathing the whole area in a harsh white glare. The waiting crowd of reporters had been promised news, and they had got news. The five who had been taken inside had returned with news of the helicopter's imminent arrival and the promise that the Press Officer would come out with a detailed Press Release later. Now they waited impatiently, speculating about the unexpected arrival of the American Secretary of State and his unconventional mode of transport.

There was a brief flurry of interest a few minutes later when two gleaming black Cadillacs, one carrying the stars and stripes on a short staff mounted on the fender, pulled round and stopped in front of the Embassy. The drivers doused their lights and remained in their seats.

If a hot dog van had arrived at that moment the proprietor could have made a fortune. As it was, if any of the reporters were hungry they were all too preoccupied to notice.

Chapter 37

IN LANGLEY THE TEAM had been making progress. Thornton, Joe and Connor had returned from Idaho. Together with Penkowski they spent most of the morning going through all the papers recovered from the Senator's hunting lodge. Many were photocopies, but some things, like used airline tickets and the bearer bonds, they had not bothered to copy and had just brought the originals.

Penkowski found three used tickets that showed the Senator had made unrecorded visits to Hong Kong during the last sixteen months. Joe checked the dates against the record of the Senator's movements he had obtained a few days previously. Each of the flight dates corresponded with periods when he was supposed to have been on vacation at his hunting lodge.

"Now why do you think he wanted to go quietly and unobserved to Hong Kong?" Penkowski was asking as Green came in to see how they were getting on.

"Who was going to Hong Kong?" he asked.

"Slippery Jeff," Penkowski answered. "And always at times when he was supposed to be hunting and fishing in the Bitter Root Mountains." He passed the ticket stubs to Green, who looked at them and tossed them over to Connor.

"Do those dates mean anything to you?"

"No. We were on particularly poor speaking terms at that time. Lois used to see him sometimes, but he wouldn't talk to me. It was only... Hold on, this one." He held up one of the tickets. "Lois's father was away at that time. He said it was a vacation, but he went on his own. He didn't take his wife. I remember it struck me as odd at the time, but he never explained. One thing that did stick in my mind was when he came back he brought Chinese firecrackers for our boys, and a length of silk for Lois. Could he and my father have been together?"

Green took the ticket and stared at it for a long time before speaking.

"Sim, get on to the Air Traffic Control people. See what kind of records they keep. If memory serves me right, that was about the time Howard took delivery of his fancy executive jet. See if they have any record of overseas flight plans being filed for that aircraft. This can of maggots could just have started to hatch." A wry smile touched Green's face as he spoke.

Thornton picked up the phone and started punching numbers.

"What's on your mind?" Penkowski asked.

"It goes like this," Green began, straddling a chair and leaning his arms on the back of it. "There have been just too many coincidences, and after a while they begin to smell of rotten fish. One," he held up his first finger, "we know that Slippery Jeff, as Penkowski has so aptly called him, is somehow tied up with the Howard Nuclear Power Corporation. Howard's goons keep a watch on his play house, which could be good neighborliness because Howard himself visits there sometimes, but it is about two hundred miles from the Howard plant, and helicopters don't come cheap just to keep a friendly eye on your buddy's play parlor. Two," he held up a second finger, "both Howard and Slippery Jeff have been dealing with foreign nuclear people. Three, one of these is a thinly disguised military scientist. Four, we have evidence that the Senator is implicated in the illegal export of classified documents and technology under the disguise of irrigation equipment. Five, even if that were a straight deal he is engaging in commercial activities incompatible with his status as a member of the United States Senate. Six, Connor has provided evidence that Mason and the Senator had a number of clandestine contacts and meetings which, among other things, resulted in this game to tie up our people in a long winded chase after fictitious guns. I think that was part of his plan that misfired. My guess is they expected Mason himself to head up the investigation, and then conveniently miss certain key bits of evidence and create a bureaucratic snafu that would divert attention from their true activities. That would account for the hostile attitudes towards our team and the pressure the Senator is putting on to keep our attention diverted." Green paused for a moment.

"Seven, Slippery Jeff, Mason and, let us assume, Howard all made secret trips to Hong Kong at the same time. We will probably find all three went on somewhere from there in Howard's jet, and it would come as no surprise at all if we find that their destination was the People's Republic of China. Eight, it looks as if our lily-white Senator arranged the early demise of his wife in order to cover up his adulterous relationship with his daughter-in-law. I think Mason knows all about that relationship. He probably even encourages it, and may have suggested it in the first place. It makes a good private communication channel between himself and Slippery Jeff. Nine, we have all the evidence from the computers and the hunting lodge tapes that he and Howard are dealing with military grade nuclear materials and making deals with the Indians. The Chinese could well be behind those, with finance. The Indians have been making a lot of friendly overtures towards the Soviets since old Mother Gandhi got shot. That is likely to make Beijing a mite nervous, but they're a cunning bunch, and instead of brandishing their spears along the border, as they have in the past, they are trying a more subtle approach. India and Pakistan have been uncomfortable neighbors for a long time and there is still a lot of friction between them. Add to that the fact that Pakistan now has a greenhorn leader – Benazir Bhutto is an untried woman in a Moslem country, and Beijing could well see ways of destabilizing the area and improving their own influence. India already has basic nuclear technology, and even some weapons, and this must grate with the folks in Islamabad. They have enough problems with their own wrecked economy and Afghanistan on their northern border. Fundamentalist Iran to the west cannot be a comfortable neighbor either. Even more so since Ayatolla Khomeini died and the leadership is now in dispute. The last thing that the Pakistanis want just now is for India to become a fully fledged nuclear power. There cannot be any doubt that if the Chinese are picking up the tab they will be getting a share of whatever nuclear technology the Indians manage to acquire. If Uncle Sam can be given a red face over a few guns in the hands of Sri Lankan dissidents, that's icing on the cake. It also distracts attention from the Indians' real goal." Green had been ticking off the points on his fingers as he spoke. Now he held up his spread hands and looked around the team to gauge their reactions.

"I'll give you numbers ten and eleven," Connor offered. "My father speaks fluent Chinese. It used to be a bit of a joke when I was a kid. He loved showing off when we went out to eat Chinese. He would jabber away to the waiters and have them all fawning over him. He hasn't done it for a long time that I'm aware of, but it is not something he would forget."

There was a stunned silence for fifteen seconds as everyone stared at Connor.

"What's number eleven?" asked Mitch.

"Lois did languages at college. No big prizes for guessing what she majored in."

"Chinese." Green sounded sick.

"Give the man a pineapple," Connor nodded. "She worked as a translator before we met and later with the resettlement program for the Vietnamese boat people as well. She even suggested adopting one of the orphaned kids at one time."

"Shit! Is there anyone who ain't involved in this mess?" Joe asked with feeling.

"Seems like the only ones we haven't run into are the IRA and the Colonel Gaddafi's Libyans," Mitch observed.

The laughter that greeted this was flat. Green looked thoughtful.

"Where do we go from here, Nose?" Penkowski asked after a pause. "Should we start to round them all up?"

"First I'd better tell the Chief. He'll probably want to bring the Bureau in before we make any move. While I'm doing that you guys find out precisely where all the players are and keep close tabs on them from now on. If we have to, we need to be able to pick them up at a moment's notice. This is now top priority." Green pushed himself off the chair, and stretched like a cat.

The communications room messenger was delivering a signal from Mike in Beijing when Green returned to his own desk. He read it while his fingers dialed Braden's number, and smiled.

"Hi, Maureen. Is Chuck there?"

"Nose! I keep telling you he hates to be called that. There is someone with him at the moment. Can I give him a message?"

"Yes. Tell him Big Chief Heavy Water has jumped the Reservation. Oh, and I just got word from Mike. Ninety nine right down the line," he said.

"Must you be so cryptic?" Maureen laughed. Green knew that she enjoyed trying to decipher his little clues, and was pleased when she succeeded. "I'll tell him as soon as he's free. Bye."

Green was still staring into space fifteen minutes later when Braden called and asked him to come over.

Chapter 38

THE AMBASSADOR LED the Secretary of State directly to his office and asked his secretary to bring the Marine commander and the helicopter pilot along immediately. The two diplomats were talking about the discussions the Secretary of State had held during the stopover in Seoul when they arrived. Taking the top seat himself, the Ambassador invited the others to join him at the conference table.

"Welcome to Beijing, gentlemen," he began. "Mr Secretary has told me about your visit to Seoul. I would now like to bring you up to date with the situation here. Firstly I must tell you there has been a mixed response to your flying direct to the Embassy compound and not landing at the airport as was expected. You cannot fail to have noticed the two gunships presently circling above this Embassy. They will almost certainly maintain a presence there until you leave. The military authorities were in fact instrumental in you being allowed to fly here direct. They originally opposed the visit altogether. The situation here means the country is not geared up to receive visiting diplomats at this time, and there appears to have been bitter argument about the visit within the inner circles of power. Since the Chinese had no knowledge that there would be United States Marines on board, apart from the crew, I expect we shall shortly receive a strong protest. They may insist that the helicopter return direct to the carrier it came from, leaving the Secretary of State to wait for the arrival of Air Force Two. If the helicopter departs first they will surely find some means of delaying the Boeing's arrival, just to show they're in full control. We sent a signal to Seoul as soon as we heard you approaching, and Air Force Two is now en route." The Ambassador looked at each man for his reaction.

They all sat impassively and waited for him to continue.

"As you may be aware there's been something of a reshuffle in the leadership of this country in the last few days. The Communist Party has a new Chairman. This man is now the one with the stick. He has agreed to a meeting with Mr Secretary, at which I shall also be present, at eight this evening. We have no way of knowing how long that meeting may last, but it is quite on the cards that it will be very brief indeed. It is now six thirty five, so you may have only an hour and a half to get your people prepared," he looked at Mike as he spoke. "John Walker is waiting in the outer office to take you to them. Officially I must have nothing to do with your operation, so I'll leave you to get on with it. Unofficially, please wish Dr Chong and his wife good luck from me. I hope they make it. John will inform you of any other developments." He stood up and held out his hand to Mike and then the pilot.

John Walker, the Company Resident, met them in the outer office and led them through to the elevator and up to the top floor. The Sergeant who had come with the escort was there ahead of them, getting the two Chinese dressed in Marine blues. During the preceding days the Embassy guards had spent long hours teaching Chong and San Kiu how to move and behave like Marines. Although he had treated it as a bit of a game they had applied themselves in earnest, and Mike and the Sergeant were impressed.

Chong and San Kiu had both had their hair cut short and Chong's mustache had been shaved off. Touches of theatrical make-up, applied by Walker, had transformed San Kiu's face to look more masculine. Walker's wife had done some tailoring to disguise her female shape and make her uniform fit better, and after the Sergeant had persuaded her to wear two sweat shirts to pad out the jacket it looked good. Chong was quite a big man and the uniform fitted him well.

Mike waited until the Sergeant was satisfied with their appearance before he went forward to speak to them. Surprise registered on both faces as he addressed them in perfect Chinese.

"You must be prepared for the unexpected," he said after greeting them. "Whatever happens, you must show no reaction at all."

They both nodded.

"We will go down to the big function room in a moment and run through the drill for our departure with the other Marines. I am putting both of you at the front of the escort when we march out to the helicopter. That will put you right next to the door when we halt. It also means you will be less visible from the road while our official passenger boards. As soon as he is inside you will follow him in and go to the seats right at the back of the cabin. After that all you have to do is sit there. We are expecting to fly to the airport where we will transfer to a big jet aircraft. All the Marines we have with us are from Chinese American families so that you will not look out of place. Just concentrate on doing the drill, exactly as you have learned it, and nobody will know you are not United States Marines." Mike smiled and asked if they had any questions.

"How long will the helicopter flight take?" San Kiu asked.

"Only about ten minutes. Anything else?"

"No," they said in unison.

"Good. Let's go down and give you a run through with the others." Mike led the way back to the elevator.

In the function room the Marines had moved aside the great banqueting table, leaving the middle of the long room clear. They had left the rich carpet in place so that the surface would feel more like marching on grass. A marine by the door handed carbines to Chong and San Kiu as they came in, before taking his place in the line.

The Sergeant took over, and for the next half hour the marines marched up and down the banqueting hall and practiced the weapons drill they would soon perform outside. Mike watched for a few minutes and then went to talk to Walker and to his brother.

In the hallway he passed the two diplomats who were leaving for their meeting with the Chairman of the Chinese Communist Party. He joined Walker and they went into an office down the hall.

"Where on earth did you find Fu Manchu's Warriors?" Walker asked, closing the door.

"In the US Marine Corps, where else?" Mike said with a dead pan face. "We thought it would make these two less conspicuous, and could always be passed off as a compliment to the Chinese people if anyone objects to their presence."

"They are more likely to call them traitors to their ancestors," Walker replied. "Many of the older ones still talk about us being foreign devils, so that sort of thing would fit. It's a neat idea, all the same."

"We thought it was worth trying. Your Embassy guards have done a good job. Provided they don't take fright at the last minute they won't look out of place. Any news of the big bird?"

"I'll check." Walker picked up his phone, dialed and, after a moment spoke to someone elsewhere in the building. "It landed ten minutes ago and is refueling now," he said, replacing the handset.

"How long do you think we have?" the pilot asked.

"It's hard to say. Either they will be back in fifteen minutes, or it will take at least an hour. This new Chairman is almost unknown to us. He's been around on the fringes of power for a long time, but foreigners have not had anything to do with him. He's reputed to be a hard liner and a bit of a fire breather. My bet is he will give them a hard time for half an hour, then request that your guys depart immediately and go direct back to the carrier."

"We must try to avoid a road trip to the airport. That would allow too many chances for things to go wrong," Mike said. "Our Mr Secretary is an unknown quantity as well, if it comes to that. I'm not sure how he will respond if they tell him to go by motorcade."

"Yeah. Did Braden say what he wants Bob Peach to do once they are out?" Walker asked.

"No. I would take him along if we could, but that might look wrong as officially he's only a tourist. I suggest you get him back to his hotel and out on a flight in a couple of days time."

"Right. I'll do that." Walker got up and went to the filing cabinet. He pulled out a neatly wrapped package and handed it to Mike. "Word is you got a new son the other day. Ellen and I would like you to take this home with you and to give Chevvy our love."

"You what?" The pilot leapt to his feet. "Congratulations! You sly old wolf! Why didn't you tell me?" He pumped Mike's hand and embraced him, and they danced round the room together.

"I didn't exactly have time for a social chat before now, and you were out playing on the deep blue sea," Mike protested. "Thanks, John. That's very kind of you both. Please tell Ellen they are both doing fine. I was there when he arrived. We've called him Thomas, after Chevvy's Dad."

They continued talking about the baby for a few more minutes until the telephone interrupted them. Walker answered it.

"That was the big bird's driver. He's ready to go when you are."

"Good." Mike passed the package he had been given to his brother, asked him to take it with him to the helicopter when he went out, while he went to check on the escort party.

The Sergeant expressed himself satisfied with their progress, and made them run through one more time to show Mike. He watched them complete the drill faultlessly and asked if there were any last questions. There were none.

"That was well done. Do it like that outside and this thing will work perfectly. Refreshments will be brought in here now, so relax until we have to move. Dismiss."

Chapter 39

IT WAS MIDNIGHT before Green finished putting his case to the Chief. When he was done Braden had a number of questions. He decided it would gain nothing to haul the local Bureau Chief or his Director of Operations out of their beds in the middle of the night, so it could wait until the morning. Braden would call them for a conference at nine thirty. That would allow them to give the Company's Director a synopsis and call the others with time for them to rearrange their schedules if necessary.

The two men parted in the parking lot and went home.

Something he could not quite pin down was niggling at the back of Green's mind. As a result he slept badly and got up three times to pace around the silent house. Near dawn he was standing in the living room staring out of the big picture window across the valley. A pair of warm arms wrapped themselves gently round him and Betty laid her head on the back of his right shoulder.

"You don't get like this, Nose. What's burning? You never missed a night's sleep in all the twenty three years we've been together. Are the ghosts finally catching up?" her soft voice asked.

He leaned back and rubbed the back of his neck against her head. Her hair smelled of flowers. Slowly he turned round and held her close.

"No, Honey. I'm just missing a trick, and it won't leave me alone, that's all. I must be getting old. Maybe it's time I gave up this game and came home to dig the garden with you."

"Old, my foot! You're not ready for that yet. You're not even fifty five until next month," Betty chided.

"Yeah, well…"

"I'm not saying I wouldn't like having you around more. I would love it, but you'd soon get bored and wishing you were back doing what you've always done well."

"Humph. You know me too well Betty Green." He gave her a squeeze.

"Come on," she said decisively. "Let's go to the kitchen and make some hot chocolate. Then I'll cook you a fancy breakfast and you can go back to the battle and win." She led him through the darkened house, turning on all the lights as she went. Green sat down at the kitchen table and watched with interest as she bustled about like a mother hen. By half past six he was ready to leave for the office, feeling refreshed if not rested. He loitered for a moment by the front door until Betty shooed him out.

"Go on. You won't find your answer hanging on our coat hooks. I'm going to spend the day with Chevvy and the baby. She wants me to teach her how to crochet." Betty pecked his cheek and opened the front door. She closed it immediately he was outside, to stop him turning back.

When he reached the office, Green went straight to the communications room to see if there was any news from Mike. Disappointed, he leafed through the general sit-rep sheets from China before going to his own office. Joe and Connor were waiting for him.

"You're early. Has something happened?" he asked.

"Yes. I rigged an alarm on the monitor on my father's place. It went off a while ago. Howard has been on the phone and we think they are about to make a move. We were about to call you to listen to the tape," Connor explained.

"OK. Let's hear it right now."

Connor pressed the play button on the recorder. There was a click followed by the ringing tone of a telephone. After five rings Senator Swingate's sleepy voice answered.

"Yes?"

"Jeff. It's Chet. My little gray wolf cubs found some goofers up by your pad, but they only just reported. The bird will call at your local in an hour. I think you should come visit some business associates with me. Bring your little blue book."

"You think someone's trying to muscle in? Any idea who?"

"I don't know, but I think you should come, and we'll find out."

"An hour, you said?"

"Yes. And don't forget your little blue book. You'll need it."

"Like that is it? Right. We'll be there." There was a click as the he cut the connection. The tape ran on for three seconds and then stopped. Another click, and a different tape, recording elsewhere in the house, started.

"Lo? Wake up, Lo."

"Whaaa…" The word turned into a soft female yawn. "What is it?"

"Chet called. His guys caught some snoopers up at the lodge. He couldn't say much, but he's worried enough to think we ought to get clear for a couple of days while they check it out. Get dressed. His aircraft is picking us up in an hour."

"Where are we going, Jeff?" She sounded wide awake now.

"Don't ask questions now. Just get dressed and put some things in a bag. We don't have time to waste."

"Oh, all right."

The tape ran on for several minutes. Nothing else was said, but there were sounds of people moving about, drawers being opened and closed, water running in the wash basin, and a zipper being closed on an overnight bag. Then the tape stopped.

Connor and Joe looked at Green.

"That all?" he asked.

They both nodded.

"OK. Let me hear it again, and then get it transcribed. Keep these tapes. I've got a meeting set up for nine thirty with the Chief, the Director, and some people from the FBI. Joe, you call all the local airports and see if Howard's plane is expected inbound at any of them. Check if there is an onward flight plan filed. If so, call Air Traffic and see if they can hold it on the ground. What time was that recording made?"

"Fifty minutes ago," Connor said, checking his watch.

"That doesn't leave us much time, so get busy, Joe. Now play that thing to me again, Connor."

Green had listened to the recording twice, and was just helping himself to coffee from the office percolator when Joe came back from the telephone.

"We've missed them. I called all the principal airports and none of them had anything. On the off chance I tried the small field up by Frederick City. The Howard plane took off from there three minutes before my call. The controller told me they had filed for Miami. Sorry about that, Nose."

"It can't be helped. We didn't know which field they were going to use and there are enough round this corner of the country. Frederick City, eh?" Green scratched his nose. "I have the feeling they are not going to Miami."

"What makes you think that?"

"Howard mentioned a little blue book, twice. What do you think that meant?"

"A notebook of some kind. A list of contacts, or an address book. He said something about visiting business associates. It could be something to do with them." Joe tossed out ideas at random.

"I don't think so," Green said. "He would have that sort of information in his head. Try again. Airplanes go places, don't they?"

Airplanes... log book, pilot's license. Does he fly?" Joe asked, looking at Connor.

"He flies a helicopter sometimes, and I guess he could fly fixed wing. He was a navy flier in the war, but I think he let his fixed wing license lapse."

"No. You're both way off base," Green said. "What color is your passport, Joe?"

"Goddamit! You think they are going to leave the country? South America, or Canada?"

"Or some other place," Green suggested. "Call ATC and see if they can follow them on radar. I think they'll skip customs formalities, so they won't land again in the US."

Joe went back to the telephone. Green went through to his own office to call Braden. Connor sat down at the word processor and began transcribing the tapes.

Chapter 40

"THEY'RE BACK," Walker said, coming into the room where Mike and his brother were catching up on their family news. They had had almost three hours in which to do so and had talked very little about the job in hand. That had been adequately covered in the briefings and any further discussion would follow the diplomats' return, should the situation warrant it.

The Ambassador's secretary put her head round the door and asked Mike and his brother to come into the Ambassador's office. They got up and followed her, taking their places around the conference table as they had done earlier.

"Gentlemen," the Secretary of State began, "Most of the discussions we have had this evening do not concern you. However, there are certain matters of which I wish you to be aware before we depart. The Chinese leadership is particularly upset by the presence of our Marines, and have protested most vigorously. They have made it very plain that their presence is seen as a hostile gesture. The fact that we brought men of Chinese American origin mollified them slightly, but they have insisted that these same individuals should leave with the helicopter, since they had not been informed that we wished to change any of our Embassy personnel. I have been instructed that the helicopter is to return directly to the USS Callistoga, after which an escort will be provided by the People's Liberation Army to accompany me and my aides to the airport. I protested this on the grounds that I require some of the Marines to accompany me on board Air Force Two. The Chinese were adamant, and a detachment of their soldiers will arrive here within the next half hour to accompany me. This changes the situation substantially. I would like your assessment of the risk of the Chongs being discovered if they have to travel in a motorcade." He looked steadily into Mike's eyes.

"Sir, I believe the chance of their being discovered is at least ninety per cent," Mike answered clearly.

"Why?"

"The Chinese will include some of their own leaders in the motorcade, some of whom may have met Chong. They will almost certainly hold a short farewell ceremony beside the aircraft for the benefit of their own television cameras who were cheated of filming your arrival. Any Marines who traveled with you will be expected to be formed up on the apron, and will certainly be inspected and filmed. Discovery at that point would be disastrous to bilateral relations, and make the United States a world laughing stock. I think we should send the Chongs with the helicopter and let Callistoga bring them to the United States."

"And what happens if they force the helicopter to land before clearing Chinese airspace, Captain Ash?"

"If they order me to land, sir, I should be obliged to do so, unless you have previously given me a direct order not to. In that case they might try to force me down with their gunships."

"Could they do that, Captain?"

"Not without causing both aircraft to crash, sir."

"Would they force him down?" the Secretary of State asked Mike.

"I believe they would try, sir. They won't mind sacrificing a gunship and its crew if they have to. It would easily be explained away as an accident due to the American pilot being unfamiliar with the terrain."

"Then we shall have to take all the Marines by road and let the helicopter fly back empty. We will have to risk discovery at the airport or else abandon the attempt. I do not intend to abandon it, providing the Chongs are willing to try. Could we have them in and ask, please?"

"Sir, before we do that, may I make a suggestion?" the pilot asked. "I have enough fuel for a direct return to the carrier, but could say that I do not. That justifies taking the helicopter to the airport. They may try to divert me to a military field, but I'm sure I could misunderstand their controller and land right next to Air Force Two in error. I still think we should stick to the original plan. I do not believe they will try to force me down whilst you are on board. After that I am prepared to face the risks, and try to out-fly their hawks on the way back to the carrier."

The Secretary of State thought about this for a moment, studying the pilot as he did so. The man sat calmly waiting his decision. He turned to Mike and raised an interrogative eyebrow.

"I agree, sir," Mike said decisively.

"Mr. Ambassador?"

"Mr. Secretary, I don't have to take the risk. They may be hostile after you leave, and may even demand my departure, but there is no actual threat to my person. They have not yet indicated any knowledge that the Chongs are in this Embassy, so we should assume that they still don't know. We cannot rely on that situation continuing much longer. Once they know Chong is here, the chances of getting him away will reduce to zero. If we are going to get these people out, I believe this is the best opportunity we will get, and the sooner it is done the greater will be the chance of success."

The Secretary of State looked from face to face while he absorbed this and realized that the decision was his alone. If he got it wrong now, his political demise would be immediate and spectacular.

Without further delay he made his decision.

"Very well. We will continue as planned. Captain Ash, please go and start your engines. The escort will board immediately, without forming up on the lawn. Mr Ambassador, you will please accompany me out, and we shall make a brief show of saying goodbye on the grass for the benefit of the press out there. Captain, you will lift off the moment I am on board, and only then radio that you have to go to the airport for fuel and that you have me on board. We will transfer everyone to the Boeing as soon as we arrive. As soon as the helicopter is refueled, you will return to the USS Callistoga, without landing en route. Thank you for your advice, Gentlemen. Good luck," he smiled and shook the Ambassador's hand as the other two departed.

"Thank you for all your personal help, Richard. I'm sorry we didn't get time to socialize. Give my love to Rosemary. Shall we go?" He stood up.

The two diplomats walked slowly from the Ambassador's office and paused in the entrance hall to permit the last of the escort to get out to the helicopter. As the engines wound up the two men walked slowly down the steps and out onto the grass, some yards in front of the helicopter, where they were in full view of the waiting correspondents outside the Embassy gates.

They had to raise their voices under the noise of the spinning rotor. There was a final handshake as the engine note deepened and the rotor wash plucked at their hair and clothes, they parted and the Secretary of State hurried aboard. Two Marines helped him inside, the steps were pulled up, and the door slid closed as the machine lifted gently from the grass.

The pilot looked down and saw the Ambassador raise his hand in salute. He nodded in acknowledgment and turned his attention to flying.

The circling Chinese gunships overhead moved aside to let the helicopter rise and formed up either side and just behind the American machine as Captain Ash headed across the city towards the airport.

The tower refused him landing permission when he called them on the radio to tell them he was coming, but he ignored their instructions to steer directly towards the coast. Within seconds one of the gunships had moved up alongside. He turned to look and saw a crewman in the open doorway gesticulating and indicating that he should turn east and climb. Ash looked away and concentrated on where he was going, increasing his speed slightly. In four minutes he could see the airport lights ahead.

He called the tower again and told them he must have fuel to reach his ship. After his third repetition, another voice intervened in Chinese as the gunship commander told the tower to give landing instructions for an isolated corner of the field. Captain Ash did not understand all the rapid Chinese, having only a smattering of the language himself, but the controller soon repeated the instruction in his sing-song English.

He was over the airfield perimeter now and could see the blue and white 747 in the floodlights. He flew straight towards it. One of the gunships crossed close in front, trying to turn him aside. When the second gunship pulled in front, Ash pulled sharply upwards, hopped over it, and kept going. The radio crackled with instructions from the tower, punctuated by excited Chinese voices from the gunship pilots.

Five hundred yards to go. Vehicles were rushing across the apron, converging on the Boeing. Three hundred yards. He turned slightly away. A gunship immediately skidded in front of him, trying to make him continue the turn. As the huge machine passed the tail of the Boeing, Ash hauled back on the stick and stopped almost dead in the air. A quick shift of the controls sent the helicopter skidding sideways, only feet above the port wing. Accustomed to landing on the crowded deck of an aircraft carrier the pilot slewed his craft round so that the door faced the boarding steps, in position at the front hatch of Air Force Two, and sank to the concrete below.

The spinning rotor was only a yard from the cab of a parked fuel tanker. Ash had a glimpse of the driver's terrified face as he leapt from his cab and ran for cover. The engine note dropped suddenly and the rotor slowed.

Nothing moved for ten seconds, which seemed to the two American helicopter pilots like ten minutes, then someone in the back slid open the door. Chinese soldiers appeared in a ring around the two American aircraft, their weapons cocked and trained.

As the rotor swung to a standstill a black limousine appeared round the nose of the Boeing and stopped a few yards from the boarding steps. Six men climbed out just as the first of the Marines began to disembark form the helicopter.

"We've got company, sir," the Sergeant said, leaning back inside. "How do you want to play it?"

"We'll have to behave formally."

"Very good, sir," he said, turning to face the Marines. "Form two ranks aft of the stairway: move!" the Sergeant barked a crisp command. The Marine escort scrambled out and formed up beside the boarding steps. There was a brief shuffling as they adjusted their positions then stood like statues, staring sightlessly ahead under the steep peaks of their caps.

The Chinese Deputy Foreign Minister and five other men approached as the Secretary of State stepped down from the helicopter.

"Ah, Mr Secretary, we understood that you were to come by road. This is most unexpected," he looked towards the helicopter.

"Deputy Minister, how nice to see you again," the American replied with a slight bow. "We were offered a motorcade, but as this has been such a brief visit, and the helicopter had to come here for fuel, I told your colleagues that we did not wish to cause inconvenience. It was most generous and helpful of your staff to have the fuel tanker ready." He made a modest gesture towards the tanker. "It is also most courteous of you to come yourself and see me off."

"You are honored guest, Mr. Secretary. We were ordered to provide a Guard of Honor, but I see your Marines have done so." He motioned to one of his aides and spoke briefly. The man turned and spoke to the nearest soldier, who ran off. Moments later twenty Chinese soldiers ran forward and formed two ranks facing the motionless Marines on the other side of the stairway. "Perhaps you would care to inspect the People's Soldiers?" He turned towards them.

"I would be honored, Deputy Minister," he replied and walked slowly along in front of the squad. "Your men are very impressive," he said, stopping at the end of the rank. "I would be honored if you would review the United States Marines."

"It is the People's Republic that is honored, Mr. Secretary. I see that your Marines share our ancestors."

The Secretary of State merely smiled as Mike fell in beside the Chinese official. He walked slowly along the line, looking closely at the men's faces. Half way along he stopped and faced one of the Marines. Mike felt his heart race. The Secretary of State's face showed nothing.

"What part of China did your ancestors come from?" the Deputy Minister asked in Chinese. The man's eyes never moved. He remained silent. Mike looked at the Secretary of State, then back at the Marine. "You may answer the Minister," he told the man.

"I'm sorry, sir. I don't know what he said. I don't speak Chinese," Chong said in very American English and Mike almost bit through his tongue.

Before the Minister could say anything else, the Secretary of State claimed his attention.

"Our country has many people whose ancestors came from almost every nation in the world, Deputy Minister. Many are fourth and fifth generation Americans and never learned their forefathers' languages."

"That is a pity, Mr Secretary," the Minister said, turning to him. "People should not lose contact with the culture of their ancestors. Perhaps during some future visit we should discuss a cultural exchange process for those whose roots lie in the People's Republic."

"You are most generous, Deputy Minister."

The party moved forwards again towards the waiting group of aides, beyond the end of the line. Mike followed two paces behind and saluted smartly when they turned.

"You may board the escort now, Captain," the Secretary of State told him.

"Thank you, sir." Mike saluted again and executed a smart about turn. "Board the escort, Sergeant."

"Sir!"

"They go with you, Mr. Secretary? I understood they were returning with their helicopter," the Chinese said.

"Ah, no, Deputy Minister. They are required to accompany me to London for a ceremonial duty. Their ship was on its way to Manila, for them to fly from there, when it was diverted to assist me because of the fault with the Boeing. With the time that it took, they would have been too late. Since we are not carrying any reporters on the flight, there is plenty of space on the aircraft for them, and they are far less troublesome than the press corps," he finished with a wry smile. The last of the Marines was just disappearing into the aircraft as he finished speaking.

The Deputy Minister looked puzzled for a moment then nodded his agreement. "That is most fortunate, Mr. Secretary," he responded.

An engine roared to life behind them and both men turned to look. The helicopter had completed refueling and the tanker was pulling away.

"Thank you for a most fruitful and constructive visit, Deputy Minister. With your permission, I shall ask my pilot to wait a few minutes until the helicopter has taken off. It will make maneuvering the big aircraft easier if the other has gone."

The two men shook hands and the Secretary of State climbed the stairs.

"Have the pilot radio the helicopter and tell him to get going immediately," he told the crewman by the door as he entered, and turned to nod a final courtesy to the Deputy Minister. The gesture was returned and the six Chinese withdrew, climbed into their limousine, and departed.

The ring of Chinese soldiers moved back as the helicopter started its engines, and the huge rotor began to turn and gather speed. After a few minutes it lifted into the air, hovered for a moment at fifty feet, then headed off eastwards, gaining height as it went. The Secretary of State went inside his aircraft. As the door closed behind him, the Captain of Air Force Two began starting his engines.

Chapter 41

GREEN CALLED HIS chief at home and informed him of the morning's events. They met in Braden's office forty minutes later to talk things through before the FBI Chief arrived. Joe had been in contact with the Air Traffic Control Center, and they were trying to identify the Howard jet in the mass of other blips on their screens. This was proving difficult. There was a lot of other traffic along the eastern seaboard at this time of the morning. They would call back if they got a definite ident on the plane. Meanwhile the controllers along the filed flight path were asked to report if the aircraft contacted them.

Green felt he was missing something, but would have to wait to find out what. Not long, as it turned out.

Joe had been casting around, trying alternatives, when a call to the airport at Buffalo, on the Canadian border, brought the first break. The Buffalo controller had heard the Howard plane call Rochester, seventy five miles to the east of him, on the shores of Lake Ontario. Buffalo holds a watch responsibility for a wide area, and therefore maintains a listening watch on all the main frequencies used in their area, the man explained. His attention had been drawn to the call because the Citation pilot had requested Customs clearance and an onward flight plan to Ottawa.

Joe asked the man at Buffalo for the phone number, thanked him, and called Rochester. For five minutes the phone rang and rang, but nobody answered. Joe was just about to put the phone down and check that he had called the correct number when a breathless voice answered.

"Sorry to keep you. I'm on my own up here."

"Is that Rochester Airport?" Joe asked.

"Sure is. This is Sam Roe. I'm the air traffic control, the ground control, the fireman, fuel pump attendant, telephone operator, airport manager and general gofer. How can I help you?"

"Hi, Sam. I'm Joe. I thought Rochester was a fair sized outfit, not a one horse field."

"Oh, we are. We got plenty staff, it's just they don't come on duty for another half hour. I open everything up mornings, and attend to the early birds seeing as how I live right by the field here. Been a mite busy this morning 'cos I had one fancy little jim-dandy of a business jet in, soon as I opened up." Sam sounded as if it were the most excitement he had seen in a month.

"Would that have been the Howard Corporation Cessna Citation, Sam?"

"Hell! I don't rightly know what it was. Bright, shiny, new looking thing, with two fan jets on the back end. Pilot was all done up in a fancy gray uniform. Looked like a fag to me."

"That sounds like the one, Sam. Have you still got him there? I need to contact one of the passengers. It's kind of important I speak with him."

"I'm sorry, Joe. You just missed them. Pilot went running off to Customs while I was gassing up the bird, then up and away almost before I got the bowser outa his way. Didn't even wait for me to get back up the tower and tell him official like that he was clear to go. You want me to call him an' see if he'll come back? I reckon he'll be half way to Ottawa by now."

"No. It sounds like he's in a hurry. I'll just call ahead and have him contact me when he lands. Thanks for all your help, Sam. It's been nice talking to you."

"My pleasure. I hope you make contact. Bye now."

"Bye." Joe sighed as he put the phone down. A moment later he picked it up again and dialed the Chief's number.

"Braden."

"Good morning, Mr. Braden. This is Joe, is Nose with you?"

"Sure, Joe. Hold the line." He heard Braden speaking to Green and a moment later he answered.

"What have you got, Joe?"

"They cleared Customs at Rochester. Filed onward to Ottawa. Do you want me to call the guys in Yogi Bear hats and see if they can hold the aircraft?" Joe said.

"No. Leave it for now, Joe. I want to think about this. Thanks for letting me know. I'll talk to you later." Green turned to explain this latest bit of news to Braden. The question of what to do next was still unresolved when the FBI Chief arrived.

Braden rang the Director to see if he was ready to join them. While they were waiting for him, the communications room messenger knocked on the door with a signal for Green.

"I hope this is meant for you, sir. It came in clear with no sender. We were not sure if it was meant for here at all," he said, handing it over.

Green took the sheet, looked at it, and burst out laughing. He did a little war dance round the room, whooping with joy.

"Good news, Nose?" Braden enquired, while the FBI man just looked curious.

Green handed Braden the signal. The message read:

COMING TO SUPPER. BRINGING CHINESE TAKE-OUT FOR TWO. DAD.

Braden looked at Green whose face bore a wide grin, and realization dawned. Braden grabbed him in a bear hug, and together they danced round the room laughing.

The Director was slightly startled by their antics when he opened the door. He lifted an enquiring eyebrow at the Bureau Chief, but saw only confusion in his face.

"Is this a private celebration, or are you two going to tell the rest of us what's got you so lit up?" he bellowed.

Green and Braden stopped their dance and passed him the signal.

"Well, waddya know! The craziest goddam idea I ever sanctioned, and it worked! You sure do pull some fancy rabbits out of your hat, Nose Green. Congratulations!" He held out his right hand.

"It was not me this time, sir. It was Mike. It was his idea. I just helped with the planning. He thought it up and carried it out," Green said.

"You mean we've got two raving crazies in this outfit? What are you trying to do, turn the Company into the Houdini Club or something? Be sure and bring him over as soon as he gets back. I want to shake that young man's hand." The Director looked exuberant. "Now, if we could get to the purpose of this meeting…" He moved to a chair and they all sat down.

"Sorry about that little show, Jack," Braden explained to the bemused FBI man. "We just heard that a game we had running made home base."

"I guessed it was something like that, and since you didn't tell me what it was, I guess it had nothing to do with the Senator and his barrel of cats. Here's a summary of all the information the Bureau has collected so far." Jack Clarke passed round a set of slim folders.

Green also passed round copies of the dossier his team had prepared. It contained copies of some of the documents they had found at the hunting lodge, together with transcripts of the recordings. The most damning evidence was the print-out from the Senator's secret computer files. This showed the steady flow of huge sums into three holding accounts. Almost all of the transfers originated overseas, and the cross references showed that each was dated two days after a long outgoing transmission of technical data. Green believed that this data had been brought up from the Howard plant on disks for transmission through Senator Swingate's computer and radio set up.

"Who actually sent these transmissions?" Jack Clarke enquired.

"We're not certain, but believe it was either one of Howard's girls or, more likely, Lois Swingate. Connor is working through the lists to see how many of the dates correspond to times when she was away from home. I think we'll find most of them do since the Senator likes to keep his group small and under his direct control," Green said. "If I hadn't misjudged Connor at the beginning, we might have got onto this a lot sooner. Now Lois has ducked out from home, and hasn't even tried to contact him, so she must realize he'll be wondering where the hell she's got to and be looking for her. We've had him make all the calls you would expect a worried husband to make, and made sure appropriate people noted him doing so. She may think he has no idea of what's really going on, but we cannot rely on that. It may be this little trip they are taking now is because Howard is getting edgy and wants them to speed up the play. The closer they come to the main event, the more tense they'll feel, so we have to be very careful not to spook them into an early stampede."

"Do you have any idea what the main event is?" enquired the Director.

"Nothing definite at this time, sir. It's really only my hunch that there is a main event," Green told him.

"Nose hunches have a track record of being right on the nail. So come clean, Nose, what are you thinking?" the Director pressed him.

"Well, sir, as far as we have been able to determine all he has sent out so far has been information, apart from a few electronic components which may be part of a fusing mechanism or some kind of targeting device. There's been no significant materiel, and I believe that will be the main event. The pay off will be proportionally bigger, so he'll play safe and almost certainly demand half in advance. That will be our indicator that the final play is running."

"Any ideas on what the materiel is?" Braden asked.

"I'm not a nuclear specialist, but given the current trends in that field, and the known research interests of the Howard Laboratories, we feel it's likely to be some sort of fissionable product. The Indians and the Chinese already have weapons capability, so it has to be an upgrade, probably for an ERW."

"What is an ERW?" asked the FBI man.

"Enhanced radiation weapons, neutron bombs," Braden explained.

There was a long silence while the four men thought about the implications of this, and the Director sighed heavily.

"Jack, we had better bring in your Director on this one. Get a wrapper put round the Howard Corporation, have people so close to Swingate and all the known players they can't even fart without us knowing the gas analysis, and plug the leak. As soon as we get all the evidence tied up we can haul them in and put the whole thing quietly to bed."

"You're right about my Director, Dan. He has to be brought in, but I wonder about the rest of it," Clarke said. "If we close up too much they might get shy and not make their play."

"That's what we want."

"No, Dan. It isn't. We have to find out how they were going to do it. If we fold them now and don't find out that, we leave it open for the future. We have to stop that as well. We need to catch them red handed so there cannot be any doubt. That way we'll get the materiel and the method. We can go on from there and see what other bits of the system are at risk. And, if we're smart, we may be able to nail down the foreign end as well."

"You're right, of course, Jack. I'm just mad that some sod-busting potato farmer can get so far in this game. I want that bastard's hide on the barn door and his pals all round the walls."

"We all do. Now, much of the evidence that Nose and his team have uncovered is rightly the Bureau's concern, not the CIA's, but I'm going to propose to my Director that Nose and I team up on this one. We'll combine resources, let them make their move, and scoop them all in one go."

"I agree. Please ask your Director to call me as soon as you've spoken to him. I'll want to be kept close to this one all the way. Charles, I want you in with Nose and Jack on this. Be their Devil's Advocate, sort of thing."

Green took Jack Clarke back to his own office, to go over a few points before he went to brief the FBI Director, and they agreed to use this as the center of operations. Then Clarke went off to get the Bureau moving.

Chapter 42

THE ATMOSPHERE aboard Air Force Two had a celebratory mood as the big jet thundered northwards high above the Mongolian desert. When the seat belt signs were turned off, permitting people to move around, the Secretary of State sent an aide back to the rear cabin to invite Mike and the two Chinese to join him.

"Welcome to the United States of America, Dr Chong and San Kiu," he said after Mike had made the introductions.

The two Chinese, still wearing their Marine uniforms, smiled shyly and shook his hand.

"Thank you, Mr. Secretary. When will we actually arrive in America?" Chong asked and the dapper little diplomat laughed.

"You have already arrived, Doctor. This aircraft is United States sovereign territory. While you are aboard you are free from interference by any other national authority. We are presently flying to England, where we will land at a United States military airfield. That is also American sovereign territory, so the same applies there. Later you will proceed to the continental United States where you will be helped to settle down to your new life. I understand from our Ambassador in Beijing that you have requested political asylum, is that correct?"

Chong and his wife both nodded their agreement.

"Good. Well, I am happy to tell you that the President has instructed me to grant you asylum and to offer both of you American citizenship, with all the rights and privileges it entails. You will be furnished with the necessary documentation after we land at Mildenhall Air Base."

A steward approached with a tray of Champagne and the group began to relax. It had been an exciting evening and everyone had felt the tension. Now it began to disperse.

"I was very afraid at the airport," San Kiu said.

"You were not the only one," Mike agreed. "I nearly had a heart seizure when that man stopped in front of Chong, and I almost bit my tongue off trying not to laugh when you said you didn't understand Chinese. That was genius, pure genius."

"I felt the same myself," the Secretary of State agreed. "You were very calm, Dr Chong. It is almost unfortunate that only this select handful of people will ever know what actually happened this evening, but if they knew, two hundred million Americans would stand to cheer your courage. I don't know how you did it."

"There was no alternative," Chong said calmly. "He thought he recognized me. If I had spoken Chinese, he would have been certain. I once attended a Jesuit school in Shanghai with that man's sons. It was a long time ago, but such men have long memories."

"Jeez! I'm glad I didn't know that at the time," Mike said with intense relief. The others all agreed.

Further discussion was interrupted by a crewman who asked the Secretary of State if he would come up to the flight deck.

"We have a situation, sir," the man said as he led the way.

"What is it all about?"

"The helicopter, sir. They have ordered it to land. We are listening on his frequency."

Many miles behind and below them the helicopter was heading east over the dark Chinese countryside.

Chapter 43

"I'M EXPECTING THESE guys to try some tricks before we make the coast, Gus," Ash told his co-pilot as the lights of the Chinese capital's conurbation fell behind.

"Why? They approved our flight. Diplomatic mission and all that."

"Something the Sec said. They told him to go by motorcade to the airport, and it sounds as if they were more than a bit pissed off at finding we had a Marine escort on board. He thinks they'll want to show Uncle Sam they're in charge here."

"And there was that little bitty show by their gunships," Gus added. "You really think they'll try something?"

"Yes. Call the carrier. Tell them we're airborne and on the way back. If they can get an AWACS up we should be visible to them in just under an hour. Call them every ten minutes and check in."

"Will do," Gus said and switched his radio to the secure frequency.

Beijing control had instructed them to fly east at six thousand feet. As they reached this height Ash trimmed the aircraft, engaged the autopilot, and turned his attention to the radar and electronic countermeasures panels.

"They're bound to follow us, so we may as well keep an eye on who's out there," Ash said.

The picture on the radar screen solidified as he made adjustments to the settings and he could see the airport on the trailing edge of the screen. He wound up the range and found two blips ten miles behind and slightly to port. He watched them for two whole minutes.

"They with us?" Gus asked.

"I guess so. They're keeping a constant position, about a thousand feet above. They won't do anything for a while yet."

"How so sure?"

"The big bird is still on the ground. They'll want him well away before messing us about. He should be off any time now."

Seconds later another blip appeared and moved away from the vicinity of the airport, going north and gaining speed. "There he goes," Ash said, noting the time on his kneepad.

The two men watched the blip move towards the edge of their screen, and a few minutes later it disappeared off the display. They continued eastwards in the humid night, the ground invisible in the darkness below and only occasional clusters of lights showing an isolated farming commune.

The moon had set two hours ago, and not even the myriad small lakes, streams, and fish breeding tanks they had seen during the inward flight showed against the absorbent blackness. A layer of thin cirrus, more than thirty thousand feet above their heads, obscured the stars, making their void complete.

For a while the two men were silent, lost in their own thoughts. Ash was thinking about the scene on the ground just before their departure. He had noticed his brother tense as the Chinese official stopped in front of a Marine. Because of the angle he wasn't able to see any of the faces clearly, but he knew it must be the escaping scientist. The noise of the fueling pumps had drowned out any chance of hearing the voices, but he had seen Mike speak and the Marine reply before the party moved on.

Mike had remained tense until the Marines were running up the steps into the aircraft. Only as they disappeared inside did Ash see his shoulders relax. Then Gus had climbed into the seat beside him, the refueling completed, and his attention had been distracted by Air Force Two relaying the Secretary of State's order to get airborne immediately.

Now the big jet was airborne too, streaking away in the darkness towards the North Pole and its landfall on the other side of the globe. The coastline crept slowly into the top of the helicopter's radar screen and the gray mass of Beijing dropped off the bottom as they reached the half-way point to the Po Hai Gulf and the USS Callistoga.

Ash felt a prickling sensation beneath his flying helmet. He looked again at the radar screen as Gus reached out and cranked in the range to enlarge the display. The two trailing blips were moving closer.

Their headphones crackled with a Chinese voice speaking in English. "Helicopter forty-two, you are entering restricted airspace. Turn north and descend. Escort helicopter will arrive shortly to guide you down. Acknowledge."

"Here we go, Gus. Those gunships are moving up fast," Ash said.

"Helicopter forty-two, acknowledge," the Chinese voice commanded again.

"Aren't you going to talk to that guy, skipper?"

"No. I think we'll keep quiet and let him assume we're on a different frequency.

The boss told me before we left to fly straight back without stopping at any roadside diners, so that's what we are going to do."

"And if they decide to play rough?"

"Then I'll scream like hell for my Daddy to come and chase the baddies away."

"Shit! You're crazy! Do you want to start a shooting war when we don't have so much as a bow and arrow to shoot back with?"

"That's up to the politicians and Admirals. I'm just the driver of this here cabbage wagon, doing what the boss told me to do. You heard the captain of the big bird as well as I did, and you can bet your sweet life the carrier did too."

"Well, no sense in us dickering about it, their boy scouts have arrived." Gus pointed outside. Ash looked out his side and saw a gunship level alongside. As he looked, a red flare was fired forwards and across their nose. A spotlight mounted in the open rear doorway stabbed its white lance across the intervening darkness and flooded the cockpit with light. Ash turned his head away and pulled down the dark visor of his helmet. The light continued to hold them, and the Chinese voice in their headphones instructed them to turn and descend.

"Wave nicely to them, Gus," Ash said, waving his right hand to the pilot of the gunship on his side.

He was answered by another red flare and the gunship moved forwards and began to slide across towards them. He was about fifteen feet higher.

Ash held his hand in front of his eyes and turned his head towards the gunship. The Chinese pilot must have understood for the searchlight moved slightly aft. Ash kept his hand up, and a couple of seconds later the light winked out.

"My guy is on the move, skipper." Gus drew his attention back.

The second gunship was moving up to take position directly in front of them, its navigation lights flashing brightly. It took up station about three hundred yards ahead and appeared to bob up and down several times before gently turning left and losing height.

Ash, still on autopilot, kept flying straight ahead.

A minute and a half later the leading gunship was ahead of them once more. The incessant voice in their ears was demanding that they follow it and turn north. The gunship did its bobbing dance once again. As it started down once more the second gunship to starboard fired another red flare across their nose.

Again Ash ignored the instruction and maintained his heading. The searchlight started flashing from his right. Morse this time. It was badly sent, but the meaning was clear, follow or else …

"They are going to stop playing in a minute," Ash told Gus as his hand went out to disengage the autopilot. "We'd better be ready to start flying this bucket of junk."

"What do you think they'll do?" Gus sounded calm.

"I don't know. It'll be like treating rabies, I guess; deal with each symptom as it appears and hope for the best. Here comes the first one." As he spoke, the lead gunship took station ahead of them for the third time.

As the bobbing dance was repeated, the lead gunship fired a flare to port. It did not start turning at once, and it took the Americans several seconds to realize that the gunship was reducing speed. They would either have to do the same or turn. Ash looked out of his side window and saw that the second gunship was closer now, above and slightly behind. The squeaky voice in his headphones was still ordering Ash, by name now, to descend. They could not go up, and with the second gunship behind, slowing down would be hazardous.

"Hold tight, Gus. They want us to go down, so we'll go down. Is the ECM warmed up?"

"Ready when you are." his co-pilot responded.

"OK. Here we go!"

Ash moved his controls as the leading gunship began his turn. He followed for a moment then rammed the collective lever down and steepened his own turn, dropping like a stone. Gus snapped a switch, and all the navigation and anti-collision lights went off. His finger hovered over the Electronic Counter-Measures switch as Ash continued his turn, converting vertical speed to horizontal after five hundred feet.

"On ECM," he said, pushing the huge machine forward at its maximum speed. The spiral turn brought them back to their original heading, and both pilots' eyes went to the radar screen as Ash straightened up.

The coast was now appreciably nearer, and the two blips that represented the gunships were falling behind. As they watched, one of them resumed the original heading while the other continued to circle. Leaning hard against the window and peering into the blackness, Gus could just distinguish the flash of an anti-collision beacon far behind.

The following gunship was putting on speed as the second completed his turn and followed the leader. Slowly the gunships started to gain. Ash let his heading fall off southwards while Gus played the ECM controls to keep the gunships on the edge of the wavering pattern that swam over the screen like an amoeba.

Ash turned five more degrees to starboard. The coast was now less than thirty miles ahead. They would pick up the carrier soon.

In the black skies to the north east of Tientsin, the cat and mouse chase continued, with the American helicopter racing for the coast and the two gunships following. The lights of the city were visible to the south west, about fifty miles behind. There were airfields down there and Gus was watching the radar in case their pursuers asked for fighter support. He had seen several aircraft take off, but they appeared to be commercial flights heading off towards other cities. So far none had come in their direction.

The second of the two chase planes had closed up and taken a track that would take him to the south of his leader, closer to them. As Gus watched, another bright blip appeared on the screen, detaching itself from the lead gunship and racing forward at tremendous speed.

"Missile," Gus said.

Ash looked quickly at the screen and put the helicopter into a steep climb, turning still further south as he clawed for height. In a few seconds they saw the exhaust trail of the missile as it streaked harmlessly past six miles north of them.

At nine thousand feet Ash leveled out. At the same moment the second gunship unleashed a missile. It was closer to their track, but well below. They watched as this next one streaked ahead and disappeared into the blackness.

Two more blips appeared at the bottom of the screen. These were moving much faster than the gunships, close together, and heading in their general direction. The coast was now visible ahead and the two fighters were closing fast.

"They really don't want us to go home," Gus commented.

"Seems so," Ash agreed. "I bet they won't stop at the territorial limit either. We'll be there in a few minutes. Maybe it's time we got some support. Can you find the carrier on the radar?"

Gus adjusted the radar range until he had a large echo out to sea on the top edge of the display. Ash switched to the ship's control frequency and pressed the transmit button.

"Daddy! Daddy! Some nasty big boys are beating up on Patty!" he cried in a sharp falsetto. Gus started to laugh.

He was cut off immediately by the Callistoga's response.

"You come on back to the garden fence, Patty. Daddy will meet you there."

"Daddy, the nasty boys are throwing fire crackers at me."

"That's OK, Patty. Daddy will make the nasty boys leave you alone."

Four bright points of light separated in a stream from the carrier's blip on the screen. Ash realized they must have had planes ready to launch, their engines running and hot. Within seconds they formed two pairs, heading towards the coast at high speed. Just before crossing the twelve mile limit, they slowed and began to orbit, one pair at low level, the others well above.

The two Chinese fighters coming up from behind were getting close now, and Ash could feel the tension in his gut as he crossed the coastline. Gus was pointing up and ahead where two sets of navigation lights were describing a circle.

"We will give it another two minutes to be certain." Ash told Gus, and it seemed like two hours before he pressed the transmit button again.

"I'm back in the garden, Daddy."

"Go on back to Momma, Patty. Daddy will be back just behind you."

The carrier was less than twenty miles ahead now. Ash brought his nose round until the carrier was directly ahead and engaged the autopilot.

"Ye gods and little fishes," he said to no one in particular. "I could even enjoy being seasick after that little ride."

"Me too," Gus agreed. "Want to turn the ECM off now, skipper?"

"No. Leave it on until we are almost there. Just wind the range in a bit and stabilize the wander. They may still be mad at us for giving them the slip, and want to have one last try."

Nine minutes later they saw the floodlights on the carrier's flight deck, just ahead and far below. The two pairs of Tomcats were still orbiting behind them. The Chinese fighters were flying a similar pattern a few miles further west.

"Let's show the ship where we are, Gus. Cancel the ECM and light this thing up like a Christmas tree." Ash shrugged himself upright in his seat and disengaged the autopilot. Gus's hands flicked a line of switches, turning on every external light on the helicopter.

"Callistoga, this is Charlie four two. Do you read me?"

"Loud and clear, forty-two. We have you visual. Come on down. Runway is one zero zero degrees at thirty. Headwind is nine. Pressure is thirty point seven eight inches. You have a clear pad on the bow."

"Thank you, Callistoga. Charlie four two is coming down." Ash set the helicopter into its descent, then turned and grinned at Gus. Both men began to relax. It was routine from here on.

The darkness below thinned as they got closer to the carrier. At two thousand feet they could see the flight deck crew moving about, the crash team taking their station in the well beside the landing pad. White capped sailors were on the open top of the superstructure.

The descent continued. At fifteen hundred feet things began to happen very fast.

"Look out, Patty. One bad boy is making a rush!" a startled voice shouted over the radio. Ash checked the descent as Gus knocked off all the lights. A bright dot was rushing across their radar screen towards them. Two more, in close formation, followed. Ten seconds later the cockpit was filled with a tremendous roar that completely swamped the sound of the helicopter's own engines and rotor. The air was suddenly full of lumps and Ash had to fight the controls as the helicopter bucked and tossed. He dived and turned away from the carrier just as all the landing pad lights were extinguished.

"What in hell was that?" Gus shouted as their turn took them into calmer air. A pair of bright orange flames were disappearing upwards into the night above them.

"Forty-two, are you OK?" the ship's controller asked.

"Yeah. We're still here. Gonna need the laundry and some clean flight suits, though. What happened?"

"One of those MiGs made a dash and laid a sonic bang right under you. He won't try again. Come on down as soon as you're ready."

The flight deck lights came on once more before the controller finished speaking. Gus put the helicopter's landing lights on again as Ash lined up for another approach.

"Welcome home, Patty," the controller said, as their wheels kissed the deck.

In the communications cabin aboard Air Force Two, the small group had listened in tense silence to the occasional snatches of radio traffic. The atmosphere had been electric for the last few minutes, since Ash had yelled for help. The listeners had scarcely dared breathe in case that very process caused them to miss some vital second of the drama.

Of the action they could see nothing as the big jet plunged over the horizon beyond the range of radar. Mike's face, already drawn and white, pulled into a rictus of pure terror when the Tomcat pilot shouted his warning, as though he too was staring Nemesis in the face. Bright, glistening drops filled his eyes and he let out a long held breath when his brother's laconic comment cut through the strings of tension that had held the whole audience enthralled. A comforting hand patted Mike's shoulder, and he leaned against the bulkhead, shaking with relief.

Chapter 44

IN THE LAST DECADE China's internal airlines had improved. Both Chong and San Kiu had flown a number of times to conferences and symposia, finding the experience relaxing. On this flight, however, neither was able to relax and sleep proved elusive. Instead they spent the time chatting with the Marines, discussing their future with Mike, or exploring the in-flight entertainment system. Chong was delighted to discover a jazz channel on his headphones.

Their arrival at Mildenhall was routine. The Secretary of State was met by the American Ambassador, who had driven up from London to escort him to the Embassy so he could continue his original itinerary. Taking his leave of Chong and his wife, the diplomat said he would look forward to meeting them again soon in Washington, and consigned them to Mike's care until then.

The Marines were marched off to a barrack block while someone figured out what to do with them. Mike and his charges were taken to the Officers' Transit Facility and given adjoining rooms. They were told an administrative officer would be over later to discuss onward travel arrangements and to provide Chong and San Kiu with the immediate necessities from the base PX.

Now they had landed the two Chinese were suddenly overcome by the combined influences of jet lag and all the tensions of the last twenty four hours. They retired to their room and slept until late afternoon.

Chapter 45

BEFORE LEAVING FOR Britain, Penkowski called some old friends in London. As a result he was met at Prestwick and found a watch had already been set up. The Howard aircraft had been identified on arrival, and from that moment on, every move, and many of the words, of the passengers were on record. Penkowski was pleased to be working with this group of friends again.

Ro and Mitch had taken a different flight, bound for London Heathrow, from where they were to pick up an Avis rental car and head west. They too were met by one of Penkowski's friends, a curious looking man called Walter Sparrow. He was tall and willowy, somewhere in his fifties, with pepper and salt hair and a beard. His gait, a combination of hops, skips and shuffles, suited his name and left his heels ground down at the back.

Sparrow had already collected their car, and during the drive to Bristol, he gave them a concisely detailed description of the area and the history of the nuclear installation that was the subject of their interest. He provided maps, lists of key staff, and details of the activities of local anti-nuclear groups, finishing off with the news that the people they were concerned about were at present making a tour of the northern plant where they would remain for the next two days. He had booked Ro and Mitch into a hotel in Bristol for the weekend and arranged for them to be given a guided tour of the Hinkley Point nuclear power station on Monday morning.

By six that evening they had made a comprehensive tour of the area including the approaches to the twin-reactor power station, the nearby port of Avonmouth, its adjacent chemical processing plants, and Lulsgate airport just to the south of the city. Posing as a secretary checking arrangements for her boss, Ro learned from the Hertz desk at the airport that a car had been reserved for the weekend by the manager of Hinkley Point. It was to be collected by an American, Mr J. Stanley, who would be bringing a party of official visitors.

After their tour, Ro and Mitch settled into their hotel. Sparrow had chosen a small establishment, near the Clifton suspension bridge, which had all the facilities they needed, yet was quiet and permitted them to come and go at whatever time they liked. It also had good road access in all directions. Sparrow was evidently well known to the management, who believed him to be a journalist. Ro asked him about this, and he said it was a cover he frequently used since it tallied with the manner in which he earned his crusts when there was a gap in the spying business. She could not decide whether to take him seriously, but Penkowski had vouched for him, and he had certainly been the model of efficiency so far.

Green called them at the hotel that evening, bringing them up to date on their quarry's activities and other events. The Howard jet was now waiting at Carlisle for its passengers' return from Selafield for the flight south. Hal Johnson had returned to Dakar, with a representative of Soper Pumping Inc., to inspect the crates seized from the Mathilde K. Green's nose told him the equipment would be unrecognizable to the Soper man, but the Senegal Customs Authority had already agreed to release the crates and return them to the United States. Green had arrived at Mildenhall and decided he would stay there overnight and be down in Bristol by the following evening. He had spent most of the day with Mike, handling the initial debrief of the Chongs.

Green's first conversation with the two Chinese had confirmed his suspicions about Swingate, Mason, Howard and the Indians. Chong's access to information while he had been the Director of his research institute had paid off. It enabled him and San Kiu to provide the names of all the nuclear scientists at their research center, together with their particular research interests.

Green felt all the threads were coming together neatly. Connor called during the morning to say he had located the secret bank accounts and found that a credit of twelve million dollars had been made to each one three days ago, immediately after the last transmission from the Senator's hunting lodge. Connor reported that there was one account each for Swingate, Howard and Mason.

"So what does Lois get out of it?" Green asked.

"We cannot say at this stage. Maybe she gets a cut from each of the other three," Connor said. "There must be something to hold her, especially if your guess about my mother turns out to be true. Mr Green, you don't think he's intending to dump Lois, do you?"

"It's a possibility. He can't afford to leave her loose to talk," Green observed.

"Provided he's caught in the act, and he does it somewhere where it's still a capital offence, I hope he goes through with it," Connor said coldly.

"Yeah. Where are these accounts located, Connor?"

"Malaysia."

"Oh, what!" Green sounded delighted. "That couldn't be better. It's perfect from all points, as long as they can be made to go there."

"They can," Connor said with quiet satisfaction. "I will inject a command into the bank's computer that will make it impossible to draw from or modify any of these accounts unless the account holder does it in person in the branch where the account is held. They will have to go there to get their loot. I can do this without it being traceable to us."

"Do it." Green did not need to think about it. He had already made his plans. Now it was time to act.

When he had finished with Ro and Mitch, Green asked to speak to Sparrow. Mitch called him over, laid the receiver on the bar and returned to their table. Consequently only the Englishman heard the terse instructions.

"Hello Green old fruit," he said, picking up the instrument.

"Howard's plane will be going to Malaysia when it leaves Bristol. Neither it nor its passengers must be allowed to go on from there. Can you fix that?"

"Of course, old boy. Delighted. Usual terms?" Sparrow's manner was expansive.

"Agreed. I'll see you tomorrow night."

"Looking forward to it. We'll all go out on the town together. Cheerio then." Nodding his thanks to the barman, Sparrow returned the handset to its cradle and rejoined his American guests. He felt marvelous. This business had just taken a most profitable turn for him.

Chapter 46

CAPTAIN HELEN SNYDER, the base Welfare Officer, arrived at six and took the two new arrivals to the PX. Having gathered a selection of essential items to see them through their first few days, she asked Chong and his wife to wait while she arranged payment for the goods from her welfare fund. Chong wandered over to study the cluttered notice board on the wall by the checkout. When the Welfare Officer had completed the formalities, she found Chong in a dreamlike state, staring at a poster announcing a jazz concert to be held that night in the base recreation hangar. Bomb Bay Billy and the Ground Zero Jazzmen were to perform.

"Is it permitted that we attend this concert?" Chong asked, tapping the poster with his forefinger.

The Welfare Officer scanned the poster. "Tonight? I don't see why not, if you really want to and if you are not required for debriefing. Do you like jazz?"

"Oh yes! Please, if you can, make it possible to attend." Chong almost pleaded.

"Wait a moment while I call and ask," Captain Snyder said, and went in search of a base phone. She came back ten minutes later with a smile on her face. "Mr. Green said yes," she announced to the delight of both her charges.

There was just enough time to return to the Officers' Transit Facility for a quick meal before the concert began. Chong was too excited to eat.

Bomb Bay Billy turned out to be an armorer with the Tactical Bombing Wing stationed on the base. The Ground Zero Jazzmen were all members of his weapons handling team who serviced the tools of Armageddon by day and by night sought, and found, release in the brash, bawling rhythms of their music.

None of this mattered to Chong. This was the first truly American jazz band he had ever seen. Memories of his childhood days on the Shanghai waterfront came flooding back. The sounds and smells that used to pour out of open doors and windows awoke again in his mind, brought to a rich reality by the rhythms that surrounded him and the heavy velvet tones of the tenor saxophone.

Captain Helen Snyder took her responsibilities as Base Welfare Officer seriously and remained closely attentive to her guests, regardless of the presence of Mike and Green. When the music produced an almost trance like response, she thought Chong was ill and wanted to send for a doctor. Mike persuaded her not to. At the end of the evening Chong waded through the crowd and pushed his way up to the stage. It was many years since he had last touched an instrument, and the last time still held bitter memories. But this was a new world. Freedom of expression was actively encouraged here and no less a person than the Secretary of State had told him that it was now his absolute right. Chong wanted to exercise that right, to shake Bomb Bay Billy by the hand and to thank him. Helen Snyder's plaintive calls for him to come back went unheard in the geyser of emotion the music had unleashed in Chong.

The sax player was at first confused, then amazed, then flattered by Chong's attention. He always considered himself part of the background of the band; always there but never out front on his own. Now this crazy guy thought his saxophone was God's chosen horn, and even claimed to be able to play. He shook his head, laughing when one of the other Jazzmen suggested he let the guy have a blow on his horn. He looked back at Chong, whose face wore the same expression you see on a kid who's a penny short of the price of an ice cream. He knows it won't happen, but there is no charge for a dream, and he dreams that the ice cream seller will give him one anyway. Not a begging, but a wishing look.

The man was about to put his instrument away in its case, but shook his head, turned, fitted a fresh reed to the mouthpiece and offered it to Chong instead. Chong did not understand at first until the man asked him, "Don't you want to play it?"

"Who? Me? You will let me?" Chong stuttered.

""You said you used to play. Go ahead, have a blow," the musician thrust his instrument into Chong's hands and looped its supporting strap over his neck. Chong's hands caressed the polished brass and his fingers found their place on the keys. He looked up at the instrument's owner, not daring to speak, enquiring with his eyes. The lanky Texan understood and his mouth twisted into a soft smile as he nodded faintly. Slowly Chong raised the instrument and brought the mouthpiece to his lips. Drawing a long steady breath, he pressed his lip to the reed and felt as though he had been reborn.

One by one the other members of the band paused in their packing up and turned to listen to this stranger. Instead of the few squawks they had expected, they heard something startlingly original. His playing had no polish, but was raw and vital. It was obvious that he had not touched an instrument for a long time, and some of the fingering was old fashioned or just plain wrong, but the notes were vibrant and rich. He filled the vast hangar with raw emotion that silenced the crowd and held everyone spellbound. The departing audience stopped in the aisles and turned back, every eye focused on the tall Chinaman who was not even aware they existed.

When he stopped playing, the silence that followed was so intense it felt solid. Chong unhooked the strap and placed the instrument back in its owner's hands with a small bow.

"It has been a long time. Thank you. Thank you," he bowed again and moved towards the steps leading down from the stage.

The crowded hangar erupted in applause as the audience gave vent to their appreciation for the unexpected encore. Bomb Bay Billy came lumbering across the stage and caught Chong's arm. He had no idea where he had come from but wanted to recruit him to the band. He was disappointed to hear that Chong was only in transit. The band was going to play at a jazz festival in Bristol at the weekend, and he wanted Chong to come with them. Chong was flattered but explained that he was likely to be in the States by then. He thanked the band leader again for the kindness and turned to rejoin his wife and their new friends.

There was a glint in Chong's eye as he returned. Mike noticed that he seemed to be bigger in an indefinable way. He had a new certainty about him. Looking at San Kiu he was surprised to see the same things in her also. It was as though each had broken out of a chrysalis and could never be put back in.

The three Americans were amazed by Chong's performance. Even San Kiu, who had known him far longer, was surprised. Chong had told her, in their early days together, about his childhood in Shanghai and the humiliation the Red Guards had forced on him when they made him publicly smash his own saxophone. She understood that tonight her husband had fulfilled part of a lifelong dream. The ghost he had harbored for years had been exorcised, and he was still excited about the experience when they arrived back at the Officers' Transit Quarters.

Feeling slightly left out because the conversation was all in Chinese, Helen Snyder excused herself early and left her charges in the care of Mike and Green. The four sat talking in the lounge for another hour or so, as Chong told tales of his early life and how he had secretly tuned in to Western radio broadcasts both to learn English, and to listen to his beloved jazz. Listening to the passion in Chong's account, an idea began to form in Green's mind.

"You told me earlier that you used to write to other scientists in the West. Were any of them in this country?" he asked.

"Of course. There were two at Oxford University and one in a place called Bath. That man came from Germany and he came to a scientific congress in China two years ago. I gave him a paper to bring back for publication." Chong smiled at the memory.

"And was it published?" Mike asked.

"Oh yes! That was my second paper in a Western journal. Is Bath very far from here? Would it be possible to see this man? He is called Dr. Heinemann."

"It is not very far. Only a hundred and fifty miles or so, but we have to get you some papers before you can move about freely", Green said.

"Perhaps it would be possible to talk to him on the telephone?" San Kiu suggested.

"Yes indeed, but let Mike and me make a few calls in the morning and see if we can get permission for you to go and see him. Otherwise we may be able to bring him here. It would be good for you to start picking up contacts in the West. It will help you establish yourselves in your profession. No promises, but we'll try for you."

"That is a most kind offer. Thank you Mr. Green." Chong was courtly in his manner as the two Americans took their leave and went next door to Mike's room.

"What are you scheming, Nose?" Mike asked as he closed the door.

"I was just thinking that if we can get Chong down to see this Heinemann guy he could maybe go the extra few miles to Bristol."

"The jazz festival? How is that going to help? Apart from keeping the Chongs happy, which does not seem to present many difficulties anyway."

"Chong knows Swingate and Howard. If we could somehow bring them face to face it might just make our wayward birds feel guilty enough to fly."

"And then?"

"They fly to where they think their money is, try to get it, and get caught red handed." Green's smile almost turned into a leer of anticipation. "Get on the phone please, Mike. Find out where Hal and that Soper guy are and get them over here soonest. I want them in Bristol by Saturday morning at the latest. Get them installed in the Holiday Inn. If you meet any problems, get the marvelous Miss Connaught onto it. I'll get onto the other side of it first thing after I've had some shuteye." Green headed off in search of his bed, and Mike reached for the phone.

The Company resident in London pulled out all the stops after Green called him the next morning. By nine he was on his way to Mildenhall accompanied by the US Consul with a pile of papers and forms. By noon they had produced a passport each for Chong and San Kiu, with all the necessary stamps and visas to permit them to move freely around Europe for the next three months. There would still be paperwork to do once they reached Washington, but that could wait.

Dr. Heinemann was more difficult to contact, but Green eventually found him in a laboratory in Cheshire. As soon as he heard that Chong was in England, he wanted to drop everything and drive down. Green explained that this would not get them together any sooner as Chong would be busy until Saturday morning. Heinemann agreed to a meeting in Bath on Saturday afternoon and, when he heard that they were hoping to visit the jazz festival, eagerly offered to come along. Green agreed.

Next Green called Walter Sparrow and talked through some points of his plan, arranging to meet him with Ro and Mitch the following afternoon. Everything seemed to be falling neatly into place.

Over lunch Green handed Chong a crisp white envelope embossed with the seal of the United States of America. He gave another to San Kiu and watched with genuine pleasure as they opened them and found crisp new passports inside. Their delight was complete when he informed them that he had managed to arrange a meeting with Dr Heinemann.

While they were eating, Helen Snyder arrived and with her came Bomb Bay Billy. He had asked Captain Snyder who the Chinaman was and, on hearing a carefully edited version of the truth, invited him to return to the hangar and join the band's rehearsal later that day. If he was not able to join them at the festival Billy was determined that Chong should play with the Jazzmen at least once more. He towed the unresisting Chong away from the dining table, leaving Helen Snyder to take San Kiu on a ladies only shopping expedition in the nearby town.

Mike was looking at Green as they left and noticed the glint in his eyes and the small smile of anticipation that fluttered round the corners of his mouth.

"You sly old devil. What else have you cooked up, Nose?"

"Oh, just a little something to welcome them. After all, they had to leave everything behind. We got ourselves a pair of first rate scientists, so they ought to be given a fair start."

"And does Uncle Sam know that he's paying for all this?"

"Hell! Uncle Sam ain't paying! Senator Jefferson Stanley Swingate and his buddies have just donated about forty four million dollars of the Chinese Government's money to the US Treasury. I thought they could pay. That money will also cover every nickel of our two operations and some more. Braden and the Director agreed to give Chong two hundred and fifty thousand bucks to get himself set up. Uncle Sam still gets over forty million when all the bills are paid."

"But I thought you said that money was in a Malaysian bank."

"Was, yes. I had Connor do some of his computer twiddling. The money is now in a seizure account belonging to the US Customs Department. They use it for captured narcotics money and that sort of thing. The quarter mill has been put aside in a different account for Chong once he arrives stateside. The accounts in Malaysia have been rigged so that the holders will have to go there to access them. Until they do that they'll remain unaware that the money is gone. By then it'll be too late, we'll have nailed them." Green looked smug.

"It sounds great if it works."

"It will. Now, what happened with Hal?"

"He called back earlier," Mike said. "He will be in London tonight, with Mr. Hollings, the man from Soper, and drive direct to Bristol. Hollings confirmed that nothing in any of the crates had been manufactured by Soper Pumping and Hal has managed to persuade the Senegalese to release not only those crates but the whole ship to us. We have to send over a crew since they are holding the original crew on a narcotics bust. They found three hundred kilos of crack during a full scale rummage search after Hal's tip off. I talked to Joe. He's fixed things with Marshall in the Customs Department to send over a prize crew. Marshall is also going to have that tame professor inspect the cargo as soon as the ship reaches Galveston. He'll probably have to get someone in from Howard's engineering division to confirm, but it looks as though you guessed right again."

"Guessed?" Green sounded indignant. "That was pure deductive intuition, Mike," he grinned.

"Yeah! A damned good guess!" They both laughed. Mike stood up, "Now I'm going to call my wife and son. After that I am going to listen to the new maestro rehearsing."

"Give my love to Chevvy and Thomas and tell them you'll be home Monday. See you later."

That evening Chong was like a dog with two tails. He had played with the band all afternoon and still was not tired. The other musicians had given him lots of helpful advice and also asked him to play again the tunes he had played the previous evening. They were fascinated by the unusual tones he produced with apparent ease, even though some of them were obviously the result of fundamental errors from when he had first learned to play. The fact that his hands had been too small when he learned explained some of the fingering errors, but didn't account for the originality of Chong's improvisations.

When the rehearsal ended and the band were packing up, the sax player approached Chong with a large box wrapped in brown paper. On top lay a card signed by all the Jazzmen, wishing him well for the future and giving a standing invitation to play with them any time he was in the area. Chong was going to take the package back to his room, but his new friends wanted him to open it immediately. As he raised the lid, his eyes brimmed with tears of joy. Inside, bedded on padded red velvet, was a brand new tenor saxophone. It had even been engraved with the signatures of the whole band and the words 'Play it from the heart'.

Realizing that Chong was lost for words, Bomb Bay Billy took up his trumpet and began to play the band's signature tune, a ragtime piece called Ground Zero. One by one the others joined in. As the tears cleared from Chong's eyes, he saw they had placed a music stand beside him with his part on it. The rag had never been played with so much feeling as it was that evening.

San Kiu had also had a momentous day. Helen Snyder brought along two of her female colleagues and together they had taken San Kiu to all the best shops. She came back laden with clothes for herself and Chong, feeling slightly guilty that she had got so much, but reassured by the encouragement of the American women. They were all surprised by the sophistication of her taste, and only ran into problems looking for shoes because San Kiu's feet were so small.

After such a day, it was hardly surprising they wanted to turn in early. Later that evening, before turning in himself, Mike picked up the phone and dialed a number on the base. "It worked like a dream, Billy. Thanks," he said when the call was answered.

"That was entirely our pleasure, Mike. He did something special to our music. We just wish he could stick around."

"Oh, you'll see him again, don't worry. Thanks anyway. There's a case of whiskey with the band's name on it waiting collection from the PX, as a small token. See you soon. Billy." Mike too slept well that night.

Chapter 47

SATURDAY DAWNED bright and clear. Ro was up and about early and called up the airport to check on the arrival time of the Howard jet from Carlisle. It was due in at eleven thirty. She had spent part of the previous afternoon checking bookings at the main hotels in the city and discovered three rooms had been reserved for Mr. Stanley's party at the Holiday Inn. The two pilots were booked into a pub near the airport, and they had requested that the plane be cleaned and refueled immediately on arrival.

Ro called Green at Mildenhall and brought him up to date. He outlined what he was hoping to achieve and roughly how, then asked for Mitch to meet Hal and Mr. Hollings when they reached Bristol. After talking to Ro, Green called Walter Sparrow and talked for half an hour. Sparrow left the hotel, putting a note under Ro's door to say he would meet her at the airport at ten forty five.

Ro was sitting on the spectators' terrace sipping cold orange juice when Sparrow appeared. He dumped a heavy toolkit onto the terrace with a clank and slumped untidily into a chair opposite her.

"Hello dear girl. Is that orange juice I see before you?"

"Yes. I'll get you some." Ro signaled to the waiter who was lounging against the counter trying to chat up the girl who dispensed refreshments.

When the orange juice arrived, Sparrow took a long, slow drink and sighed with contentment, leaning back in his chair and closing his eyes as though he was about to doze off. Without opening his eyes he said: "I'll take over here. As soon as they taxi in to the apron, you go down and get the car ready. They'll be taking the dark red sedan parked just outside the arrivals door. Just in case they don't go directly to the hotel, I have arranged a little dingus to help you keep track of them. Here," he pulled a small device from the cavernous inside pocket of his coat and leaned across the table towards Ro. "It has a range of about three miles. Instructions on the back."

Ro turned it over and read the instructions. They seemed simple enough, but she was puzzled. "How on earth did you manage this?"

"Easily really," Sparrow grinned. "A bit of natural nosiness and an insatiable desire to be helpful. While the Hertz girl was checking the oil, water and screen wash bottle, I simply mooched over and started chatting to her about the car and its engine, that sort of thing. Being a helpful sort of fellow, and a natural gent, I naturally offered to lower the bonnet for her. To save her getting her lily-whites grubby, you know. Stuck the bug underneath just before I slammed the lid."

"You're quite something, dickie bird," Ro shook her head with a wry smile. "If you ever come over to the States, remind me to introduce you to a man I know. He's also something of an entomologist."

Sparrow laughed "Entomologist. That's good. I like that, Ro. Now, here they come. Off to the car with you," he waved her away as the waiter came over to enquire if they would require anything else.

Sparrow declined and paid for their drinks.

Chapter 48

GREEN HAD ARRANGED for a US Air Force helicopter to fly him, Mike and the Chongs from Mildenhall to Fairford where one of Penkowski's contacts was waiting with a car. It made sense to have a driver with local knowledge; one, moreover, accustomed to driving on the left side of the road. Comfortably chauffeured, they arrived at Dr Heinemann's house just after two, having stopped at a small pub for lunch and to introduce Chong and San Kiu to English beer. Somewhat to the Americans' surprise they both loved it and insisted on drinking a pint each.

Once the arrival courtesies had been observed with Dr Heinemann, Green and the driver, Dave Bonner, continued to Bristol in order to spy out the land and get the feel of the place where the jazz was being played. Mike stayed with the Chongs, and Bonner was to return and collect them at six. Dr Heinemann would have none of this and insisted on bringing his guests to Bristol himself.

"It will not be an inconvenience for me as I am also wishing to go there for the music," he insisted. "We shall meet at the lighthouse boat at six thirty, if that would be suitable. I know well where it is."

Mike and Green looked doubtful and looked at Bonner for his advice.

"There is an old lightship, moored to the quay right next to the street where the music is played. That's a good place to meet." Bonner explained.

Green thought for a moment, and agreed. He and Bonner headed back to their car while Heinemann and the Chongs were lost in scientific discussion before the car turned the corner.

BONNER DROVE THROUGH Bristol as though he had been born there, and soon found a good parking place near the quay in a small street just off Queen Square. They could hear music as they climbed from the car. For the next hour Bonner led Green on a detailed tour of the neighborhood and made him blindfold familiar with the streets surrounding the quay, many of which had been closed to traffic.

Wooden staging for the musicians had been erected in the street between two pubs. One of these was an old black and white timber framed building with leaded windows cast wide. The upper storeys of the building leaned out crazily over the street, its three levels overflowing with people, many of whom were hanging out of the windows to watch the scene below.

The pub opposite was called the Duke, with a swinging picture sign portraying a famous jazz musician hanging out from the wall. Is inside walls, where they were visible at all, were stained dark from the smoke of a million cigarettes. The rest were hung with a vast collection of old instruments and posters advertising past events and concerts. This building was equally full and the part of the bar that served as a stage during normal times was packed with beer swilling enthusiasts, listening to the music blaring in through the open windows whilst trying to converse over the noise.

In the street outside, five bands were taking it in turn to play twenty minute sets, surrounded by an enthusiastic crowd.

After walking round the immediate area of the festival, Green and Bonner walked through to Baldwin Street and hailed a taxi. Green gave the driver a twenty pound note and asked him to take them on a tour of the city center streets. Bonner pointed out landmarks and occasionally asked the driver to take them past certain chosen places. Half an hour later the taxi dropped them back at the end of the quay where he had picked them up. Green thanked him sincerely and gave him another fiver. The driver was loud in his thanks as he drove off.

Green and Bonner walked along the waterfront and stopped by the old red lightship. It was tied to the quay, converted now into a club, and badly in need of a coat of paint. The vessel was a sad sight with the top of the lamp tower whitened by pigeon droppings, the red hull paint fading, and moss and weeds starting to grow in the scuppers. Several other old vessels, similarly converted into floating restaurants, were moored nearby. At the far end of a neighboring quay, beyond the Arts Center, was an old steamer. Retired from years of service as a ferry plying between the Hebridean islands, it too had been converted into a floating watering hole. The lightship was moored directly opposite the end of the street where the bands were playing.

The crowd grew steadily through the afternoon. By six it was spilling over into surrounding streets. These also held their share of clubs, bars and eating places, and trade in all of them was vigorous. The crowd was good natured and in constant motion, shuffling round to accommodate newcomers, and to let the thirsty reach the bars. Green was surprised to note how few policemen were around, and that those who were there seemed to have adopted the relaxed party mood, laughing and chatting easily with the crowd. Some had paper party hats jammed over their helmets by merry revelers, and one even wore a festoon of colored streamers draped round his neck.

Green sat on a bollard beside the water and looked across at the old warehouse opposite. The building was being converted into apartments by an enterprising developer. He hoped they were fitting good double glazing; if this sort of event was usual it would be needed if the residents ever hoped to get any sleep.

His reverie was interrupted by Heinemann's arrival with the Chongs and Mike. They had left their car in a car park several streets away and walked through the gardens and over the bridge. The two Chinese seemed excited by the energetic atmosphere and Heinemann looked pleased.

Bonner went in search of drinks for the new arrivals while Mike and Green brought each other up to date. Mike had used a call box on the other side of the river and contacted Hal at the Holiday inn. He reported that Swingate and the others had arrived and were congregated in the hotel bar. Mason was also in the hotel, but still in his room.

As soon as Mason joined the others Hal would launch the next phase of the operation. He would leave a message for Mike at the desk when the party left the hotel, and Mike was to call again in forty five minutes. Walter Sparrow had joined Hal, reporting that everything had gone as planned at the airport.

Chapter 49

WHEN THE HOWARD Corporation jet landed at Bristol airport, the controller directed the pilot to a stand behind a parked Airbus. From the terminal building and the control office it was impossible to see more than the tail of the Cessna. The three passengers disembarked immediately and went out to find their car, each carrying a light bag. As the crew descended to the apron, a white electric powered vehicle drove up and stopped next to the doorway. A middle-aged man in white overalls, bearing the legend 'Business Hospitality Services' across the back, stepped down from the driver's position.

"Welcome to Bristol, Gentlemen," he greeted the pilots cheerily. "We offer a free service to all visiting business aircraft, Captain. It will be our pleasure to clean the cabin for you. We vacuum the floor, clean ashtrays, polish all the windows, replenish your fresh water supply and empty the waste tank. My name is Harold and it would be my pleasure to perform this service for you while your aircraft is being refueled."

The two pilots looked at each other in surprise.

"I thought this sort of thing only happened in the States," the Captain remarked.

"It's fairly new here, sir, but we do like to make our visitors feel welcome," Harold said.

The Captain snorted and smiled. "Sure. You go right ahead. Seen one of these birds before? You know where everything is?"

"Oh yes, sir. I know what I have to do. She'll be all ship shape and Bristol fashion in no time. If you gentlemen would like some refreshment, you'll find we have excellent facilities in the terminal, and the Control Office is just round the corner of the building over there," he pointed towards the terminal. He turned to his converted milk float and began unloading his cleaning equipment. The crew walked off towards the airport buildings.

The cleaner carried his equipment inside and took a quick look around. Checking that the two pilots were out of sight, he moved forward to the cockpit, reached under the pilot's seat and removed the lifejacket. Pulling the pouch open he removed the contents and replaced it with a yellow, rubber wrapped package from his trolley. The lifejacket he dropped into a black rubbish sack. The pouch was soon replaced under the seat and three others were treated in a similar way before the man turned his attention to cleaning the cabin. It was not dirty and didn't take long. Only one of the ashtrays had been used. A scented aerosol and cotton cloth removed the smears from inside the windows and freshened the air. Inside twenty minutes the interior cleaning was completed.

Harold removed his equipment and stacked it on the rear platform of his cart before driving it round to park under the aircraft's tail near a small hatch with 'WASTE' printed on it in stiff red letters. A recessed clip released the hatch to reveal a screw cap inside. He removed this and attached a hose connected to a small electric pump. This whined for a moment when it was switched on, then settled down to a steady whirr as the contents of the waste tank were pumped into a large blue plastic bin on the back of the cart. When the pump began to whine again he switched off, disconnected the hose and stowed it back on the cart. From a pocket he took a plastic cylinder and pushed it into the open mouth of the waste pipe, connecting the end of a thin wire that protruded from the cylinder to the small retaining chain that held the cap before screwing this back in place and closing the hatch.

Moving round the other side of the aircraft he opened a similar hatch and replenished the fresh water tank. With this task completed, he walked round the aircraft giving the outside of all the windows a clean wipe before he climbed back onto his cart and drove away, disappearing round the back of the airport buildings.

Ten minutes later Walter Sparrow drove his car out of the airport car park and turned left towards the city. Traffic was building up, and it took him almost half an hour to reach the center and find a space in the Lower Castle Street multi-storey car park. From there he walked to the hotel next door, enquired for Mr Johnson, and spent the afternoon stretched out on the spare bed in Hal's room reading a paperback copy of Homer's Odyssey in Greek.

Chapter 50

THE PUBLIC PHONES in Queen Square were busy when Mike went to call Hal at the hotel, and he had to wait. As a result his call was almost half an hour late.

"I'm very sorry Mr. Ashton, but Mr. Johnson is not in the hotel. He did warn me that you might call, and asked me to tell you that he has met some other friends and gone with them down to the waterfront to listen to the music. He said that you would be able to find them near the front of the Duke. Do you know where that is, sir?" The hotel operator sounded polite and helpful.

"Yes, I know where that is, thank you. I'll find him. Bye."

"Good bye, sir."

When Mike got back to the others he found that Bomb Bay Billy had already seen them. The Ground Zero Jazzmen were due to play another set in a few minutes and he was trying to persuade Chong to go on stage with them. Chong protested he would have loved to but did not have his beautiful new sax with him. Green said the car was parked only a few streets away, with all the luggage in the back. If Chong really wanted to play he saw no reason why he shouldn't. Dave Bonner offered to fetch the instrument and disappeared into the throng. The previous band was into their finale when he came back a few minutes later.

During the interval many of the audience dived into the adjacent bars. This allowed those who had been at the back of the crowd to move closer and a general reshuffle of the audience took place while the band set up. Bomb Bay Billy led the Ground Zero Jazzmen onto the stage amid loud cheers.

The light was fading and floodlights on the surrounding buildings had been turned on. The stage was brightly lit as the Jazzmen took their places. Chong stood next to the other sax player, on one side. He fingered his treasured instrument lovingly as Bomb Bay Billy stepped forward and the crowd hushed.

On the count of three, music filled the street. The audience, most of whom had been there all afternoon, noticed the difference at once. It was not simply that there was another player in the band, but the music had a different quality about it. There was a new energy flowing through it and the musicians' faces reflected a special enthusiasm. This subtle quality reached into people's minds and touched emotional chords that had not been felt earlier. The wave of applause that followed the first number went on and on, completely drowning the opening bars of the next piece. The crush of bodies increased as people returned from the bars.

During the changeover Green and Bonner worked their way along the side of the street to take up positions near the front of the Duke. Mike, San Kiu and Heinemann stayed fifty yards away near the lightship. From there the two groups were in view of each other and would be able to see when Hal brought their quarry into the arena.

After the fourth number Bomb Bay Billy announced that the Jazzmen would play one more piece before taking a breather. He led the band into a lusty rendering of the Hiawatha Rag and the crowd loved it. As the number was coming to an end Billy glanced at Green who was staring intently at a group of people just coming out of the front door of the pub.

The music ended and the crowd loudly demanded more. Their cries became more insistent as Billy moved to leave the stage and those at the front packed closer to stop him leaving. He looked at Green again, his eyebrows raised in enquiry. Green nodded once.

Bomb Bay Billy stepped back onto the stage amid tumultuous applause and raised his hands for quiet. Slowly the noise died down. "We gonna play one more this time round, then we gotta take a break else we don't get to drink no beer," he bellowed. The crowd laughed. "Now, y'all saw we got another man on the line this time, and he all don't come from Texas like the rest of us." The crowd cheered. "This one's for him. It ain't never bin played afore seein' as how we only writ it last night over a case of whiskey, so we have to use the sheet music fer the first performance less'n we gets lost."

There were whistles and catcalls among the general laughter from the audience as the Jazzmen put out their music stands. Chong looked at the sheets his neighbor had placed before him, then looked at Billy in surprise.

"We hoped you'd like it, Chong. Stole the idea from you," Billy said with a grin. Chong grinned back.

"Here we go folks, with the Chinese Take-out Rag. Take it away Chong." Billy gave the beat. Pearls of rich sound cascaded into the street from a single gleaming saxophone. Glasses on their way to mouths paused in their rising arcs as the intensity of the sound gripped the audience.

The background hum of conversation died as every head turned towards the stage. Slowly, subtly, one at a time, the rest of the Jazzmen joined in, the harmonies took shape and developed. After the first few bars Chong hardly even looked at the music. Closing his eyes, he did as the inscription on his instrument enjoined and played it from the heart.

The party of Americans who had emerged from the pub at the moment the music began stood in a close group. The three men stared in open disbelief at the tall man on the stage in front of them. As the Ground Zero Jazzmen took the melody into a vigorous variation, the dark haired, heavy set man nudged his neighbor and muttered something out of the side of his mouth. The other grunted, nodding, and would have turned to leave had not the press of bodies behind prevented him.

The tall Chinese sax player opened his eyes and stared right at the dark haired man. Their eyes locked and the American saw recognition in the musician's eyes.

The Jazzmen reached a massive, heart stopping crescendo and suddenly there were only the velvet tones of a solitary instrument pouring its passion into the street. Nobody was quite sure when the music actually finished. It was followed by a roar of appreciation loud enough to shake the surrounding buildings.

Eventually the band managed to climb down from the stage and began to move through the crowd towards the pub door.

During the final number Mike had left Heinemann and San Kiu and worked his way round via adjoining streets to the front of the Duke. He was standing just behind the group of Americans as the music finally ended.

Bomb Bay Billy stood aside and motioned for Chong to lead the way. Chong came to a halt in front of a heavily built, swarthy man. He looked quickly at the people either side of him, surprise showing on his face.

"Why, Mr. Stanley. What a surprise. Mr. Howard and Mr. Mason as well; I did not expect to see you here," he said. Swingate was making goldfish faces, his mouth opening but no sound came out. The other two went bright red.

"Don't you remember me? Last year you all visited the research center where I used to work in China, surely you remember that visit?" His face reinforced the question. "You came to see..."

He was interrupted by a screaming woman barging into the group.

"Get away from them, you filthy yellow fiend! They never saw you before, and don't want anything to do with you now!" Her voice was a band-saw screech.

As she forced her way in front of the three men she pulled something from her purse. The crowd around them hushed and turned to look.

"Look out, she's got a gun!" a voice said in alarm.

The crowd pressed nervously backwards. There was a movement to her left and, as she lifted the gun to point it at Chong, a man lunged forward and grabbed her arm. There was a sharp crack and the man slumped.

The crowd shied back further, leaving a gap. The woman let go of the gun and dived for the gap. People shouted for her to stop as she raced off along the street, and the man who had tackled her fell to the ground. One of the Americans turned as if to follow the woman, calling "Lo! Stop!"

The woman ignored him and fled, dodging round scaffolding, parked cars and a skip full of builders' rubble. Some people on the edge of the crowd started after her, but she already had a ten yard start. Charging blindly on towards the main street ahead, she lunged across. A squeal of brakes, a rasping grinding sound and a sickening, body crushing thump. She was propelled thirty feet down the street by the impact. More brakes squealed as oncoming cars swerved to avoid the crash.

When her pursuers emerged into Baldwin Street they found the rear wheel of the motorcycle still spinning. The rider's leg was trapped under his machine; the sharp end of the clutch lever was embedded in the side of his helmetless head. The woman's twisted body slumped against a stationary bus across of the road.

A stunned, whispering crowd gathered. A man laid his jacket over the motorcyclist. Somebody else covered the woman as the wail of approaching sirens smothered the faint sound of a jazz band floating down the street.

Outside the pub, the three Americans, surrounded now by the Ground Zero Jazzmen, stared in numbed shock at the man who had been shot. The one who had shouted at the woman looked again in the direction she had fled, turned and started to follow, calling his companions to go with him.

Green grabbed Hal by the arm. "Stay with Mike. Send Mitch and Bonner along to find Heinemann and San Kiu. Tell them to take Chong with them and go back to Ro at their hotel. I'll call there later. You call there and tell Ro which emergency unit Mike's been taken to."

Weaving his way through the crowd, Green ran after the three Americans. He caught up with them as they reached the main street.

"Swingate, Howard, stop," he gasped, grabbing each by the arm.

"Mr. Green. What are you doing here?"

"Never mind that now, I'll explain later. We've got to get you three away from here. Mr. Howard, there's nothing he can do for her, so get Mason away from the girl and bring him this way." Green pointed to the edge of the crowd and pulled Swingate after him as he moved in that direction himself.

Howard grabbed Mason and pulled him, struggling, in the same direction. The four men pushed through the gathering mass of sightseers who flowed past them, eager to gaze on the carnage in the street. Green saw a taxi and hailed it, waving frantically as it slowed.

"Where are you staying?" he demanded and Howard told him.

Green bundled the other men into the taxi and gave the driver instructions, climbing in with them and slamming his door as the cab moved off. At the hotel entrance Green gave the cabby a twenty pound note, told him to keep the change, and ushered the three dazed men into the building. The taxi driver looked at the money and shook his head in wonder.

Green found the Senator still had his room key in his pocket so he hurried the three men into the elevator and pressed the button for the sixth floor. He hustled them along the corridor and into Swingate's room, followed them in, closed the door and leaned against it to regain his breath.

Swingate recovered first and started to demand an explanation. Green pushed him savagely into a chair. "Just shut up, all of you. You'll get your explanation, and I'm damned well going to have one from you as well. You're the last people I either expected or wanted to see here. You and that crazy bitch have just screwed up one hell of an important operation."

"That was my daughter," Mason snapped at him.

"You'd better hope 'was' is the correct term, Gerry. You keep damned well clear till we find out. Fine load of trouble that's going to cause if it gets out. Company man's daughter interferes in covert operation on our premier ally's territory. Tries to murder a top grade scientist on whom we're making a snatch, and then kills one of the Company's agents by mistake. Yep, you'd better hope she's dead, buddy, and that nobody makes the connection. You're supposed to be grounded stateside anyway, so you're going to have some sharp questions to answer when you get home." He eased a snub nosed revolver from his pocket as he spoke. "And just in case any of you idiots is thinking of trying something clever, don't. If any of you has a gun you'd better tell me now."

Swingate shook his head, Mason did the same. Howard's hand moved towards his inside pocket but Green stopped him. "Hold it. Just walk slowly over here," he pointed to a spot on the floor. "Now take off your coat and drop it. Now go back and sit down." Howard did as he was told. "Now you two," Green told the others. "Coats off, and drop them on the floor in front of you. Slowly."

They complied, glaring sullenly at Green as he moved forward and hooked the coats towards him with a foot, keeping his eyes on the three seated men all the time. He lifted each coat and felt the pockets, removing a small-bore automatic from Howard's and another from Mason's.

"I told you not to do anything stupid, Gerry. That was very stupid," he said, pocketing the weapons and leaning back against the door. "OK, now we'll have your explanations. That Chinaman recognized all three of you. Where and when have you met him before, Senator?"

"I've never seen him before. He was mistaken and took me for someone else." Swingate mumbled uncomfortably and ran his finger round his collar.

"Sure, sure. You used your middle name when he met you. That's what he called you by down there; Mr. Stanley," Green came back sharply. Swingate looked sick. "He said you visited the research center in China where he used to work. When was that, Senator? You are not on record as having ever made an official, or even a private visit, to China."

"He's mistaken, I tell you. I've never met him anywhere before tonight."

"Senator, you're already in deep shit, don't make it any worse. That guy is a top research scientist. People like him are trained to observe and recognize the familiar from the unusual. They don't get to see many westerners and they don't make mistakes like that. When and where, Senator?"

Swingate stared at his feet for a long time. "A year and a half, maybe two years ago, in China," he finally admitted with great reluctance.

"Now we are getting somewhere," Green said. "What were you doing in China?"

"We were trying to fix up a trade deal." The Senator's reply was subdued.

"All three of you? Crap! Howard I could understand. He is in business, but you are a United States Senator and debarred from any form of private business interest. Gerry here is an employee of the CIA. His section is not even remotely concerned with China, and you can bet your life I would have known all about it if he had been brought in for a covert op. How do you explain that, Senator?"

"Chester was trying to persuade Gerry to leave the CIA and join his corporation. He came along to see if he liked the job."

"That's a nice pat answer, Senator. Why don't you answer for yourself, Gerry?" Green stared at Mason who remained mute. "You don't have an answer, do you? Well, we'll leave that to be sorted out by the enquiry after we get home. Now, what were you all doing here in England?"

"Chester had business. He offered me a ride in his plane so I came along for a short vacation." Swingate was ready with another pat reply.

"Which you are equally not allowed to accept because of your position, Senator. You're more full of shit today than usual. So, Gerry, how do you just happen to be here as well? I suppose you also came along for the ride, with Howard trying to entice you into the business; that it?"

"No, I came here on vacation, last week. I brought my daughter to see my sister who lives near this city, and we came in for the jazz festival."

"And just happened to meet the two men you went to China with, one of whom is trying to sign you up and the other just happens to be the father of the man your daughter is married to. That's a whole bucket full of coincidences, don't you think?" Green asked acidly.

"That's the way it is, however odd you find it," Mason insisted flatly. "Sure, I was supposed to stay home, and I'll have to answer for that. We've told you the rest. We didn't know that Chinaman was going to be here and cause all this trouble."

Green stared at them all for several minutes before he spoke again. None of them had the nerve to break the silence as their obvious discomfort grew.

"No, I don't suppose you did expect him to turn up, but if you had all been doing what you were supposed to be doing, this situation would never have come about. And you wouldn't have screwed up my operation," he hooked the dressing table chair towards him with his toe, turned it round and lowered himself onto the seat. "What a mess. It's just about crazy enough to have some truth in it." Green ran his hand back through his hair. "Supposing I accept this crap you three have been pushing at me, I still have a screwed up operation to patch up and try to recover without causing an international incident. Always assuming that it's not already too late. Each of you is bound to have some questions to answer here; how do we handle that?" He put the pistol in his pocket.

The others began to relax at his apparent acceptance of their story.

"We have to leave immediately, and get back where we are expected to be," Swingate offered.

"That won't wash. You are too well known, Senator. Your presence in this country will have been noted by the immigration authorities when you arrived, and there were press photographers in that crowd, snapping off pictures like sharpshooters, in case you failed to notice."

"They won't know it was me. I have a passport in the name of Stanley, for private travel."

"That's kind of irregular, Senator. Does the Immigration Department know about it? Even if you do hold it with their knowledge, it will have an arrival stamp on it. Then, when they get round to identifying your daughter-in-law, there are going to be some juicy headlines back home. Your position ain't going to be any too good," Green finished on a thoughtful note.

"I will have to resign," Swingate said.

"Yeah, but how do we get you home without anyone knowing."

"That's no problem. We'll fly back through Canada. They don't check US passports coming in that way. Howard has been on a legitimate business trip. Mason has been on vacation and caught a ride home. Immigration won't ask questions with his ID, and they don't know he's grounded anyhow. He can always say that was cover for an unspecified covert operation. By the time anyone gets round to checking he'll have ducked out." The Senator was warming to the lie.

Green sat, as if considering the idea, and said nothing. Then he shrugged and sighed as if with resignation. "It might work. You'll have to leave the girl and I'll try to hush up that connection at this end. I'll put an advert in the New York Times, on a Thursday, when it's all cleared up. I'll put something which includes ' I forgive you Daddy, Lois.' By the way, Gerry, just tell me one thing: were you selling guns to the Tamil Tigers?" Green stared him in the eyes.

Mason looked flustered. Before he could reply Swingate coughed. "I think I was a bit hasty on that. You effectively showed there is no substantive evidence. I'll use that as my reason for resignation and say something about making a grave error that has not served the interests of my electorate and therefore feel I should go."

"That should fix that one," Green said, nodding his agreement. "You'd better write that out right now, Senator, and I will see that it gets to the right place faster than you can get it there. At least this might keep the lid on things long enough for me to finish my mission. Just in case any of you think of trying to pull another stunt, let me tell you there were nine of my agents in that crowd this evening. They all know you, Senator, and Gerry, maybe not Howard, and they will have registered and recorded your presence. If I hadn't been watching the Chinaman so closely, I might have noticed you as well and warned you off. The fact remains that all my agents will have seen you; one had a video camera going, and another was the man who got shot."

Swingate gasped and went pale.

Green stared at each man in turn. "I can keep them quiet, but just remember, if you're thinking of pulling another stupid stunt, they all know who you are and you have no idea who they are." He looked again from face to face.

"Now then," Green continued mildly, "where is your aircraft and do you have any flight crew with it?"

Howard heaved himself upright in his chair. "It's at the airport four miles out of town. There are two pilots staying at a hotel in the village nearby."

"How soon can the plane leave?"

"The aircraft is ready to go. It only requires everyone to get out there and the pilot to file a flight plan." Howard was back on familiar ground.

"What about air movements at night?" Green looked at his watch and was surprised to see that it was only just after ten.

"They fly all hours from here. We'll be headed for Prestwick so there's no customs clearance, no reason to hold us up. Once we are off we'll sneak out to Shannon in Ireland and go home from there."

"Right." Green put on a decisive manner. "Senator, you use some of the hotel's paper and write that resignation letter, now. Mr Howard, you pick up that phone and call your pilots. Tell them to get out to the aircraft and be ready with their flight plan filed by the time we arrive. I will take you to the airport. The pilot can tell Movements you are going back to Scotland. Once you're airborne you are on your own." He waited while Howard made the call, listening to make sure the instructions were relayed correctly.

Swingate took paper from the hotel courtesy folder, chose a blank sheet and began writing his resignation from the Senate.

"Now make another call," Green told Howard. "Call the front desk and have them make up your bills. Say that urgent business is taking you back to Scotland. Ask them to make new reservations for three days time. You won't arrive, but it will allay any suspicion about your hasty departure, and in three days time it won't matter anymore. Ask them to have the Bell Captain bring the bills up here with the correct credit card slips, and find some pounds to tip him. Ask them also to have your bags taken down and call a cab to take us to the airport. Do it now."

Swingate finished writing his letter, folded the sheet, put it in an envelope and handed it to Green. Green tore the envelope open and read the letter. He noted it was dated two days previously. When he finished he grunted, replaced the letter in the envelope and folded it into the inside pocket of his jacket.

"I think that covers everything. If not, I shall just have to do the best I can later." Green told them. "Now all we have to do is wait for the bills."

"What about your agent, the one who got shot?" Mason asked.

"He was dead. You had better hope that girl of yours is too." Green's expression was grim.

They sat in silence for several minutes until there was a discreet knock at the door. The Bell Captain entered with their bills on a silver tray. The three men each signed and handed over their credit cards.

"I will have your cards and receipts ready when you come down, gentlemen. The other gentlemen's bags are already downstairs," he picked up Swingate's bag, accepted the ten pound note held out to him, and left.

Green waited a full five minutes after he had left, then stood up.

"OK. Put your coats on and let's go. Just relax, this is the easy part."

In the lobby the Bell Captain stood with the three credit cards and receipted bills on a tray. The hotel's courtesy coach was at the entrance with its door open. The driver was putting their bags into the back. The four men got in and the driver climbed into his seat and pressed a button to close the door behind him.

"To the airport, I believe, gentlemen?" he said, setting the vehicle in motion.

"That's right, thank you," Green acknowledged.

"I didn't know there was a flight this late, sir," the driver seemed chatty.

"We have a company aircraft waiting," Green told him, aware that the conversation was making the other three feel uncomfortable and smiling to himself in the darkness. He maintained a companionable banter with the driver all the way to the airport and pressed a ten pound note into his grateful hand when he dropped them off.

The pilots were in the aircraft and ready to go as the four men walked across the apron. The Airbus that had been parked there earlier was gone. As they reached the steps the second pilot came out, took their bags and stowed them in the baggage hold. He walked round the aircraft checking that all the external hatches were secure while his passengers took their seats, and then boarded himself.

Before the crewman secured the hatch, Green took the two automatics from his pocket, removed the magazines and tossed the guns on the cabin floor. He stuffed the magazines into the seat pocket by the door, turned and walked back towards the terminal building as the crewman closed and locked the door.

By the entrance he turned and waited. The engines of the small jet had started and it was soon taxiing towards the end of the runway. It stopped and waited. Green lifted his hand and stood clicking his thumbnail against his front teeth, listening to the distant sound of the aircraft's engines. It was almost a minute before the sound increased. The aircraft lined up with the runway centerline, its two engines screaming their last defiance at the black night. The pilot released his brakes and it rolled forward, gathering speed, its anti collision lights flashing angrily. Green saw the racing lights lift and climb steeply in a graceful arc to merge and lose themselves amid the myriad twinkling pinpoints of the stars.

He stood staring into the darkness until the final rumble of the jets had faded before he turned to leave.

Walter Sparrow was sitting at the wheel of a rented car when Green emerged from the terminal's front door. He started the engine and pushed open the passenger door. "Can I offer you a lift, Mr. Green?"

Chapter 51

ON TUESDAY AFTERNOON Mike woke to find Chevvy sitting beside his bed, holding his hand.

"Chevvy, how did you get here?" He tried to sit up, but she pushed him back against the pillows.

"In an airplane, silly. How else do you think I'd come, on a broomstick?"

"I didn't mean that. I mean..."

"I know that, silly. When you didn't turn up on Monday as I expected, I rang the office. Joe told me that instead of coming home to your wife, you were gallivanting about over here playing at being Sir Walter Raleigh, only you'd fallen over your own big feet and got a few bruises," her eyes reflected the fun in her voice.

"Sir what?"

"Sir Walter Raleigh. He was an English gentleman who took off his cloak and laid it over the puddles so that Queen Bess wouldn't get her pretty feet wet. The only trouble is your Chinaman stepped into a different puddle." She was laughing now.

"What? Chong's not hurt is he?" Mike pushed himself upright.

"No, silly. He's fine, and sitting in the waiting room along the passage. There's a whole mob of them out there, and the nurse made them all wait until you woke up. Chong has got Dr. Heinemann on one side trying to persuade him to stay here, and work with him, and a whole lot of wild Texans on the other side trying to get him to join their jazz band. That's all."

With great relief Mike leaned over and pulled his wife to him, wrapping his arms around her and burying his face in her hair.

"Oh, Misha," she said, "I was worried, and I missed you."

Mike held her away and looked at her.

"You haven't called me that for ages, Chevvy. I've missed you too," he pulled her close again and they held each other in silence for a long time.

At last Chevvy let go, kissed him, and pushed Mike back against his pillows.

"Now, the nurse said you only got a scratch along your ribs and the bullet got stuck in your wallet, so they'll let you out tomorrow. Nose has given you five days sick leave, so we're going to Wales. I want to take my son to the Brecon Beacons and show him where I found his father."

"Thomas! Where is he?" Mike tried to sit up again.

"He's perfectly all right. He's being cuddled by San Kiu, and loving every minute of it. I like her, she's special, and she'll be having a baby of her own in a few months. So you lie there while I go and bring Thomas. Then I expect they'll all want to come in and see you."

"Chevvy, I love you."

"Mmm. I love you too, my hero." Chevvy said, heading for the door.

She was back in a minute with the baby and laid him in his father's arms. A moment later the door opened and a wave of smiling people swept into the room.

The next half hour was chaos.

Eventually a nurse came in and chased most of the visitors out. Only Chong, San Kiu, Penkowski and Chevvy remained.

"We seem to have given you a crazy introduction to Western life," Mike said to Chong, "Have you thought what you are going to do next?"

"So many different offers, and I want to accept them all," the tall Chinaman replied. "So I have decided that I shall be a part-time scientist and a part-time jazz musician. But I will also be a full time father, like you," he turned to look proudly at San Kiu who was again holding Thomas. "Mr. Green has offered me a job too, so I shall also work for the Company and help the country that has given us so much."

"And you can both come and stay with us until you find your own home," Chevvy said decisively.

Penkowski pulled a folded newspaper from his pocket.

"Nose has gone back to Langley to tidy up. You can bring Chong and San Kiu back with you next week. Meanwhile they are invited to spend some time with Dr Heinemann. I thought you would like to see this," he opened the paper and laid it across the bed, pointing to an item at the bottom of page three.

Under a small headline announcing a narcotics arrest it read:

Malaysian authorities arrested five Americans when their business jet landed at Kuala Lumpur yesterday. They were found to be in possession of fifteen kilos of heroin and two kilos of crack-cocaine. Narcotics trafficking

is a capital offence in Malaysia and carries a mandatory death penalty.
A police spokesman said the evidence was conclusive and the five would
undoubtedly face the hangman's noose. A British man was hanged last week
for a similar offence, committed seven years ago, involving only four ounces
of heroin. One of the five Americans is believed to be a former United States
Senator whose daughter-in-law was killed in a road accident in Bristol last
weekend. Another is said to be the head of a substantial American business
empire.

Mike looked up from the paper and stared at Penkowski.

"How on earth … ?"

"We wanted to fix their bags, but the hotel security was too tight," the big Pole said with a grin. "A sparrow somehow left its droppings in their aircraft. Now, if you folks will excuse me, I have to go. I promised to tell a little boy back home a story about some bears, and he's been kept waiting a long time."

Acknowledgements

IN LATE MAY AND EARLY June of 1989, the Chinese authorities flirted with democracy. In Tiananmen Square, students were permitted to gather in unprecedented numbers, and to paste political posters on the Democracy Wall. Tolerance, and a measure of free speech, seemed to be emerging from behind the bamboo veil. For a week the mandarins did nothing, while the army sat in their trucks and watched. Then, one evening, the troops were withdrawn. Overnight new regiments were brought in, equipped with tanks, tear gas and orders to disperse the demonstrators. As the clampdown began on 4 June, an outspoken Chinese astrophysicist, Fang Lizhi, and his wife, Li Shuizian, took refuge in the US embassy in Beijing, and so began an uncomfortable standoff.

I went to the pub that evening with a wildlife artist friend, Guy Troughton, (www.guytroughton.com) and we fell to talking about the dilemma this imposed. The problem of getting Fang out of the embassy had the makings of a good thriller; something out of Alistair Maclean, or Hammond Innes. Guy said I should write it. "Okay," I said, "I'll do that." It was only beer talk, and we moved on to talk about a delightful Australian girl he was becoming rather fond of.

At three the following morning, I woke up with a solution to the US embassy dilemma clear in my mind, put paper in the typewriter – I had no computer in those days – and began typing.

Thus I am indebted to Guy for nudging me into writing in the first place.

The contribution of many others should be acknowledged too, among them: Larry Berkowiz, Chas Dyman, Harry Coombs and Slim Beck, for insights into some of the crazy schemes enacted by the CIA, and Ted Minetti for sharing his first-hand knowledge of the FBI.

Sally Parkes spent hours checking facts for me, and proofread the first manuscript, picking up over twelve hundred typos. Her diligence and patience is much appreciated.

Noel Phillips briefed me on the corporate world of the nuclear industry, and the ins and outs of exporting technology from the USA, while Mike Carson spent hours explaining and demonstrating a variety of covert electronic listening devices. To all of these my sincere thanks.

In more recent times, my thanks go to a number of readers for helpful comments, and for assisting me in adjusting the story to fit modern tastes and sensibilities. Also for asking awkward questions about bits which didn't fit too comfortably in the story. Particularly among these, Rosanne Dingli, who persuaded me to take the plunge and write fiction; Sharon Lippincott, whose writing skill and constructive criticism has helped me enormously; and Wendy Reis, for insightful editorial suggestions.

My thanks to Melissa Brayford for an engaging cover design, and for being patient with the numerous changes she had to make in order to satisfy an imprecise brief.

To my publisher, Chuck Grieve, my thanks for his usual patience, interesting talks throughout the publishing process, and the many cups of excellent coffee which fuelled our discussions.

And finally, thanks to my lovely wife, Gay, for endless love and support, and for putting up with the hours I spent in front of a screen, polishing the manuscript.

Lightning Source UK Ltd.
Milton Keynes UK
UKOW07f0758301214

243722UK00007B/79/P